International Praise for Alex Miller

'Alex Miller is a wonderful writer, one that Australia has been keeping secret from the rest of us for too long.'—John Banville

'Few writers since Joseph Conrad have had so fine an appreciation of the equivocations of the individual conscience and their relationship to the long processes of history . . . [*Landscape of Farewell* is] a very human story, passionately told.'
—*Australian Book Review*

'As readers of his previous novels will know, Miller is keenly interested in inner lives . . . As one expects from the best fiction, *Landscape of Farewell* transforms the reader's own inner life. Twice winner of the Miles Franklin Award, it is only a matter of time before Miller wins a Nobel.'—*Daily News*, New Zealand

'Miller is a master storyteller.'—*The Monthly*

'The most impressive and satisfying novel of recent years. It gave me all the kinds of pleasure a reader can hope for.'
—Tim Winton on *Journey to the Stone Country*

'A terrific tale of love and redemption that captivates from the first line.'
—Nicholas Shakespeare on *Journey to the Stone Country*

'Miller's fiction has a mystifying power that is always far more than the sum of its parts . . . His footsteps—softly, deftly, steadily—take you places you may not have been, and their sound resonates for a long time.'
—Andrea Stretton, *The Sydney Morning Herald*

'A wonderful novel of stunning intricacy and great beauty.'
—Michael Ondaatje on *The Ancestor Game*

'In a virtuoso exhibition, Miller's control never once falters.'
—*Canberra Times* on *The Tivington Nott*

Lovesong

Also by ALEX MILLER

Landscape of Farewell
Prochownik's Dream
Journey to the Stone Country
Conditions of Faith
The Sitters
The Ancestor Game
The Tivington Nott
Watching the Climbers on the Mountain

ALEX MILLER

Lovesong

HarperCollins Publishers Ltd

Lovesong
Copyright © 2009 by Alex Miller.
All rights reserved.

Published by HarperCollins Publishers Ltd

First published by Allen & Unwin: 2009
First published in Canada by HarperCollins Publishers Ltd in this original trade
paperback edition: 2011

First Canadian edition

HarperCollins books may be purchased for educational, business,
or sales promotional use through our Special Markets Department.

HarperCollins Publishers Ltd
2 Bloor Street East, 20th Floor
Toronto, Ontario, Canada
M4W 1A8

www.harpercollins.ca

Library and Archives Canada Cataloguing in Publication
information is available upon request

ISBN 978-1-55468-803-6

Text design by Emily O'Neill

Printed and bound in the United States
RRD 9 8 7 6 5 4 3 2 1

For Stephanie
and for our children
Ross and Kate

And for Erin

I adjure you, O daughters of Jerusalem,
by the gazelles or the wild does:
do not stir up or awaken love
until it is ready!

THE SONG OF SOLOMON

One

*W*hen we first came to live in this area in the seventies there was a drycleaners next door to the bottle shop. The drycleaners was run by a Maltese couple, Andrea and Tumas Galasso. My wife and I got to know them well. A few years ago the Galassos closed up. There was no explanation for why they had closed, no notice on the door regretting the inconvenience to customers, nothing to reassure us that the business was to open again soon. The premises that had been the drycleaners for all those years remained abandoned for a very long time, junk mail and unpaid bills piling up inside the front door.

I live with my daughter. She's thirty-eight. She came to stay with me when her marriage broke up. It was to be for a week or two, until she sorted herself out. That was five years ago. I was in Venice during this last Australian winter and came home to an empty refrigerator. I don't know why Clare doesn't buy food, she is a very successful designer and has plenty of money, so it's not that. When I ask her why she doesn't buy food, she says she does. But she doesn't. Where is it? I took a taxi from the airport and I walked into my house and there was no milk in the refrigerator. I was exhausted from the interminable flight from Venice and I probably said something harsh to her. Clare cries more readily even than her mother used to. I said I was sorry, and so she cried some more. 'Oh, that's all right, Dad. I know you didn't mean it.' I don't understand her.

Even with our enormous modern airliners, Venice is still a world away from Melbourne. You have to adjust. Venice and Melbourne are not on the same planet. No matter how fast our airliners go, or how comfortable and entertaining they become to ride in, Venice will never be any closer to Melbourne than it was at the time of the Doges. It was spring here and everything seemed very dry and barren to me. I'd come home to an empty refrigerator. That's what I remember. I couldn't even make myself a cup of tea. So two minutes after I got out of the taxi from the airport I was walking to the shops.

When I turned the corner by the bottle shop, I hadn't yet decided whether I was glad to be home or was regretting not staying on in Venice for another month or two. Or for a year or two. Or forever. Why not? I was passing the shop where the drycleaners had once been and was asking myself gloomily why I'd bothered to come home, when the delicious smell of pastry fresh from the oven hit me. For twenty years we'd walked past the Galassos' on our way to the shops and there was the smell of dry-cleaning chemicals. I stopped and stood looking in through the open door of the shop. It was new. I suppose I was smiling. It was such a lovely surprise. The woman behind the counter caught my eye and smiled back at me, as if it made her happy to see a stranger standing out in the street admiring her lovely shop. It was Saturday morning; the shop was full of customers and she was busy, so it was the briefest of acknowledgments that passed between us. But all the same her smile gave my spirits a lift and I went on along the street feeling glad I'd come home and hadn't stayed in Venice for the rest of my life.

Venice brings out the melancholy in me, inducing the overriding conviction that effort is pointless. Doesn't it do that to everybody? I walk around in that timeless city feeling like the untouchable Victor Maskell. Which I don't actually mind all that much. I've always enjoyed indulging my gloom. Don't ask me why. It's probably my father's side of the family that does it, the dour Scottish influence, so I've been told. I've never visited Scotland. As I searched the aisles of the supermarket that dry spring morning, my gloom had vanished and I felt as if I'd been welcomed home by the smile of the beautiful and rather exotic-looking woman in the new pastry shop. While I was trying to remember which aisle things were in at the supermarket I was thinking about the woman's lovely smile and I probably had a look of secretive pleasure on my face, as if I knew something no one else knew; the kind of look that infuriates me when I see it on someone else's face.

Sweet pastries were not part of our regular diet, but on my way back from the supermarket I went into the pastry shop. I had to wait quite some time to be served. I didn't mind waiting. As well as the woman behind the counter there was a man in his late forties and a little girl of no more than five or six years of age. The man and the girl were bringing trays of pastries in from the kitchen at the back of the shop, the man encouraging the girl and pausing every now and then to serve a customer. The mood among the customers was unusually good-humoured. There was none of the regular Saturday morning impatience, no one trying to get served before their turn. Nothing like that. As I stood there enjoying the pastry smells and the friendliness of the place, I felt as if I'd stepped into a generous little haven of old-fashioned goodwill. This, I decided, was due to the family that was running the shop, something to do with the sane modesty of their contentment, but more than anything it was due to the manner and style of the woman.

When my turn came to be served I asked her for half a dozen sesame biscuits. I watched her select the biscuits with the crocodile tongs. Separately and without hurry, she placed each biscuit in the paper bag in her other hand, her grave manner implying that this simple act of serving me deserved all her care. She was in her early forties, perhaps forty-three or -four. She was dark and very beautiful, North African probably. But what impressed me even more than her physical beauty was her self-possession. I was reminded of the refined courtesy once regularly encountered among the Spanish, particularly among the Madrileños, a reserved respect that speaks of a belief in the dignity of humanity; a quality rarely encountered in Madrid these days, and then only among the elderly. It was this woman's fine sense of courtesy to which the customers in her shop were responding. When she handed me the bag of sesame biscuits I thanked her and she smiled. Before she turned away I saw a sadness in the depths of her dark brown eyes, a hint of some ancient buried sorrow there. And on my way home I began to wonder about her story.

When I was telling Clare about the pastry shop later I said something like, 'There's a kind of innocence about those people, don't you think?' Clare was sitting at the kitchen table reading the newspaper and eating a third sesame biscuit, taking a little bite from the biscuit and looking at it, then dipping it into her coffee. She had been into the pastry shop several times while I was away, she told me, but had seen nothing especially interesting about it or the people who were running it. 'He's a schoolteacher,' she said, as if this meant they couldn't possibly be interesting, and went on reading her paper. I added some thought or other about the possibility of a simple love story between them, this Aussie bloke and his exotic bride. Clare didn't look up from her paper, but said with that quiet conviction of hers, 'Love's never simple. *You* know that, Dad.' She was right of course. I *did* know it. Only too well. So did she.

A week or so later I saw the man from the pastry shop in the library. He was with his little girl. Over the following weeks I saw him at the library several times. He was sometimes alone, sitting at one of the tables hunched over a book. There were usually children running around dropping things and making a noise, and I was impressed by the way nothing seemed to distract him from his reading. He read the way young people read, lost to the world around him. Surely, I said to myself—defending my opinion against Clare's cynicism—surely there is a kind of innocence in the way this man reads? I tried to get a look at the books he was reading but could never quite make out a title. I greeted him on a couple of occasions. But he just gave me a very cool nod. I thought he hadn't recognised me. He had big hands, the veins prominent. Beautiful hands they were, the hands of a capable man. He seemed more like an artisan than a teacher to me; not a workman but a craftsman of some kind. Perhaps a woodworker. A musical-instrument maker would not have surprised me. I could imagine the harpsichord his hands might lovingly fashion for his beautiful wife.

When he closed his book and got up, he was tall and a little stooped. I watched him going out of the library, his books under his arm, his gaze on the ground ahead of him, and I wondered what had brought him together with his darkly exotic wife.

One warm Sunday afternoon in October, when the weather was more like summer than spring, I met him at our open-air public baths. For several lengths of the pool I'd been aware of another swimmer keeping pace with me in the next lane, doing the crawl as I was, arms lifting and driving down as my arms lifted in turn and drove down into the water. I completed my twenty lengths and stood up at the shallow end. I was resting my back against the edge of the pool and taking my goggles off when the man who'd been swimming in the lane beside me also stood up. I saw at once it was the man from the pastry shop. I wasn't going to say anything, as he'd seemed quite determined not to recognise me. So I was surprised when he said g'day and asked me if I was a regular swimmer. I said I was hoping to become one. I was glad he was being friendly but I did wonder what had changed his mind about me.

That's how John Patterner and I met. Side-by-side swimmers. After our swim he invited me to have a coffee with him in the pool café. While we drank our coffee we watched his daughter having her swimming lesson with two of her friends from her prep class. She kept calling out to him, 'Watch me, Daddy!' and he kept calling back, 'I *am* watching you, darling.' I said, 'She's very beautiful.' His eyes shone with his pride and love and I remembered how Clare and I had been when she was that age, how infinitely close we had been in those days, how filled with emotion and love and delicacy our friendship had been. And I saw all this again in John Patterner and his daughter. Her name, he told me, was Houria. When he introduced her she looked at me gravely, and I saw she had her mother's eyes. I don't remember what John and I talked about that day, but I do remember that the coffee, in its cardboard cups, had somehow managed to become flavoured with the taste of the pool water. Two weeks later I saw him at the library on his own and suggested we have a coffee at the Paradiso. He seemed pleased to see me.

After that we met for coffee every week or two at the Paradiso. Slowly at first, hesitantly, little by little, he began to tell me their story. The story of himself and his wife, Sabiha, the beautiful woman from Tunisia whom he had married in Paris when he was a young man and she was little more than a girl. And the beautiful and terrible story of their little daughter Houria. They lived now in the two or three rooms above the pastry shop. There couldn't have been a lot of space for them up there. Their family kitchen was the kitchen on the ground floor behind the shop where Sabiha made her delicious pastries. You could see the kitchen from the street. When I walked past late at night, taking Clare's kelpie, Stubby, for a last walk for the day, the light in the pastry shop kitchen was usually on.

From the day we'd had our pool-flavoured coffee together at the baths, I had detected his need to talk.

But he was a modest and very private man and it took me some time to convince him that his story interested me. Time and again he said to me, 'I hope I'm not boring you,' and laughed. It was a laugh that implied all kinds of reservations and uncertainties. This laugh of his made me anxious. I was afraid he might decide he'd revealed too much and say no more. But I was the perfect listener for him. I told him so. I was the best listener he'd ever had or was ever likely to have.

My last novel was always going to be my last novel. I'd had enough. 'That's it,' I said to Clare when I finished the last one. 'No more novels.' She asked me what I would do. I said, 'Retire. People retire. They travel and enjoy themselves and sleep in in the mornings.' She looked at me sceptically and said, 'And will you play bowls, Dad?' I'm her father and she's entitled to these little witticisms. I was so sure that book was my last I had called it *The Farewell*. I thought this was a pretty direct hint for reviewers and interviewers, who are always on the lookout for metaphor and meaning in what we do. I waited for the first interviewer to ask me, 'So, is this your last book then?' I was ready to say, 'Yes, it is.' Simple as that, and have done with it. But no one asked. They asked instead, 'Is it autobiographical?' I quoted Lucian Freud: *Everything is autobiographical and everything is a portrait.* The trouble with this was they took Freud's radiant little metaphor literally. So I went to Venice to enjoy my solitary gloom for a month or two. When I got home I realised I didn't know *how* to do nothing. During my life I had acquired no skills for not working and I soon found that not writing a book was harder than writing one was. How to stop? It was a problem. For a while I concealed my panic by doing things like going to the National Gallery in the middle of the morning during the week. It was pretty demoralising. The place was haunted by do-nothings like myself. I watched them, solitaries all of them. Then I met John Patterner, and suddenly I had something to do. I could listen to him telling me his story. More than anything, I wanted to know by what means sorrow had found its home in the eyes of his beautiful wife. That was what I listened for, to find that out.

If it was fine we took a table on the footpath under the plane trees outside Café Paradiso. John liked to smoke. 'I'm having a spell at the moment,' I told him when he insisted he was keeping me from my work. He sat a while, playing with the unlit cigarette between his fingers, then he straightened and began to tell me about himself, the cigarette unlit in his hand until he finished talking and we'd got up and were walking back to the shop together. Only then did he finally light his cigarette. I suppose he was trying to give them up.

He told me he was originally from a farming family somewhere up on the south coast of New South Wales. And Clare had been right, he was a schoolteacher these days, teaching English as a second language to boys and girls at the local secondary college, kids who for the most part came from homes where the language spoken was not English, which is about half the population around here. He spoke of his students with great respect, but I had the feeling he was not content in his job. He loved his wife and his daughter, but he also loved to lose himself in a book. I picked him for a passionate reader.

So, to his story then. I soon began to realise that it was, in its way, a confession. But isn't that what all stories are? Confessions? Aren't we compelled to tell our stories by our craving for absolution?

*D*om Pakos was in his narrow kitchen at the back of the café serving up his usual midweek offering of overcooked pieces of stringy beef from the abattoirs down the road, mixed with a couple of dozen boiled zucchinis and one or two spices, a dish he dignified with the name *sfougato*. Dom was a man of short stature with a nose that had been broken so often in his youth it looked as if it might have been trodden on by an elephant. Despite the hard bulk of his torso, Dom, at that time in his fiftieth year, was quick and confident in his movements. He was ladling the *sfougato* into bowls, the big saucepan set on the gas stove in front of him, the bowls laid out in a line on the marble bench to his right. Dom let go of the big iron ladle, which dropped into the saucepan, splashing the front of his white shirt with gravy, and he gave a short gasp, as if he had suddenly remembered an urgent appointment. And with that he collapsed onto the tiles.

The café, Chez Dom, was in the narrow street known in those days as rue des Esclaves, opposite Arnoul Fort's drapery and next door to André and Simone's stationers. If you turned left outside the café and walked past the stationers to the corner, then crossed the square and walked down the slope on the far side of the square for a hundred metres or so, you crossed the railway line and came to the source of the nose-tingling smell that pervaded the locality in those days: the great abattoirs of Vaugirard. For the locals, the distinctive smell of the slaughterhouse signified work and home. Some days the smell was sharper than others, and there were days when it was scarcely noticeable at all. Like the weather, the smell was always there, day and night, winter and summer. And, as with most things, familiarity had rendered it innocuous to the people who lived in the area. It was newcomers who wrinkled their noses.

The red checked curtains that Dom's wife Houria had strung across the lower half of the café's window were always drawn aside, allowing the daylight to enter the modest dining room and permitting the patrons to see who was coming and going on the street outside. Inside, a plain varnished timber bar stood across from the front door, and here Houria dealt with the bread and the wine and the coffee. The wooden trims around the window and door were painted green, and the walls were a calm faded old pink, rather like the underside of a freshly picked mushroom. Houria always had laundered red or green checked cloths spread over the six tables. And, depending on the time of year, there was usually a generous bunch of yellow daisies or russet chrysanthemums in a green ceramic jug at the end of the bar nearest the door. The only sign advertising the café was painted in a less than professional hand in red letters across the window above the door. At the back of the dining room, opposite the door and to the right of the bar, a bead curtain led through to the kitchen, where Dom Pakos did his work. Chez Dom's customers were from the immediate locality, many of them from the lower levels of management at the abattoirs. It was rare that a customer enjoying a midday meal in the little dining room did not know all the other diners. Strangers did not, as a rule, find their way to Chez Dom.

The café had been established twenty years earlier by Dom Pakos and his Tunisian wife, during the winter of 1946, in those chaotic days immediately after the war, when everyone was scrambling to find their feet. Dom Pakos had been a merchant seaman before the war and a ship's cook during the war and had found himself stranded in Paris when the peace was signed. It was meeting Houria, who was twenty-eight at the time, that decided Dom to give café life a try. He was always to claim afterwards, with a combination of surprise and pride, that it was Houria who had made sense of his life for him. They were both misfits the day they met, and each knew at once, with a fierce instinct, that they would cleave to the other for life. Neither ever required children from their union to make it complete. Dom and Houria completed each other.

Dom thought he was a great cook, but he was not even a middling to good one. The café thrived not on Dom's cooking but because he was an energetic and cheerful man who enjoyed the company of his customers. For Dom Pakos all people were pretty much equal; the good, the bad, the ugly and the beautiful, the old and the young, the infirm and the agile, they were all much of a muchness to Dom. He had sailed to the wildest ports of the world and seen everything of the human parade on offer. If you were even half-human, you felt Dom loved you. And if you were a stray dog or cat, he fed you scraps at the back door of his kitchen, where the defile of the cobbled laneway to this day arrives at its abrupt destination. Dom's tolerance had its limits, to be sure, but generally he was open to the world and indiscriminate in his affections. He was not a religious man, but neither was he averse to the company of those who were. Dom's gift was the gift of happiness. He had it from his mother. His ease and generosity of manner could strike a smile from the sourest soul.

It was a pity he died the way he did. Less than two minutes elapsed between Dom's collapse and Houria's return to the kitchen from the dining room. She pushed in through the bead curtain, some comment or other ready on her lips, expecting to find the bowls filled and ready for her to carry out to the waiting diners. She saw at once that Dom Pakos was dead. But Houria did not scream or react in any way as if she was witnessing something terrifying. She knelt on the old cracked tiles beside her husband and took his head gently in her hands. 'Dom!' she pleaded softly, as if she expected to wake him. She *knew* he was dead. Death is unmistakable. But she could not *believe* he was dead. It was the first time she had ever seen a grimace of discontent on her husband's face, and it was this she remembered afterwards.

When the surgeon conducted a post-mortem on Dom's corpse two days later at the hospital mortuary he found that an aneurism in the wall of Dom's abdominal aorta had burst. 'Dom scarcely suffered at all,' the surgeon reassured Houria when she went to the hospital to receive his report. The surgeon was tall and had drooping, sad eyes, as if he carried the weight of the world on his shoulders, and a small moustache beneath a large nose. He reminded Houria of the saviour of France's dignity, Le Général himself. She felt safe with him, and half believed, even as she sat in his office next door to the mortuary, where Dom's remains were lying, that the surgeon was going to tell her Dom was not dead after all.

'So he *is* dead, then?' she said, the tiny little hope she had kept alive until now winking and going out as she spoke it.

'Oh yes, Madame Pakos, your husband has passed to the other side, we can have no doubt of that.' The surgeon smiled and touched his small moustache, which had begun to remind her of Hitler's moustache. 'Your husband was a very fit man for his age, Madame Pakos.' The surgeon said this with such an air of comforting surprise she thought for a flickering instant he was telling her good news. 'You must have been taking very good care of him. When your man's aorta burst he exsanguinated in a matter of seconds.' The surgeon fell silent, deep in thought for a moment, then he suddenly went 'Whoosh!', making the sound through his pursed lips and at the same time throwing out his hands towards Houria across his desk in a bursting motion.

Houria jumped.

The surgeon regarded her closely, then announced in a grave voice, 'Once the gate was open, Madame Pakos, his big heart pumped his blood into his abdominal cavity at a terrifying rate as it struggled heroically to do its job. But to no avail.' He paused and drew breath, then leaned towards Houria, conspiratorial in his intensity. 'When the body's Canal Grande bursts its banks, the more powerful the heart the more abrupt the decease of the man.' He sat back. His expression indicated to Houria that something greatly to his satisfaction had just been expressed and she wondered if she should offer him some kind of congratulation. But the interview was over. The surgeon had other fish to fry.

•

Her interview with the surgeon signified for Houria the official end of twenty years of happiness with Dom Pakos. She was forty-seven and from now on she was to be alone. She thanked the surgeon and got up from her chair and went home to the café, which was very silent and very still. A lonely empty place without her Dom.

She sat on their bed in their room above the café and stared out the window at the upstairs windows of Arnoul Fort's shop across the street. She had not taken off her coat and she still clutched her bag in her lap with both hands, as if she was expecting to be called at any minute to get up and go somewhere urgently. But the minutes went by and no one called. The voices of children playing in the street beneath her window, cars hooting their horns, and every now and then a voice raised in greeting or farewell, the tight, sharp smell of the abattoirs. This was her home. She would have liked to reach back into the antique past and have her own grieving voice joined in lamentation with the voices of the women of the tribe. But all that was lost to her long ago. After staring out the window for quite a long time, Houria suddenly remembered that Dom was never coming home again. She began to sob helplessly, the wrenching pain of his loss like an iron band around her chest.

When she at last stopped weeping, she got off the bed and went downstairs and hung her coat in the alcove and put her bag on the bench in the kitchen. She made a glass of sweet mint tea, clasping it in both hands close under her nose to comfort herself with its familiar fragrance. She could see Dom's shadow through the bead curtain. He was standing by a table in the dining room looking out the window, gesturing with his cloth in his hand, talking to a customer. He was so real she could have reached out and touched him. 'Dom!' she whispered, the emptiness of despair in her now. 'Do you remember, you promised you would always love me and would never leave me?'

She closed the café and put a notice on the door, and for several days she went about aimlessly, picking up a saucepan then putting it down again, going to the back door and looking along the lane, not knowing what to do with herself. She cried a good deal and was not able to settle to anything. André's grey ghost of a dog, Tolstoy, a big old borzoi, came to the back door and pressed its head against her and gazed up at her with its great melancholy eyes. She caressed the head of the beautiful beast and it stood close and attentive while she told it of her sorrow, the faint sour animal smell of its damp pelt rising pleasantly to her nostrils.

One evening, when the children on the street had all gone home and the cars had ceased going by hooting their horns, she sat in the absorbed silence of the little sitting room they had made together under the stairs and she wrote a letter to her brother in El Djem. An unaccustomed longing for home and family had risen in her as the evening had come on, like the waters of a long-dry spring returning and bubbling to the surface.

Dearest Hakim, she wrote. *My man is dead and now I am alone. I have decided to come home, but first I must put our affairs in order here and sell the business if I can find a buyer for it. The freehold is not ours but André, our landlord, is a good man and will give me time to do the best I can for myself.*

She wrote some more about herself, then asked how everyone was at home, struggling all the while to form a clear picture in her mind of the place she had not seen since she left it with her mother as a girl of seventeen, thirty years earlier.

•

In El Djem a few days later Houria's brother, Hakim, came home from his day's work on the road gang. His wife took his jacket at the door and his two unmarried daughters, Sabiha and Zahira, stood beside her looking at him. Hakim's moustache was whitened from the dust of the road. His wife handed him his reading glasses and the letter and he stood angling the envelope to the light in the doorway, examining the writing. Hakim opened the envelope by running the disfigured nail of his thumb under the flap and he took out the single sheet of paper and unfolded it. He read his sister's letter aloud to them, reading slowly, pronouncing each word with care, lingering in a small silence at the end of each phrase. Hakim had lost his government job when he joined the Communist Party, but he had not lost his ideals or his self-respect. When he finished reading his sister's letter he looked up at his wife and daughters. 'Dom Pakos is dead,' he said, surveying their faces. He had never met his sister's husband. 'My sister is coming home.'

Hakim washed, then went out into the courtyard and sat on the bench under the pomegranate tree and smoked a cigarette in the last of the sun, the ruined amphitheatre visible above the wall of the courtyard, its ancient stones golden in the evening light. His wife brought him a glass of mint tea and he thanked her. She withdrew into the house to prepare the evening meal and he sat in the quiet alone, sipping his tea with little slurping noises and taking an occasional drag on his cigarette. He had read the despair in his sister's words and her pain had touched him. They had not seen each other for thirty years. He decided to send his youngest daughter, Sabiha, to Paris to keep Houria company and help her until Houria could sell her business and organise her move back to El Djem. He could not bear the thought of his sister grieving alone in the distant city of her exile. Even as this decision was forming in Hakim's mind, he was thinking how patterns form in families, repeating themselves like patterns in the weave of a carpet, from one generation to the next. He was thinking of Houria leaving on the bus with his mother all those years ago, he and his father and two brothers standing by as the bus pulled away from the post office, his sister's and his mother's faces pressed to the window, their hands waving. He was not yet a man then and had never understood why his mother had gone away, but had accepted it.

Sabiha came out of the house. She was the favourite of his two daughters. She stepped across to him and took her aunt's letter from the bench beside him where he had laid it. He watched her read it, seeing the eagerness in her. The Difficult One, he called her. Two daughters, and on this one destiny had placed its mark. Why this should be so, no one could know, but he had known from the day of her birth that she was not to be as his other daughter was. He and Sabiha understood each other in ways neither of them could explain. He knew Sabiha would manage Houria's grief, and would even manage the whole of Paris, and the world, if she was called upon to do so. What is it, he asked himself, looking with love at his beautiful daughter reading the letter, that makes some people so different from others that they cannot share a common fortune with them?

Sabiha sat on the narrow bench beside her father and leaned her head against his shoulder. 'Do you miss your sister?' she asked him. She was dreaming of her aunt Houria in Paris. She longed to meet her aunt and to know Paris.

Since Dom's death Houria had been worrying about her hair. Dom had liked her to keep her hair long, so that she could uncoil it in front of the dressing-table mirror at night and brush it out while he lay in bed admiring her. 'Long hair,' he told her, reaching his arm around her as she climbed naked into the bed beside him, 'is the true grace of a woman.' They slept naked. Winter and summer. As long as Dom was alive there had never been a chance of even talking about getting her hair cut short. But Houria had been secretly envying women with short hair for some time.

While no one, and certainly not Houria herself, would have come straight out and said that Dom's death was a blessing in disguise for Houria, his absence did nevertheless bring certain liberties into her days. There were even odd moments when she caught herself guiltily enjoying being without him, the thought teasing her that she was entering a new and interesting phase of her life. She had begun letting the grey grow out, but that was all, so far. It was a start. She was not standing still. She saw women of her own age, and even older, going about the streets with fashionably short grey hair and she envied them. It wasn't so much that they looked smarter, though they did, as that they seemed to her to be freer and more confident. As if they were living in a world of their own choosing. Their *own* world, that's what she envied these women. Something to do with a decision they had made. Their step was lighter, she noticed, than the step of older women like herself who still wore their hair long and had the grey disguised by the hairdresser every few weeks. Now that Dom was gone, she was impatient to join the short-haired women of Paris before it was too late to enjoy it. She was agonising now over whether Dom had been dead long enough yet for her to get her hair cut short without offering a slight to the dignity of his memory. If she were to suddenly appear on the street and in the café with short hair, mightn't it seem to everyone that she was *glad* to be rid of him? Mightn't it even seem like that to herself? This possibility was all that was holding her back.

She was standing in the doorway between the kitchen and the dining room, holding the bead curtain aside and watching Sabiha lay the tables. Sabiha was wearing a pretty blue and white dress with a belted waist. Her long dark hair was tied back with a blue ribbon. When Sabiha straightened and turned around, Houria said, 'How do you think I'd look with short hair, darling?'

Sabiha considered her aunt, holding the bunch of knives and forks and the cloth in her hands, seeing a woman nearing fifty, her thick coil of hair growing out at the roots into a strong iron grey. 'Really short? Or just shorter?' she asked. Houria had a broad, handsome face, her hair pinned in a double coil and sitting like a cowpat on top of her head. It looked very unnatural and heavy. And it made her aunt look like an old woman. Like a woman who had given up trying, or who was maybe trying too hard. When Houria had complained to her of getting old, Sabiha told her, 'You don't seem old to me. You seem really young for someone your age.' Houria had laughed and hugged her.

'No, *really* short,' Houria said, reaching her hands up and pushing at the heavy cowpat with her fingers, dusting her hair with flour—for she was in the middle of making a batch of filo. 'Down to an inch or two.' She held up her hand, thumb and forefinger indicating the length of hair she was aiming for. 'Two, maybe three at the most. What do you think? Tell me the truth.' She was longing to get out from under her hair. If Sabiha approved, she would step into the hairdressers this afternoon and have it done. Sabiha herself had beautiful hair, long and glossy and black as . . . well, *very* black. It would be a terrible pity if Sabiha were to cut her hair short. But that was not the point. Sabiha was twenty-one and would soon have to find herself a husband and start a family. At Sabiha's age, long hair was as much a necessity of life for a woman as a moustache was for any half-decent sort of man. There was a time for everything.

Sabiha smiled. Her aunt stood before her in her enormous blue apron and those heavy black shoes she always wore. Houria was not a beautiful woman. In fact she was short and fat. She was a lovely woman. But she was not beautiful. Those vast breasts and her strong arms and sturdy legs could not be called beautiful. A good and capable woman she was, to be sure, and kind and generous. All those things. She was surprised now by her aunt's vanity. Sabiha's own mother was not vain. Or at least Sabiha had never noticed her mother being vain, not about her appearance at any rate. Her mother was delicate, thoughtful and intensely proud of her husband, but she was not vain. Sabiha tried to think of her mother with short hair but couldn't imagine it. Houria was very different from her mother. Sabiha's mother *was* beautiful. She was sad and beautiful and she had wept when Sabiha left on the bus from outside the post office. Her father had definitely not married his sister's look-alike. It amused Sabiha to see this anxiety in Houria about her appearance. 'Why don't you just go and get it cut,' she said. 'If you don't like it, you can let it grow again.'

Houria patted her hair. 'Do you really think I should?' She knew in her heart that to cut her hair short now would be a kind of divorce from Dom. She wanted a divorce from him, was that it? She wanted a divorce from their past. *That* was it. To hope for something good in her future, that was what she wanted now. To set out again. With his death, if she was not to begin living in the past, divorce from the old days with Dom was a necessity. It was very unexpected and she did not quite know what to make of herself for thinking in this way. Was it good or bad? She was not sure. But it excited her and she could not help secretly admiring herself for it. She understood there was a kind of courage in it.

'It will grow again,' Sabiha said lightly, setting down the knives and forks again on the red checked cloths. 'Just get it cut if you want to. *I* would.'

'Would you really?' This wasn't the answer Houria had been hoping for. She wanted enthusiasm from her niece. She said glumly, 'Dom liked it long.'

Sabiha paused again and they stood looking at each other across the small dining room.

Sabiha wanted to say, Listen, Dom's dead. Okay? So just get your hair cut if you want to. What's the difference? She smiled and said nothing. She had never met Dom of course. And there was evidently a complication she did not understand. People were funny. She loved her aunt and didn't want to say anything that might offend her.

Houria lifted her shoulders. 'I just don't know what to do!'

•

The very first evening Sabiha arrived in Paris, they were standing in the back room upstairs that Houria had prepared for her. It was a sweet little room, under the sloping roof, intimate, safe and homely. A bed with a flowered cover and a hard-backed chair beside the bed, an old black trunk from Dom's seafaring days pushed up under the slope of the roof to keep her clothes in. A pot of some lovely fragrant spice mixture on the deep windowsill, like a blessing on the air.

Sabiha felt she was wanted. Houria apologised for the lack of a mirror.

'I'll get you a mirror, darling, as soon as I have a minute.' She asked her then if there was something special she wanted to do in Paris.

Sabiha said, 'I've imagined going up the Eiffel Tower and seeing the whole of Paris laid out below me.'

Houria leaned and pointed through the single-paned window above the bed. 'See that red light? Way over to the north of us there?' Sabiha bent to look and their heads touched. 'That's the light on the top of the Eiffel Tower.' They leaned there together, looking out the narrow window into the glowing sky above the great city.

Sabiha said, 'It's so beautiful.' And it was, for there is no more beautiful sight in the whole world than the rooftops of Paris at night.

'We'll go together,' Houria said. 'I've never done it. Dom wasn't one for the sights.' Houria kissed Sabiha's cheek, then straightened and said, 'I've changed my mind about selling the business and going home to El Djem. El Djem's no longer my home.' They looked at each other. 'Yes. I was panicking when I wrote to your father. Dom's death was such a shock. I didn't know what I was doing. I didn't know what I was saying or thinking or anything.' She took Sabiha's hand and held it and led her downstairs and into the kitchen, where she set about making hot chocolate for them both. 'The minute I stopped and faced the reality of going back to Tunisia, I knew *this* was my real home. Paris is where I'll die.'

'Don't say that. You're never going to die.'

Sabiha was secretly thrilled. She had already decided not to go home unless she was absolutely forced to.

'This is where my memories are,' Houria said, looking around the kitchen at the worn pots and pans and the crocks and piles of bowls and old brown *pichets* and wine bottles and all the paraphernalia she and Dom had gathered together over the years. 'If I went back now, what I'd have would be just those old threadbare childhood memories. I'd be sitting with the old women being a widow, listening to them gossiping about lives and times I know nothing about. What could I say to them? If I went back now, I'd be more alone than I am here. I'd just be waiting to die. Well I'm not ready for that. Not yet.'

Sabiha said. 'You're still young, Aunty.'

Houria put her arms around Sabiha and drew her close. 'You smell wonderful. I'm going to keep you.'

•

Sabiha went on laying the tables.

'Get your hair cut this afternoon,' she said definitely. She liked to see all the knives and forks and the jugs of water and the glasses sitting exactly in their correct places before the men started arriving for their midday meal. She looked around at her handiwork with pride, then back over at Houria.

'I'll come with you to the hairdressers and watch. I'll hold your hand.'

Both women laughed.

Houria said, 'What would I do without you?'

*H*ouria had a far subtler understanding of spices than Dom, which was why her cooking was of another order altogether than his had been. Her secret had been well kept all those years. Her light hidden under a bushel. A necessary modesty in a woman. Now she brought her secrets out and displayed them, and it wasn't long before the immigrant working men of the district heard about Chez Dom and began to come to the café for their midday meal. With Houria cooking and Sabiha waiting on the tables, the men could speak their Tunisian dialect, and the spicy cooking smells in the café were the smells of home. For an hour in the middle of their working day the men might almost have been with their own wives and daughters. In Chez Dom it was possible to forget the smell of the slaughterhouse. The young men smiled shyly at Sabiha and were gracious in their manners. The older men followed her with their eyes and thought of their own daughters and were moved by the grace of this young woman from home.

Within a year of the death of Dom Pakos the customers at the café were exclusively North African workmen. There were a few among them who had also managed to start their own small businesses. Chez Dom became their meeting place. Some of them drank wine but many of them did not, so on the whole it was cheaper for Houria to run the café than it had been when all their customers had drunk a good many glasses of wine with their midday meal. As well as this, Houria expanded the business. Her sweet pastries were rapidly becoming famous. She sold them through her friend Sonja at the market and took orders from local shops and businesses. When she wasn't busy preparing the lunch, Houria was shopping for supplies or cooking sweet pastries. The pastries were a profitable sideline and Sabiha was her willing apprentice in the enterprise. The two of them were always laughing and singing as they worked together in the kitchen of Chez Dom.

'I will teach you everything,' Houria told her. 'For a woman to understand the art of spices is as important as it is for her to understand the arts of love. With these accomplishments she will never lose her man, even when she loses her youth and her looks. I promise you!' Sabiha blushed and Houria laughed and kissed her. 'One day your man will come into your life and you will know him at once. That is how it is. It was like that for Dom and me. It has always been the way of all true love.'

With short hair Houria looked more confident than she ever had before. It was her manner as much as anything. After she had her hair cut she became the dignified *patronne* of the 'house' and was no longer just Dom Pakos's widow carrying on the business as best she could. Now she was her own woman. The position grew on her. She adopted it. She became *someone*. Something in Houria was completed by the death of her husband. Something of herself was released. It took time for her to acknowledge this to herself. But it was true. After Dom's death she began to have ideas and to put her ideas into practice. And her ideas worked. She was successful. She had not expected any of this and was excited by her success.

Now that the heavy cowpat was gone, Houria's smile was broader and more generous, and she walked with that lighter step she had envied in other women, catching herself being more happy than she had ever been when her beloved Dom was alive, and needing to remind herself from time to time that her man's death must be memorialised with dignity and gratitude in her daily life. Dom had not left *nothing* behind him, after all. It was on the modest foundation of what he had left behind him that she and Sabiha had built their new business. It was different. *Life* was different without him. But Dom was still around. At night he was with her. When she needed him, he *found* her. Dom still had his place in her life. But gradually, day by day, Dom's influence was becoming subordinate to her realities and she spoke of him less and less often to Sabiha. She never visited his grave. That was not how she wished to remember him.

The workmen who came to eat at the café, Tunisian men who had once been her own people in the distant past, knew nothing of Dom, but she knew. She still slept in their bed at night, didn't she? And she still talked to him, and made love with him, giving him pleasure and taking her pleasure with him. And while Sabiha slept and dreamed her dreams in the back room with its single-pane window looking out onto the laneway, a distant glimpse of the light winking on the top of a building behind the Montparnasse railway station—which had nothing at all to do with the Eiffel Tower—Houria was still Dom's princess in the arts of love.

They were happy, these two women. As happy as they could be. It was true, there were times when Houria missed Dom with a sudden chill gust of fear and a sense of helpless loss, as if he called to her from the void. And there were moments when she felt guilty about his death, as if she had lost him through her own neglect. But on the whole she was content that he was gone and she would not have wished him back if she had been given the chance to make such a wish. She had her new life. Her own expanding life. And she had her brother's beautiful daughter by her side.

'You are the daughter I never had,' she told Sabiha.

'Are you terribly lonely, Aunty?' Sabiha asked her. The two of them were cuddled up on the green couch in the little sitting room under the stairs, both of them tired from their long day, the blue and yellow flames of the gas fire murmuring comfortingly.

'I've got *you*,' Houria said, kissing Sabiha's cheek. 'How could I be lonely?' She loved the soft feel of Sabiha's cheeks against her lips. 'You would have loved my Dom, and he would have loved you. You would have been his daughter too.'

'Did you never want a child?' Sabiha asked her shyly. She was curious about Houria's childlessness, for secretly Sabiha believed herself destined to be a mother and knew she would never be whole as a woman

41

until she held her own child to her breasts. It was not a man she dreamed of, but a child. She could not imagine a contentment such as Houria's without a child. Sabiha's secret child was a comfort to her, it was a warmth, a presence; deep within her, it waited patiently for the moment of its birth. She was sure of it. The child had been there since she was a little girl. The child *was* herself, this inner, secret child of hers. She had spoken of it to no one, not even to her sister Zahira. One day she would have the child with her, and on that day she would become a woman.

'No, darling. Dom and I were enough for each other. We were both wanderers in this world until the day we met. And from that day we were home for each other.' She stroked Sabiha's hair, André's dog barking at the cat in the back lane, the fire hissing and burping. 'But you will have children,' Houria said. 'And you will love them. And they will love you.' Sabiha snuggled closer and closed her eyes. She loved her aunt's smell, her touch, her motherly intimacy; Houria's smell was so very different to her mother's. It was not a brood of children she wanted but was just one child. Her child. There *was* only one. She knew it without knowing how she knew it.

When Sabiha asked Houria why she and her own mother had originally left Tunisia and come to France,

Houria said, 'Your grandmother needed medical treatment. It wasn't available in Tunisia at that time.' She was silent then. 'That was her official reason for going. My mother's life was hard. She was not like your other grandmother. My mother was a restless woman. She was always looking for something she never found. She was never happy. She couldn't find the happiness she was looking for. It's like that for some people. That's all there is to it. It's not a great mystery. Some people are discontented and some people are not.'

As a child Sabiha had been close to her grandmother on her mother's side, but her grandmother on her father's side, Houria's mother, had never been spoken of in the family. No one had ever said 'your grandmother' to her before this and meant her *other* grandmother. She would have liked to know more, but felt that Houria did not wish to talk about her childhood alone in Paris with her discontented mother. She said to Houria, 'Do you think *I'm* discontented?'

Houria laughed. 'You? No, darling. You're as contented as a kitten. Life suits you. You're like me.'

But although she loved her aunt Houria, Sabiha knew in her heart she was not like her. She feared to be discontented. How did you keep such feelings from your mind if they came to you?

•

Sabiha never spoke of going home to El Djem. She wrote a letter to her mother every week, giving her mother the news in detail, and reassuring her that she was happy and in good health and would come home for a holiday soon. Sabiha knew her father understood that she was never coming home. Perhaps not even for a holiday. How was she to find the time? Her life was going on without them. After little more than a year in Paris she was already not the person she had been when she was living at home in El Djem. She knew her father accepted this. Her father didn't need reassuring. He didn't need explanations from her. He knew that people go away and never return. His own mother had done so. And she herself was now moving away from her past at such a speed she could sometimes scarcely recall her old life. She didn't have the time to think about it. She was going to the market on her own these days, buying the spices Houria required, being initiated by Houria into the mysteries of mixing spices and many other things. She loved her new life with her aunt Houria in Paris. It was too exciting to think of home with regret. Travelling alone on the *métro*, being a young woman walking along the streets of Paris with all the other people, Houria trusting her and making sure she always had money in her purse. This was her life now. It was a real life. Not the waiting life she had lived at home.

She lay in her bed at night under the sloping roof, looking at the distant light winking in the sky, and she repeated the astonishing claim to herself again and again: 'I am a young woman living in Paris with my aunt.' It was a fact. A magical fact. There were a hundred, no, there were a thousand things she was going to do as soon as she had the free time. She was determined to see all the great sights of Paris and to miss nothing. She wanted to know everything.

It is true that there were also times when she would have liked to sit with her father under the pomegranate tree in the courtyard at evening and tell him everything she had seen, and to share with him some of the secret misgivings that stole into her heart at times. She never wrote to him, but sent him and Zahira her news through her regular letters to her mother. She was *too* close to her father to write to him. And he did not write to her either. If they were to write to each other they would write things that could not be shared with her mother and sister. They *knew*, she and her father. That was all they needed from each other. To know. A time would come when they would need more than this knowing from each other. Then they would ask. Then each would give to the other what was asked.

*I*t was a rainy summer afternoon, a year and a half
since Sabiha had come to live with her aunt. The
café was quiet, the dining room empty. The men had
finished their midday meal and gone back to work
an hour ago. The door to the street was open, a drift
of rain darkening the boards, the door creaking in
the breeze. Houria and Sabiha were in the kitchen
baking pastries and singing along to the music on the
radio. The breeze died, suddenly, and the rain came on
heavier. People in the street were ducking and hurrying
now, a young couple laughing and grabbing at each
other as they ran past the window.

Houria stopped singing and said over her shoulder,
'Someone came in.'

Sabiha looked out through the bead curtain. A
stranger was sitting at the table under the window to

the right of the door, the table where she and Houria regularly ate their own midday meal. The window looked directly onto rue des Esclaves. The stranger appeared settled and had evidently been sitting there for a minute or two already. He was holding a book open on the table in front of him, his fingers spread across the pages, but he wasn't reading. He was looking out at the squall and the people hurrying to get to shelter, some with umbrellas, others with their coats over their heads. He had taken his wet jacket off and hung it over the back of the chair opposite him. The jacket was a dark brown woollen weave with lighter tan leather patches on the elbows. Sabiha noticed that the stitching on the patch of the right sleeve had come adrift. It was the first thing she really noticed about him, and she would always remember it. He looked as if he was expecting someone to join him. He had fair hair and no moustache and was wearing blue jeans and a white open-necked shirt. On his feet he had brown elastic-sided boots. One boot crossed over the other under his chair.

The two women watched the man. His wet hair straggled over his shirt collar. He was tall. In his late twenties. His shoulders rounded with the way he was sitting forward over the table. He looked away from the street then and sat back and eased his shoulders, gazing about, examining the empty dining room, his eyes sliding over the bead curtain, his expression serious, self-contained, confident, as if he felt no unease at finding himself in a strange place. He reached across the table to his jacket and took a pair of glasses from the inside pocket, put them on and began to read his book.

Houria and Sabiha looked at each other.

Houria said, 'You'd better go and see what he wants.'

Sabiha pushed at a tray of biscuits. The tray was hot and she whipped her hand away and sucked her finger. She felt suddenly inarticulate.

'Go on!' Houria urged her gently, grinning.

Sabiha looked out through the curtain again. 'We're closed,' she said. 'He'll leave in a minute.'

'Chez Dom has never turned away a hungry traveller.' Houria said this as if it was a principle enshrined in the traditions of the café since the founding days of her beloved Dom Pakos. 'Go on!' She gave Sabiha a shove with her elbow. 'He's not going to bite you.'

Sabiha gave her a look then lifted aside the bead curtain and stepped out into the dining room. She walked across to the man. She was wearing her sandals and the man did not hear her crossing the wooden boards. She stood behind his right shoulder, waiting for him to lift his head from his book. The rain was thrashing down outside, the street deserted now. She should close the front door. She lifted a hand and pushed back a strand of loose hair.

At her movement the man turned and looked up at her. 'I'm sorry,' he said. 'I didn't see you there.' His French was correct but spoken as if each word was a separate shape that he had to force across the reluctance of his tongue. For a couple of seconds she did not realise he had spoken French, but imagined him to have spoken in an unfamiliar language.

His eyes were grey and reminded her of the eyes of André's borzoi, Tolstoy. This man has gazed into vast distances and witnessed strange sights, she thought. 'We're closed,' she said. 'We close at two o'clock.' She spoke slowly so he would understand her. She imagined him to have returned from a long journey lasting many years, so long ago that he had forgotten her and the café, only the most distant echo of his old life in his memory. She smiled at this gentle fantasy.

'The door was open,' he said.

'I leave the door open for fresh air after the men have gone.'

'Can I wait in here until the rain eases off?' His eyes remained on hers.

'Would you like something to eat while you wait?'

'Thank you,' he said. 'I was going to Chartres. I got on the wrong train. I got off at the meatworks and

walked up here.' He laughed and held up his book.
'I was reading.'

She asked him, 'Were you going to Chartres for a
visit, or to live there?'

'Henry Adams,' he said, holding the book for her to
see its cover. 'I was told I ought to read it before I went.'

She said, 'I'll see what we've got.'

'Thank you.'

She turned away and walked across and closed the
street door. As she walked back across the floor and
went into the kitchen she felt the stranger's eyes on her,
as if he shared her fantasy, and was trying to remember
where they had met all those years ago before he set
out on his travels.

Houria laughed at her and filled a bowl with left-
over *harira*. She put the bowl and two of the freshly
baked honey-dipped briouats on a tray. 'Here, take this
out to your friend.'

Sabiha said, 'Don't be silly! He's not my friend.'

•

The following day the stranger came into the café
while the midday meal was in full swing. Sabiha was
busy and didn't see him until she stopped at the table
by the window.

He looked up at her and smiled. 'Hi. I came back.'

She felt the blood coming up along her neck and into her cheeks. She said, 'Did you get on the wrong train again?'

'Today I got on the right train,' he said. 'What do you think? Was that a good idea?'

'I don't know what you mean.' But she did know what he meant and she was pleased. 'Will you still go to Chartres?'

They looked at each other. She didn't know what to say. She reached and straightened the tablecloth. 'There's what you had yesterday,' she said. 'Or there's fish balls.' She could not hold his gaze. She waited for him to give his order and looked over his head and out the window at the street. Old Arnoul Fort was standing in the doorway of his drapery shop across the road smoking a cigarette. He was watching her. Their eyes met and he waved. She lifted her hand in acknowledgment.

'I'll have the fish balls, thank you,' the man said.

She turned away to fetch his order.

He called after her, 'And can I have some wine?'

She turned back.

'Please,' he said.

'Red or white? We serve a half-litre or a litre.' She indicated the brown earthenware jug on the next table.

The two workmen at the table were watching. They both looked at the jug on their table.

'A half-litre, thank you. Red.'

She realised that every man in the dining room had been watching her and the stranger.

•

They were in the little sitting room under the stairs. Houria was ironing blouses and aprons and tablecloths. Sabiha was watching the television. It was a week since they had seen the stranger. They had not been talking about him when Sabiha suddenly said, 'I wonder if he'll ever come back again?'

Houria said, 'Yes, I wonder.'

The singer on the television sang into the microphone, her eyes closed. Sabiha watched the singer. She might have done with the conversation. It wasn't that she *wanted* to see the stranger again, she told herself, she just couldn't get him off her mind. When she woke up in the morning she lay in bed thinking about him. Not fine romantic thoughts, just *thinking*, pointlessly, stupidly, annoyingly. Seeing him sitting there at the table under the window reading his book. She wished she could forget him. She said, 'He just came in to get out of the rain the first time.'

Houria turned the apron over and ran the iron along the piping. 'Then he came back to see *you*.'

Sabiha made a scoffing noise and shifted on the couch. She looked up at her aunt. 'It's good to be just us, isn't it? It's the best thing.'

Houria said, 'Just us, yes,' and went on ironing. 'Yes, darling, it is very good.'

Sabiha watched the screen. She wished she hadn't said that. They *were* just themselves, weren't they? But she couldn't leave it at that. 'So, if he was coming to see me, why did he stop coming?' It wasn't a question. It was an attempt to have done with him.

Houria folded the apron and laid it on the ironed pile and looked at her niece.

Sabiha swung her feet off the couch and stood up. She went out to the kitchen and put the kettle on the gas. She put the mint leaves and lumps of brown sugar in the two glasses and stood waiting for the water to heat. Tolstoy stood in the open doorway watching her. A grey ghost in the pale light of the laneway. She went across and patted his head and said goodnight to him. Then she closed the door. She was angry. It was stupid. Why couldn't she just be happy and content, as she had been before the stranger came in? It *was* stupid. The whole thing. He was just a man, after all. The streets were full of them every day. What was so special about *him*? She watched the steam starting to come out of the spout of the kettle in little pouting curls. It was an old kettle. As battered and loved as her mother's kettle had been. He was a foreigner and a stranger. He could hardly speak French. And he had just been passing through. She hated him for disrupting everything. The wooden grip on the handle had split and the two halves had been bound neatly together with wire years ago, the wire worn to a smooth polish. She ran her fingers lightly over the wire, feeling the soft ripples against her skin. Dom's handiwork. Had the stranger really come back after that first day just to see her? She poured the water slowly into the glasses, breathing the fragrance of the fresh mint.

With a perfectly equal intensity of feeling, Sabiha wanted to forget about the stranger and to see him again. Her days in the café felt empty without his visits. As if something was missing now, where before he came everything had been perfectly in place. While she was serving lunch she found herself watching out for him, hoping to see him coming along the street from the direction of the railway station. The days were flat and uneventful without the disturbance of his visits. Every day now, by two o'clock in the afternoon, when she and Houria were sitting down to their own midday meal, she felt grumpy and discontented. It wasn't fair.

It was no good talking to Houria about it. She and Dom had decided to live together for the rest of their lives on the very first day they met. Anyway it wasn't about that. She didn't know what it was about. She didn't *want* to know. It would just have been good to see him come into the café and smile at her with his lovely calm grey eyes, as if everything was understood between them.

She placed the glasses of amber tea on saucers and put a sesame biscuit with each, then she picked them up and carried them into the sitting room. The sitting room smelled of Houria's ironing and the warmth of the gas fire. The television was still going. She loved her home here with her aunt. She loved it so much she felt the tears welling up. She didn't want anything to change. Was she like Houria's mother, her *other* grandmother, a discontented person? Was that who she took after? The thought terrified her. Did she have a choice to be who she wanted to be, or did she have to be the person fate had decided she would be?

Houria turned around from the ironing board and smiled to see the tears in her niece's eyes. 'Don't worry. He'll come back.'

Sabiha set the glasses down on the table in front of the couch. 'I don't care. I hope he *never* comes back.' She went up to Houria and put her arms around her and burst into tears. 'I don't know what's the matter with me!'

Houria held her close and stroked her hair and said, 'You have a good cry, darling. You'll feel better.'

Saturday morning, and Houria and Sabiha were at the kitchen bench preparing the evening meal— another of Houria's ideas for expanding the scope of the business, a Saturday evening for the men, a time for relaxing instead of the rush of their workday meals. The lamb had been in the oven since before dawn and the kitchen was filled with the delicious smell of its roasting flesh. Houria was preparing the chickens and Sabiha was chopping carrots, the stock simmering in the big boiler on the stove beside her, the narrow kitchen window to the back lane steamed up, old Tolstoy lifting his snout and howling to an ancestral memory of the steppes, or maybe to a bitch on heat up the road.

Houria paused and watched her niece chopping the carrots, and she thought once again how beautiful

Sabiha was and how deep and gentle was the friendship which had grown between them. How greatly her own life had been enriched by her brother's generous gift of his favourite daughter! She resumed pushing the warm spicy stuffing into the cavity of the chicken. The change had slipped over the happy simplicity of their lives like the change of a season, the moment when you turn and quietly close a door and retreat a little into yourself. She had watched Sabiha falling in love and not knowing she was falling in love. Now she watched her dealing with the stranger's absence, her struggle to forget him and to be content again. Houria knew that what she was witnessing was Sabiha's struggle not to believe in her heart that this man had wilfully disappointed her or, in some obscure and unaccountable way, betrayed her, the deep irrationality of her feelings troubling her and putting a cloud over her days. That was Sabiha's torment, to know one thing and to passionately believe another. Houria herself had known this blank enmity of time before she met Dom, the interminable passage of the hours, the hope of each day rising then failing, the inability to reason it all away. For what is there in life, she asked herself as she rammed the stuffing into the cold carcass of the bird, that is more sublime than the finding of a mate?

She knew that Dom, in his new life on the other side, agreed with her.

She looked at the six prepared carcasses ranged on the bench and hoped she wasn't overdoing things. What if none of the men turned up tonight? Some of the midday regulars wouldn't be able to afford an evening meal, and others just wouldn't be bothered to come. Saturday evening was a risk. Everything was a risk. She took up the first chicken and rammed the steel spit through it. She felt for Sabiha and prayed the stranger would return for her, but in her heart she feared they had probably seen the last of him. Her impression had been of a style of man who could be trusted, a calm man, without great disturbing ambitions, a man who might become a reliable husband and father. A man, in other words, whose life waited to be completed by a good woman and children. And wasn't he also strong and healthy and not *too* good-looking? Such a man, with this certain sturdy plainness about him, would be faithful. Dom had been faithful. She cherished the memory of his faithfulness. She would cherish it till the end of her days. His gift. His manly homage to her. She sighed and wiped her eyes and grabbed another chicken and rammed it through with the big steel skewer and she went, 'Yai! Yai! Yai!'

Sabiha looked up quickly. 'What's the matter, Aunty?'

Houria said, 'My beautiful Dom just visited me.'

An hour later she lifted her head from her pastry and saw the stranger coming through the door into the empty dining room from the street. It was the sunlight falling across the boards as he opened the door that made her look up, his long shadow before him. She did not feel surprised. *So, here he is!* Such things are written. She watched him turn and close the door with care, as if he feared to wake the house. He was carrying a small khaki rucksack across one shoulder. The leather patch on the sleeve of his jacket had not been mended. So, there was no woman attending to his needs!

She turned to Sabiha and touched her arm.

Sabiha looked up, the big vegetable knife in her hand.

Houria raised her chin. 'See who's here.'

He stood at the bar, not looking around, but waiting, as if he knew himself watched.

Sabiha looked and said nothing.

Houria said softly, 'You could go and tell him we're closed, darling.'

Sabiha looked through the bead curtain at him. She was certain he would leave and would never come back ever again if she did not go out to him at once.

'Should I take my apron off?'

'Go and speak to him. Just the way you are.'

Sabiha went out through the curtain and walked across to the stranger.

He turned and saw her. 'Good morning,' he said.

'Good morning.' She stood before him.

'I had to go back to London to get my things,' he said.

The awkward earnestness of his manner made him seem like a boy. She wanted to laugh at him. And suddenly it was he, not she, who was vulnerable and ill at ease.

'I meant to come back straightaway but other things happened and I was delayed. I should have told you I was going to be away for a while.'

She shrugged. 'It's not my business what you do.'

He looked down at his boots, then up at her. 'I wondered if you'd like to go to Chartres for the day? I still haven't been. We can go there and back today. Just for an excursion. Just for that.' He stood frowning at her. 'If you don't want to go, it's okay. I just thought I'd call in and ask you. Just in case you did feel like going. That's all.'

'We're busy today,' she said. She was delighted to see how nervous he was.

'Yeah. Well, okay then. It's all right. I'm sorry. Another day maybe. I shouldn't have asked.'

She knew he was about to leave and she did not know how she could keep him there. Why could she not find it in herself to be generous and say to him, 'I'm glad you came back'? He would surely not return a second time. He was probably ten years older than her. If he were Tunisian he would be married by now. She wondered why he wasn't married.

He looked at her helplessly. 'I only came to Paris for an overnight stay last time. I was going to Chartres then back to London in the morning.'

'But you took the wrong train. I know. You told me.'

'Yes. I took the wrong train.' He held her gaze. 'I'm glad I did.' A little light of defiance was in his grey eyes now, as if he would not accept defeat.

'Will you stay longer this time?' she asked.

'It depends.' He gestured towards the door. 'I'm booked in for two nights at the pension across the square. Madame du Bartas.' He laughed. 'She says she knows you and your aunt.'

'You asked her about us?'

'I'm sorry. Was that wrong? She asked me why I was here. She seems nice enough. Her place is clean. And it's not expensive.'

'Nothing's expensive in Vaugirard,' she said. So it was true. He had come back to see her. 'What did Madame du Bartas tell you about us?'

The bead curtain rattled and they both turned. Houria was coming across the room, wiping her hands on her apron. 'Good morning, *monsieur*,' she said. 'It's nice to see you here in Chez Dom again. We don't do lunch on Saturdays but we can offer you coffee and a sweet pastry.' She walked right up to him and shook his hand. 'I'm Houria Pakos.' She turned to Sabiha. 'This is my niece, Sabiha.'

The stranger said how do you do as he shook Houria's hand. Sabiha did not offer him her hand. 'I'm John Patterner,' he said.

'Are you on holiday, Monsieur Patterner? We don't get many tourists out here. The abattoirs keep them away.' She laughed. 'There's not a lot to bring visitors to our little corner of Paris. It's not the Paris they're looking for.' Houria looked him up and down. 'So, where are you from, *monsieur*?'

'Australia,' he said. 'I'm from Australia.'

'Whereabouts in Australia? My husband sailed there many times when he was in the merchant navy.'

'New South Wales originally, but Melbourne these days,' John Patterner said.

'Dom visited the Dandenong mountains. Do you know them?'

John Patterner laughed. 'Of course! The Dandenongs, for sure. They're just hills really. They're not mountains.'

'So you know them?'

'Of course, yes. Everyone in Melbourne knows the Dandenongs.' He kept glancing at Sabiha.

Houria looked at him with satisfaction, her eyes bright. 'So,' she said with deliberation, putting her hands on her broad hips and taking a step back the more fully to see John Patterner. 'You know the Dandenongs and my Dom knew the Dandenongs.' She smiled and said, 'The Dandenongs,' as if it were an important code for some deeper meaning that had been established between herself and this stranger from the other side of the world. An understanding between grown-up people. 'And what is your profession, Monsieur Patterner, when you are in Melbourne?'

'I'm a high school teacher. But I grew up on a farm.' He looked quickly at Sabiha again. 'I can turn my hand to anything. I'm a pretty good carpenter. I've done the lot. Everything. You name it, I've had a go at it.'

'My Dom could turn his hand to anything too. And they've given you a holiday from teaching?'

'I've taken some leave without pay. I was going to Scotland. I've been staying in London for a couple of months. I thought I'd come over here and have a look at Chartres before I went north.'

'And when your leave is finished, then you will go back to Melbourne and start teaching again?'

He was looking at Sabiha. 'That was more or less the idea, Madame Pakos.' He turned back to Houria. 'I was just asking your niece if she'd like to come to Chartres with me today. But if you're busy, perhaps another day would be better.'

Houria said, 'I'll ask Adrienne, our landlord's daughter, to lend a hand. She sits in there watching the television all day. André will be glad to have her off his hands for a few hours.' She turned to Sabiha. 'Why don't you make some coffee?' She smiled at John Patterner and touched Sabiha's arm. 'Take good care of my niece today, Monsieur Patterner. She is all I have in the world. I shall expect her back before dark.'

*T*he summer grass was cool against Sabiha's bare feet. She sat in the broken shadows under the willow tree. The great old tree leaned far out over the river. It formed a canopy of restless shade on the water, the water glinting and delayed in its smooth run against the bank, the ducks looking about as they sailed upstream. John Patterner lay on his back behind her, his big hands clasped under his head. He was looking at her, his eyes half closed. She was watching the vivid green weeds trailing in the water, imagining them to be the long tails of exotic fish. She broke another piece from the remains of the baguette and crumbled the soft bread between her palms. She tossed the crumbs out onto the sparkling water. The two adult ducks with their five chicks paddled after the crumbs. Sabiha hugged her knees and watched the ducks feeding on her offering. The river's breath was cold, metallic in the shade of the tree, as if the water carried the approaching evening. She hugged her knees tighter to her chest.

John Patterner's voice came from behind her softly. 'I love you.'

She turned and looked at him. 'You mustn't keep saying that. You can't love someone you've known for less than a day.'

'I've known you forever.'

She smiled at the idea, knowing it carried its own mysterious truth for them. It *was* forever. This morning on the train was a faraway time. Those two people sitting beside each other in the carriage like awkward strangers this morning were not these two people lying under the willows by the river. And at the door of the cathedral, when he stopped her as they were about to enter and said solemnly, 'Through this portal is the way to eternal life.' Not yet certain of him, she asked, 'Are you religious?' His mother, he said, had been brought up Catholic, but had not bothered with religion after she met his father. 'And you?' he asked her. She told him proudly of her father's hopes for the people, and of his devout atheism. 'I've never been inside a mosque.'

'You're glowing in this light,' he said.

She lifted her head and pushed back her hair with both hands, and she closed her eyes and declaimed in her mother tongue, 'I am the colour of the sands of the desert at evening.'

He was awed by her, enchanted by the mysterious sound of her language. 'That's beautiful,' he said. 'What does it mean?'

She told him the meaning of the words. 'That is their meaning and it is *not* their meaning,' she said. 'Their meaning is in the Arabic only. It is not in the French. In French these words mean something else. Something less.' It was from her grandmother she had received these words, from her mother's mother. The opening line of an antique song. She felt his admiration like sunlight on her body and she wanted to sing for him, but she was too shy.

'I'll always love only you,' he said seriously.

She laughed at him. 'How do you know that? You might meet a beautiful woman one day who will seduce you.'

'Don't joke about it,' he said. He reached and gently pulled her down beside him.

She was unresisting and lay back on the grass with him. 'I'll sing my songs for you one day.'

He took her in his arms. 'I'll learn your language,' he said. 'So that I will understand them.'

She loved the feeling of his strong body against her.

'My language is too difficult for you. You will never understand it,' she said. 'It is better not to try.'

They were silent in each other's arms, the whispering of the breeze in the branches of willow overhead.

'There will never be anyone else, Sabiha,' he said. 'That's my pledge to you.'

She said nothing to his earnestness, his desire to impress her with his belief, his urgent need to acknowledge between them a binding commitment. She was thrilled to hear it on his lips. But it was too much. It was too soon. It weighed her down. She wanted to hear it and she didn't want to hear it. What she wanted was to laugh with him. To run and play and hide with him, the way children play and hide and tease each other. 'Your eyes are the colour of Tolstoy's eyes,' she said.

He laughed at this and took her hand in his and kissed her fingertips. 'So how do you know what colour Tolstoy's eyes were?'

'You can take a look for yourself later,' she said. 'He's our landlord's old wolfhound. His eyes have seen into vast distances, like yours. His ancestors hunted wolves on the steppes of Russia.' She kissed him quickly on the cheek and said, 'Is that one of the things you can turn your hand to, Monsieur Patterner—hunting wolves on the steppes of Australia?'

He bent his head to her and their lips met in a long, gentle kiss. Afterwards they lay side by side on the grass holding hands.

She removed her hand from his and raised herself on her elbow and looked down at him. 'You didn't tell me yet why you wanted to go to Scotland?' Would he still go? she wondered. Or had he really changed all his plans now?

He opened his eyes. The hanging willows moved in the breeze above her head, back and forth, like the emerald weed in the river. 'We could stay here forever,' he said. 'We could disappear from our old lives and live here together. Just you and me, till the end of our days.'

'Houria would be upset. She'd miss me.' She stroked his cheek. It was rough and unshaved. 'You didn't shave this morning before you came to see me,' she said, playfully reproving him.

'I was in a hurry. Do you mind?'

'I like it. Isn't there someone who'd be upset if you disappeared?'

He thought about it. 'My mother. Dad too, for sure. And I suppose my sister. And one particular friend. I don't think anyone else would notice.'

'You are so serious,' she said. 'So why did you leave your home and go so far away if they miss you? Why did you want to go to Scotland? You haven't told me anything yet.'

He laughed. How could he tell her of his need to get away from Australia? His feeling of being stifled by everything. His French wasn't good enough for it. His longing just to *be* somewhere else. How could he make sense of that for her? Taking himself halfway around the world. 'Everybody does it,' he said. 'It's what Australians do.' He had been getting away from himself as much as going to Scotland. She might think he was subject to sudden irrational changes of heart if he told her this. 'I've got a good friend who was born in Glasgow,' he said. 'Harold Robinson. Harold was the librarian at my school. He's an old man. Harold's always been an old man. Ever since I met him. He collects books on Scotland and lives in Melbourne these days. He's been retired for ages. He told me all about Scotland when I was a boy. We've been friends since I was thirteen. I wanted to see the place he came from.'

She ran her fingers lightly over his lips, then leaned down and brushed her own lips against his, then withdrew, teasing him. 'I wish we could just stay here all night. Not forever. Just for tonight. And watch the moon come up.' She touched his lips with her fingers, then his unshaved cheeks and his forehead, and ran her forefinger along the bridge of his nose. 'You've got a beautiful nose, John Patterner,' she said. 'It's strong and confident. Are you sure you're not one of us?'

He took her in his arms and kissed her.

There was a fluttering in her belly and she thought of the child waiting inside her. She gasped and, suddenly, she could not hold back her tears.

He drew away. 'What is it? What's wrong? What did I do? I'm sorry, Sabiha.'

She shook her head. 'It's not you. It's nothing.' She wiped at her tears. 'I'm just happy. I often cry. Mostly I don't know why I cry.' Was this man to be the father of her child? Did her body know something already? She felt a sudden sharp fear that she would lose him. A shift of his desire, a failure of the mood between them, and he would be gone, off on his travelling, and they would never see each other again. She pulled him against her strongly and ran her hands along his flanks. 'You are so beautiful, John Patterner!' She kissed him hard on the mouth, then drew away, releasing him abruptly, abashed by her clumsiness.

He smiled and touched her cheek. 'You're crazy,' he said gently. 'I love you being crazy.'

'Am I? Do you?'

'I love you.' He kissed her lips. 'Come on! We'll miss the train,' he said. 'You'd better get your shoes on.

I promised your aunt I'd get you home before dark.'
He looked at his watch. 'We've got seven minutes to
get to the station.'

She wanted to be meek now, obedient and under
his command if that was what he wanted from her. She
sat up and put on her shoes. She wanted it to be real
between them, not just a dream.

He stood up and held out his hand and she took it
and he helped her up.

'We've got the rest of our lives,' he said.

They held hands and hurried across the bridge.
'What will we do?' she asked him. So they had made
their pledge to each other after all. It frightened her and
moved her all at once. 'I'm happy,' she said, hoping it
was true, and she kissed him on the cheek.

'We'll have a wonderful life,' he said. 'Whatever we
do. I just know we will. It doesn't matter what we do.'

They walked through the town and around the
bottom of the hill to the railway station; breaking into a
run, their laughter floating up the hill behind them.

•

As she saw them coming through the door of the café
Houria said to herself with satisfaction, John Patterner
is a man to be relied on. And that is how John came

to be there in Chez Dom for their first Saturday night, proving himself a useful man to have about the place, rearranging tables and chairs and serving coffee and wine and taking the initiative with this and that as he saw a need for it. He was at ease with the men, his manner polite and respectful, making them smile with his peculiar French. And Houria and Sabiha were glad to have his help, for more men turned up for the evening meal than the dining room of Chez Dom could comfortably accommodate. Houria had to send him next door to André's to borrow two folding tables and some extra chairs, leaving him to find a way to squeeze them all in somehow, which he did.

After the last customer had gone home and the three of them had finished cleaning up, they sat in the little sitting room under the stairs and drank coffee with a drop of brandy in it and laughed about the mad rush of the evening and how it had all gone so well, the three of them working together like a practised team. Houria counted the money and offered to pay John for his time. But he refused it and would not hear any more about it from her. She saw he was offended by the offer of the money and she was pleased. By the time John finally got up off the couch to return to Madame du Bartas's boarding house, it was after one o'clock in the morning. At the front door Houria squeezed his arm and told him to be sure to come back for his breakfast in the morning. 'But don't be too early,' she said.

She and Sabiha stood at the door and watched him walking down the deserted street until he reached the empty square. He turned under the light and looked back and waved, and they waved to him. Houria said, 'It doesn't seem right to be sending him off into the night on his own like this.'

When he'd gone they went back inside the café and closed the door. Houria turned to Sabiha and they hugged each other. 'He's a lovely man,' she said. 'It was good to have a man about the place again.' And then both of them shed a few tears, for they were overtired and rather excited. And anyway it was nice to have a cry. It had been a very long day.

There was just the one little thing clouding the perfection of all this for Sabiha. On the landing at the top of the stairs, after she'd said goodnight to Houria, she paused at the door of her bedroom and, with considerable concern in her voice, said, 'I just don't know what we're going to do.'

Houria smiled and told her, 'Don't try sorting out the rest of your life tonight, darling. You'll see, it'll all work out in the most unexpected ways.'

And so they went off to bed in their separate rooms and both of them lay awake thinking about everything for a very long time. Houria was the first to go to sleep—Sabiha heard her snoring through the door. Then Sabiha herself went to sleep. She dreamed she was at home in El Djem in her own bed, her sister Zahira sleeping in the bed next to her. She was comforted by the crack of light coming under the door just the way it used to when she was a little girl, knowing it signified that her dear father was sitting up late composing one of his pamphlets for the movement. She wanted to get up and go out to him and put her arms around his shoulders and kiss him on his unshaved cheek and tell him she was happy. But she couldn't move.

Two

A bitterly cold January morning, two and a half years after Sabiha and John had spent their day together in Chartres. Sabiha was holding the back door of the café open for John. It was still dark outside, the light from the kitchen spilling into the laneway. A blast of frigid air drove down the lane and Sabiha drew back, almost losing her grip on the door.

John leaned down and kissed her on the cheek as he went past, raising his voice against the wind. 'See you later, darling.' He stepped out into the lane, turning his head aside from the needles of sleet whipping against his cheeks. His overcoat collar was turned up and he was wearing a green woollen scarf around his neck and a black cap on his head, the shiny peak of the cap catching the light like a startled eye as he went by her. John had not shaved and he looked older, a man with cares and responsibilities that did not sit easily with him just at this moment. He bent forward and hurried across to the van, carrying the last tray of the day's orders, the white cloth lifting and flapping, pinned at two corners by his thumbs.

Sabiha watched him struggling to slide the tray into the back of the van. The runners he had made to take the trays were not perfectly square and there was always a bit of jiggling to be done to get the trays to slide in. He was forever promising to take the runners out and realign them. But he never did. His skill at carpentry, it had turned out, was more make-do than pretty good. He knocked things together and declared them near enough. His heart wasn't in it. It was all temporary for him. Not part of a life's work, but measures for the time being. He stood back and closed the van doors, turned and gave her a wave, then went around to the driver's side. He yanked the door open and climbed in. His tall frame was too big for the tiny cabin and he had to hunch himself up to fit in.

Crouched in the cab, John was evidently a man in some kind of diving bell about to descend into the solitary depths. His mother, had she been able to see him at this moment, would have laughed at him; her laughter fond, loving, good-natured, amused and pained by the lanky fool her boy had turned into.

'Look at yourself, John!' she would have shouted at him. As she often had. 'Look at yourself!' So he did, seeing himself through his mother's eyes more readily than through his own—and laughed, too, at the man he was, the man he had *become*. A puzzle not only to his mother but to himself as well. His mother had seen herself in him and encouraged him to travel, imagining the remedy might lie in seeing the world: 'Get out and see the world or you'll end up like your father, stuck here in the back blocks for the rest of your days.' His father grinned to hear her say such things. His father loved the farm. His father was a contented man and had no need of the great world; it was enough for Jim Patterner to have his thirty breeders and a good bull and to grow his crops of pumpkins and tomatoes on the narrow acres of the creek flats. They had been happy, the pair of them, giving each other a hard time for the fun of it, believing all sound friendships improve for a good rubbishing. She would have loved to see the world herself. It was she who had bought the cartons of old *National Geographics* from the Salvos' op shop in Moruya. When John was teaching in Melbourne she sent him cuttings from them, pictures of Patagonian glaciers and bird-eating spiders in the Brazilian jungle, just to encourage in her son the pursuit of the exotic. 'Off you go then!' she cried, delighted when he came home for Christmas and told them he was going to Scotland. Glasgow wasn't Patagonia, but it was a start. 'Don't you worry about me and your father. We'll be right as rain.'

This morning, before driving off to make his deliveries, John lit a cigarette then switched on the single headlamp of the van and looked along the faltering beam of weak yellow light, the black cobbles of the laneway glistening, the rain whipping across the beam. It was all beautiful and strange still, all of it, and he loved it in a quite painful way and wanted to hold it forever in his memory. It was sacred, to be sure, but even if he lived in this place for the rest of his life it would never be real. He could not *enter* the reality of it. It stood away from him, and he was not admitted to it. It was joy enough most times to be helping his wife and her aunt to run Chez Dom, making himself useful with the handy skills he'd learned as a boy on the farm, and even to find his anxieties subdued by the routine of it at times, but he was not getting on with his own life. His reading was falling behind and the new theories of education were passing him by. Events were going on without him. He would be thirty this year and a new generation was already coming up behind him at home and getting on with it. He could feel the deepening of his isolation, his absence, his drifting.

And at times it frightened him. His reality was waiting for him, his friends getting on with it without him. But how long would it wait? In Paris he would never be more than a transient. A man passing through. An accidental man. A man who got on the wrong train one day and fell in love. He cherished Chez Dom and his friendship with Houria, and he loved his wife, but Chez Dom and Paris were not his life. He often had the feeling he was living another man's story. One life, he kept reminding himself. You've only got one life, John Patterner. For God's sake don't let it slip through your fingers. André, Houria's landlord, was the only one he felt understood his predicament, and when they were fishing together at night on André's boat on the Seine he sometimes felt at liberty to confide his anxiety to the older man. And perhaps it was because André felt he'd let his own life slip through his fingers that there was this sympathy between the two of them.

John screwed himself around now, his cap pushing into the fabric of the roof, and he squinted back at the door of the café. Sabiha standing in the light waiting for him to get going, clutching her cardigan around her and watching to see him off. If only she would come home with him to Australia, his life would be perfect. Or near enough to perfect. There would still be the problem of the lack of children. He wanted children too, but, unlike Sabiha, he was relaxed about having them, confident their children would come when they were ready to come. Whenever he thought of their children, which was more often than Sabiha gave him credit for, John imagined them running around the playground of the school he'd been teaching at before he came to Europe. He couldn't imagine their children going to school in Paris. He had no images in his mind for schools in Paris. He didn't know what the children of Paris did from day to day. He didn't know their games, their slang, their secret signs. He had never been inside a school in Paris. He didn't want his children growing up thinking they were French. France was okay. He didn't have a problem with France or the French, but he didn't want his kids missing out on growing up Australian. He wanted his children to be like him. If they grew up in Paris they would not understand their father's love for Australia. Whenever he tried to explain this to Sabiha she got upset. It had reached a point recently where they couldn't talk to each other about children without one of them getting upset. For Sabiha it wasn't just children, it was *one* child, a daughter. 'Why not a son as well?' he asked her. John didn't care what sex their children were so long as they were healthy, happy Australian kids growing up in the sun, the way he had. He wanted to take them to the farm, and for them to know and love his mother and father and the country where he had grown up. He dreamed of showing them the fishing holes along the river, and the good swimming holes. The places where he and Kathy had swum when they were children. If his children grew up in France they would be strangers to him and to his country, and he couldn't bear the thought of that.

In her most recent letter his mother had asked him the question which he knew she had been wanting to ask ever since he'd called her that day and yelled down the phone at her, 'I just got married!'

'Oh, that's lovely, darling, that's really lovely! What's her name? She must be a treasure to have taken *you* on. Give her a cuddle from the pair of us.'

Now at last, almost two years on, she had brought herself to ask him the big question: *Is there any sign of a little one yet? Your father and I can't wait to be Granny and Grandad. I don't think your sister's ever going to meet a man good enough for her, is she? You know what I mean. So you're our only hope. How does that make you feel? It's a stupid question and I shouldn't ask it. But we do wonder, that's all. Neither of us is getting any younger. Your father wants to put a deposit on a unit in Moruya, but I'm not keen on the idea. It feels like planning our own funeral to me. We've had one of our best years since you left. The trout have come into the creek again and the eelers are coming by every night with their lamps and driving the dogs crazy. I shall hate to leave the old place when the time comes. Your father amazes me. He's more realistic than I am. You and I always were the dreamers, darling. I hope you're still dreaming. I know I am. Silly me.*

There was something about the tone of his mother's letter that made John wonder if everything was really going quite as well as she said it was. The idea of his mother and father living out the end of their days in an old people's unit in Moruya, the farm in the hands of strangers, depressed him.

He engaged first gear and let out the clutch. There was a high-pitched screech and the van moved off with a jolt. He was away. The smell of his cigarette and the warm pastries in the back of the van. He took a last quick look at Sabiha in the doorway, his hand raised.

Sabiha shut the back door against the cold and walked across the kitchen to the stove, the smell of the van's exhaust sharp in her nostrils. She was frozen. The oven was still warm from the morning's baking and she stood with her back to it, listening to the rattling of the van's unsteady old motorcycle engine receding down the lane. Then it was gone, suddenly, as John turned into rue des Esclaves. She had a moment to herself. The kitchen was quiet, the tapping of a loose windowpane against the timber frame. She closed her eyes and stood warming herself. Houria was singing in the bathroom. Houria had a big velvety contralto voice. She was singing a French song. Houria never sang the old songs of her people. She did not know the songs of her people as Sabiha knew them. They were not hers. She had not received them from her mother, that mysterious discontented woman who had been Sabiha's *other* grandmother. Houria sang for Dom. For the two of them. For the life they had made together in Paris. And sometimes she hummed a tune, not quite breaking into song, but humming to herself.

Sabiha was in the middle of washing up the pile of pastry trays and mixing equipment when Houria came into the kitchen and put the coffee on. Houria's spiky grey hair was standing on end, still wet from the bath, her plump cheeks rosy, her beautiful dark eyes bright with wellbeing. They had both been up for hours before her bath, baking the biscuits and sweet pastries for John to deliver in the little three-wheeler he had bought last winter, when the cold was keeping a lot of their customers away and the baking business had begun to go downhill. Orders had picked up once they had the van and customers no longer needed to come to the café to collect their pastries.

Sabiha kept her head down when Houria came in, scrubbing at the hard pastry residues on the trays in silence, going at it as if the job needed all her strength and concentration, burnishing corners that had retained their oven stains for years. Houria dried a couple of trays for her then poured their coffee. 'Come on,' she said. 'That can wait. Come and have your coffee.'

She carried the two bowls of coffee through the bead curtain into the dining room.

Sabiha straightened up and stood a moment at the sink, her hands at rest in the water, as if she might not follow Houria. Then she snatched up a tea towel and wiped her hands and went out through the curtain. John had set the big iron gas fire going an hour ago and the small dining room was cosy. They sat at their usual table, the sleet rattling against the window, beads of ice melting as they slid down the glass. Early risers hurrying by along the narrow street, heads bent against the weather.

Sabiha held the bowl of steaming coffee close to her lips with both hands, her elbows on the table. She was looking at the people going by on the street and feeling guilty about John out there in the terrible weather delivering the day's orders, making an effort to be cheerful with their customers and hating every minute of it. She was regretting having been quite so grim with him in the middle of the night. She longed for them to be close and loving. She felt Houria's gaze on her and turned from the window. 'We were awake half the night arguing about the same old thing,' she said, answering Houria's unasked question. 'It's not interesting.' She drank her coffee.

She had asked John that day in Chartres, holding his hand in hers, a girl then filled with astonishment and apprehension, *What will we do?* It was she who had foreseen this. She should have persisted that day. She should have stood her ground and insisted they make a real decision about their lives, instead of meekly accepting John's and Houria's reassurances that everything was sure to work out for the best. John must have known even then that he had no intention of staying in France for the rest of his life. Of course he knew! She blamed herself however. And these days she *did* stand her ground. Too firmly perhaps. Too inflexibly. She knew at times she was unfair to him. It was always he who had to give way in the end. She knew herself to be a changed woman, and was not always happy with the way she was these days. She had understood that strength and determination were needed from her if their marriage was to endure. She was wishing now that she had been more loving and gentle with him this morning before sending him off into the fierce weather in that ridiculous little van of his.

Houria said, 'If Dom had asked me to go to Australia with him I would have gone.' She snapped her fingers. 'Just like that.' She laughed. 'What an adventure that would have been.'

'I'd never see my father again if I went to Australia. Or you.'

Houria shrugged. 'We have to live the lives we choose.'

'My life is here.'

'And John's?' Houria asked gently. 'Is his life here, darling?'

'John's life is with me.'

Houria looked at Sabiha steadily. 'You've changed,' she said, kindly but a little sad.

Sabiha caught the sadness in her aunt's tone. 'We've all changed, I suppose,' she said. 'It's what happens, isn't it?' She looked out the window again. Old Arnoul Fort's light had come on upstairs, his shadow passing back and forth across the red curtain. His wife had been bedridden for years and he spent his time caring for her, their drapery shop neglected and dirty, the stock old and their custom fallen away. Sabiha sighed, aware suddenly of the sadness of all lives. She turned and reached across the table and took Houria's hands in her own.

Houria lifted Sabiha's hands to her lips and kissed her fingers. 'If you two settled down in Australia in your own home you'd probably have your little girl before you knew it.'

'This is my home,' Sabiha said. She withdrew her hands. Houria's words made her feel tight and resistant.

'Well, you can't live in that little room up there forever, can you?' Houria said reasonably. 'That's all I meant. It's not fair to either of you. How would you manage if a child came along right now? The three of you in that tiny space? There's no room for a child. And I can't let you have my room. It's still Dom's room.' She grinned. 'Hey! I'd come to visit you in Australia. You could meet me at the airport. Imagine it! Me arriving at the airport and you being there to meet me! It would be so exciting. You'd be a local. You could show me everything.'

But Sabiha was only half listening to Houria now. Why *didn't* her child come? What *was* blocking it? Was it really that there was no room for it here at Chez Dom? She couldn't believe that. She didn't want to believe it. They'd had all the tests and the doctors had told them they were both perfectly healthy. John's sperm count had been a little low on one of the results, but they said not to worry about it, it was temporary and probably due to his anxiety. John said he wasn't anxious. But they said you can't always tell when you're anxious. They offered more tests but she was sick of it. She had begun to feel as if her body no longer belonged to her. And every time they had sex they were both thinking about what day of the month it was and what her temperature was. John hated it as much as she did but he had been willing to go on with it for her sake. It was she who had called a halt.

She often recalled with wonder and sadness the night she and John made love for the first time. She believed at the time that she had conceived that night. She was certain her little girl had begun the mysterious journey of her life. She had lain awake beside John until dawn, unable to sleep for excitement, knowing her body had welcomed his seed, imagining the conception of new life taking place deep inside her. She had her own secret view of all this. She lay down with John that night a girl and rose from their bed in the morning a woman. In the morning she rejoiced that she was no longer a virgin girl. The first, and the greatest, disappointment of her new life in Paris was to discover two weeks later that she was not pregnant. Nothing had happened. Nothing had changed. She wept for a week and was inconsolable. The seed of her child still waited, distant, untouched, silent within her. John had not reached it. Their love had not been enough. Something was missing. Something vital and real but hidden from them. It drove her crazy trying to think what it was.

Ever since she was a little girl, Sabiha had believed the state of womanhood and the state of motherhood composed the same order of being. To be a woman was to be a mother. She could not now rid herself of this belief. She would not *try* to rid herself of it. What would she replace it with? It went deep. It was the bedrock of her being. Her sense of her worth, the meaning of her life, these sheltered within it. Without this belief her existence would be pointless. Until she became a mother, as a woman she was only marking time. Waiting for reality to begin. The past two years had been more difficult for her than either John or Houria understood. There was loneliness for her in knowing this. It was a loneliness she shared silently with her yet-to-be-conceived child, the dependable companion of her secret interior life.

Sabiha had been closer to her grandmother than she had been to her own mother, and had not doubted it when her grandmother whispered to her as she lay dying, 'I will always be with you.' These last words meant a great deal to Sabiha. They embodied a promise that she considered sacred, a promise that when she finally needed to call on her grandmother, her grandmother would be there to provide her with the strength to meet the great challenges of her life. Sabiha was not alone, but felt herself to be accompanied through life by her grandmother and her unborn daughter. Her own promise to herself was that one day she would place her baby daughter in the arms of her beloved father.

Sabiha would never accept a life without her child. She and Houria were different. The old simplicity between them was gone. She still loved Houria, more than she could ever say, but things had changed for them. Her life was no longer as straightforward as it had been before she was married to John.

To sit with her father and her little daughter in the courtyard under the pomegranate tree, the three of them together, this was the beautiful dream Sabiha carried with her everywhere. It was her comforter. She was sure the day would come when it would become a reality. Without hope of this dream coming true, her life would be too sad to bear. To take this dream from her would be to take everything from her. John did not realise how cruel it was of him to insist she go to Australia with him, for if she went to Australia she would have to give up her dream. It was difficult for her to explain the importance of this to him. She had tried several times, but whenever she spoke of it, it sounded as if she was speaking of a small and childishly selfish thing compared to the big facts of their reality.

Sabiha noticed that the rain and wind had eased and the people on the street no longer looked as if they were being blown along. The light had come on downstairs in the back of old Arnoul Fort's shop. He would be making coffee and toast for his wife.

Houria said, 'Do you still love him?'

Sabiha came out of her reverie and for a second thought Houria was referring to her father. 'My father?'

'*John*, for God's sake,' Houria said.

'Of course I still love him! You know I do. That's not fair.'

'John's a good man. He's done everything he can to make you happy. He worships you. You'll never find another one like him.' Houria was impatient with the conversation now and didn't want to take it any further. She pushed her chair back and collected their empty coffee bowls and got up. She stood a moment looking down at Sabiha. 'I'd better get on with things,' she said, then turned and walked across the dining room and went through the bead curtain into the kitchen.

It was true what Houria said. Sabiha did not disagree with any of it. There would never be another man for her but John. But there were also things Houria could not understand. For some reason Houria's question—*Do you still love him?*—made Sabiha think of the day John took her up the Eiffel Tower. It was in the early days, when they were going out almost every Sunday to see the famous sights of Paris. He was so confident that day. So busy, so eager to be the one in charge of the excursion. It was only later that she realised he had in those days been trying to see everything before they went to Australia. He bought the wrong tickets and they were only admitted to the first stage of the tower. She had laughed at his dismay, and had hugged him and said the view was wonderful anyway and they would come back and go right to the very top the next time. 'Don't worry. The Eiffel Tower will still be here,' she had said. 'They're not going to pull it down just yet.' But they had never returned.

Later, when Houria had gone across the road to Arnoul Fort's and Sabiha was alone in the house, she ran a bath. She dropped her clothes on the bathroom floor and lay back in the steaming water. She found herself thinking about the day she and John went back to Chartres. The morning was fine when the train left Paris, John carrying their picnic in his old rucksack, just as he had the first time. They were both in good spirits and looking forward to seeing Chartres again. When they got out of the train the weather had turned grey and cold, and as they walked up the hill towards the cathedral from the railway station it began to rain. Chartres was a cold, unwelcoming place that day, with scarcely anyone on the streets; it was not the Chartres of their memories. Later, to cheer themselves up, she suggested they walk down to the river to look for 'their' willow tree. They found the tree had recently been cut down. She remembered now her shock at the sight of the white stump of the tree glistening in the rain. It was surely a portent of something terrible.

She ran more hot water into the bath and washed her hair. She was thinking about Houria taking a tray with two hot meals across the road to Arnoul and his wife in the freezing rain. It wasn't charity. For years Houria had bought fabric for the café's tablecloths and their kitchen aprons from Arnoul. His cotton was fine old stock of a quality hard to find these days. She and Arnoul and his wife were friends. Houria often sat with Arnoul's wife and told her the local gossip. And whenever she went to see them she always took pastries or hot meals. 'I need to try this recipe out on you,' she would tell them. 'You are both such fussy eaters. If *you* approve, the men will love it.' She had tried to encourage old Arnoul to take his midday meal at the café, but he had never come into Chez Dom—unlike André, their landlord, who needed no encouraging. André often came in and took his midday meal with the men, and quite often he just popped in at odd moments without any warning and sat with John and had a brandy and a cigarette or a coffee. But he always insisted on paying, leaving his money under his plate or his glass, in the old-fashioned way. And before he left he always put his head through the bead curtain and wished Houria and Sabiha a good day.

André usually managed to find something to say about the lack of maintenance around the café. John had been serving him a brandy the day before when André picked a flake of paint from the windowsill.

'I know,' John said. 'Yes, I know. I'm going to repaint in the spring.'

André said gloomily, 'Once the weather gets into a building, John, you may as well forget it.' As if his property was going to fall into ruin if John didn't repaint the windowsill immediately.

After her bath Sabiha went upstairs and sat at Houria's dressing-table and brushed out her hair. She put on a fresh blouse and went down to the kitchen. It was not long before she heard the noise of the van coming down the lane. She was a little nervous now, anticipating putting her plan into action. She had never tried Houria's arts of love on John. She had been too shy. And anyway there had been no need. They had soon invented their own language of love. With sex she had never taken the initiative with John, as Houria had advised her to. There had never seemed to be a need for it. She went out into the lane and Tolstoy came out from André's back door and stood beside her, looking along the lane with her. She saw it was one of those days when it was never going to get properly light. John still had the headlight on. She stood in the beam of the headlight waiting for him. When he uncoiled himself from the van she stepped across to him and put her arms around him and kissed him on the mouth. 'I love you,' she said and she took his hand and led him through the kitchen and up the stairs to their room. She closed the door and turned to him. 'Make love to me,' she said.

They lay in each other's arms after they had made love. She thought he had gone to sleep and raised herself on her elbow and looked down at him, studying his features in the dim grey light that was being let into the room through the small window behind her. He opened his eyes and looked at her. He put his arms around her and drew her against him.

She pushed back, holding herself away from him, tears in her eyes. 'Will you promise me, darling? Please? That you'll never again ask me to go to Australia with you until my father has seen our child?'

John frowned. He hated to see her crying. And he hated this business of their first child having to meet her father. 'Don't cry, please. Of course I promise,' he said. There didn't seem to be any point arguing. He wondered how long he would have to keep his promise. Supposing they never had a child? What then? He wondered if he would ever get back to Australia.

*M*arie and I were in El Djem nearly forty years ago. I was there researching a book. We'd driven down to El Djem from Sidi Bou Said, where we were staying, to see the amphitheatre. Clare was conceived during that trip. It's just possible she was conceived the one night we spent in El Djem. Marie woke me in the middle of the night. It was very hot. There was no fan and no air-conditioning. I was covered in sweat. She was in a panic. She grabbed me and screeched in my ear, 'There's an animal on the bedside table!' It was pitch dark and I imagined a big hairy creature with glistening fangs. I said, 'Okay! Okay! Let go of me and I'll put the light on.' It was a cockroach, not an animal. A big one. It waved its feelers at me like an alien reading my mind. I flattened it with the sole of my shoe. It didn't see it coming.

The night was so hot and we were both too agitated to sleep after this drama. We decided to make love in the bath. It was wonderful. I still remember it. The bath was a magnificent thing. Ancient, possibly Roman, carved from a single massive slab of finely veined white marble. It was the only cool place to be. Sabiha must have been a five-year-old somewhere in that town that very night while Marie and I were making love and creating our daughter. In the morning, on the way back to Sidi Bou, we passed a road gang. The half-dozen men stood aside, shouldering arms with their picks and shovels, as we went by. The white dust of the road was thick on their moustaches. I like to think I saw Sabiha's father that day, and that our glances met and there was a brief moment of understanding between us. Of course it's hard to know these days what I remember and what I'm making up. Marie used to accuse me of making everything up and of being inherently incapable of telling the truth. 'It's a gene,' she said. 'They'll find it one of these days. The truth gene. I could tell them now, you haven't got it.'

I'm definitely not making up, however, the fact that our driver had to stop the car later to let a group of Berbers ride their camels across the road in front of us—you couldn't call it a highway, it was barely wide enough for a single lane in each direction, the edges crumbly and broken. It was lucky for us there wasn't much traffic. The Berbers rode their camels across the road in front of us at an angle to the direction of the road, as if the road wasn't there, not looking to left or right, and so completely ignoring us in our car that it felt as if either they weren't there or we weren't. The women had refused the veil and gazed straight ahead, looking at their familiar world through the coins and silver pendants jingling from their headgear. Haughty they were. Superior. Travelling some old highway of their own from the ancient days, to which they were connected through their living tissues presumably. They were very impressive and were not of our world. Their sudden presence there in the emptiness of that landscape rendered us and our car, on that narrow strip of bitumen, vulnerable and temporary; and while they passed us in stately progress, we felt just a little ashamed of being who we were. They, the Berbers, found all they required in the empty landscape. The brindle hounds travelling with them looked dangerous and our driver warned us not to get out of the car for photographs.

So I knew something of El Djem. Not much, but at least I'd been there. I wasn't sure why I didn't tell John I'd been to Sabiha's birthplace. He told me he'd never gone.

I hadn't seen him for three weeks. It was unusual. I went to the pool every Saturday morning and swam my twenty lengths, and I haunted the library during the evenings. But I didn't see him. Sabiha had a way of making me feel I was intruding if I mentioned John while buying our biscuits and sweet pastries, and I hadn't the nerve to ask her straight out where her husband was hiding himself these days.

I'd had a bad night. Not nightmares, but waking anxieties. Itchiness across my chest. My legs wanting to twitch and move. Turning over every few minutes. Switching on the light and looking at my watch and finding it was, unbelievably, still only two o'clock. Drinking all the water I'd put out for my pills in the morning. I slept towards dawn and woke with the sun streaming through the blinds. Without John I had nothing to do and was staring at another empty day. I got up and went into the study and looked at my notes. I had found it impossible not to make a few notes. There were things I could have added to his story, but I didn't want to make it up this time. The truth is, and despite Marie's insistence that I couldn't tell the truth, I have never really liked making it up. My imagination, such as it is, needs the facts to feed off. I could see directions I might go in with John and Sabiha's story, but I resisted. I wanted to hear the truth from John.

I wanted to know Sabiha's secret sorrow. I was missing my regular instalment and was annoyed with him for not showing up at any of our usual haunts.

I went downstairs in my dressing-gown. I was feeling grumpy and ready to find fault and I cautioned myself to be careful. Clare was sitting at the kitchen table drinking coffee and reading the newspaper as usual at that time of the morning. She was wearing a smart navy business suit that I'd not seen before and was eating one of Sabiha's sweet pastries, leaning over the table so the crumbs wouldn't fall into her lap.

I said, 'You've already been out then?' She didn't reply, but went on eating and reading the paper. I poured myself a cup of coffee, took one of the pastries and sat at the opposite end of the table and looked past Clare and out the back door into our narrow strip of garden. We had one tree, a silver birch Marie and I planted more than twenty years ago. I noticed the drought was beginning to have an effect on it. It was developing dieback at the tips. Marie had held the little sapling upright while I tamped the earth around it. We were new here then. Clare was in her last year at high school. I looked at Clare now. She was making little sounds of surprise and disgust with this or that piece of news as she read it. Suddenly, and without looking up, she said in a calm, matter-of-fact voice, 'Did you ever cheat on Mum?'

I said, 'What's brought that on?' I took a drink of coffee. 'It's none of your business.'

She put the paper down and licked the honey from her fingers. She met my eyes. 'That sounds like a yes to me, Dad.'

'Well it's not a yes. I never cheated on your mother.'

'Never? Not even once? Are you sure? Come on, Dad. You're a man, men cheat.'

I said, 'If they do, they cheat with a woman. So there must be as many women cheating with men as there are men cheating with women.'

She gave me a conspiratorial smile that said it was safe for me to confide my stolen pleasures to her if I wanted to.

'Not once,' I said firmly. I bit into the biscuit. 'The pair of us are going to get fat if Sabiha has her way.'

She said, 'Mum could be a handful.'

I was surprised to hear this from Clare. Despite their fierce fighting during her teenage years, Clare worshipped the memory of her mother. I'd never heard a hint of criticism of Marie from her.

'Your mother was a strong woman,' I said. 'She knew how to get what she wanted.'

'She gave you hell sometimes.'

I said, 'And you.' I was thinking of Marie having one of her strong moments with us. 'Your mother gave everyone hell sometimes.'

Marie was a social worker when we married. She made friends of her patients and suffered with them and it drove her to the edge of a breakdown. She didn't believe in professional detachment. She scoffed at the idea, and whenever it was raised said with contempt, 'It's just a way of refusing to feel.' Years later she quit her job without warning one day and began drawing and painting. To everyone's surprise she stuck to it and eventually became good at it. Our house was full of her shadowy tonal doorways and deserted streetscapes, and those terrible naked self-portraits she made when she was dying and the flesh had gone from her bones; charcoal figures of her wretched wasted body scratched onto the paper like Giacometti's last portraits. It was all she could manage by then. There was a truth about them; in the eyes. As well as the ones we've framed, there are several dozen of these last drawings in a folder in my desk. Whenever I look at them I remember Marie's courage, her will to keep going to the very end; not as if there was not going to *be* an end, but as if every moment had something to reveal to her, and it mattered. That impressed me. I doubt if I'll manage it.

Marie stayed true to her art till the last hour of her life. There were a sketchpad and broken pieces of charcoal beside her bed the afternoon she died.

She was only interested in the truth as she saw it. But she wasn't precious about it. 'It's only *my* truth,' she used to say. 'No one else need worry about it.' That was another thing she scoffed at, the idea of there being such a thing as universal truth. And she never signed anything. An artist friend, a very successful man, said to me one day, 'Marie's very good, but she's got the woman's problem.' I took him to mean Marie was too modest for her own good. But he was wrong. It only looked that way from the outside. Marie didn't want a career out of art. Her art was a private conversation to keep herself sane. She and I knew this. I respected it and never urged her to show her work. I've got drawers full of her drawings upstairs and we must have a hundred oils, gouaches, and charcoal and ink drawings hanging on our walls here. Each one of them is like a short poem in a long linked sequence of poems. Who has done something like that, I wonder? Perhaps a Chinese poet.

Marie was a very intense woman. A very private woman. And in the early days she was a very beautiful woman. When I first met her she had a lot of lovers, one after the other. We used to joke about it. She was a friend then. In those early years every man she met had to submit to her charms. Then it suddenly stopped, as if she'd become bored with sex, or bored with men, or with herself. In the end she stayed with me.

Marie and I never had a passionate love affair, but we always got along okay, and gradually it dawned on us that we were pretty good mates. Love didn't bowl us over, but over time it grew on us, and then, when we did finally fall in love, we stayed in love. To the end. Which was the best of it. It was only I who could still see her beauty at the end. Marie's soft grey eyes remained beautiful, her sardonic humour, her determined candour, and her belief. These things stayed with her. I miss her terribly some days. If she were here now she would scoff at my so-called retirement. It would madden her. I can hear her shouting down the stairs, 'That's bullshit! Writers don't retire!' Perhaps she's right. Who knows? We'll see.

I looked up at Clare. Her mother is in her eyes and her hands. 'What made you ask me that?' I said. 'Are you having an affair with a married man?'

Clare said, 'Jesus, Dad, you're a bastard.'

'So that's a yes, is it?'

She folded the newspaper and came over, leaned down and kissed my cheek. 'You're a bastard, Dad,' she said fondly, then she turned and went out the door. 'See you later,' she called back.

'See you, darling,' I called.

So was it a business meeting or a business*man* she was wearing the suit for?

Later I went down the street and called in at the Paradiso. John was sitting on his own at the back of the café. He was reading a book. I was glad to see him, but I was a bit uncertain of my reception, not sure if he was keeping out of my way. I said hello and he looked up. Then he smiled and said g'day and closed his book.

'So how are things, John?' I said.

He said, 'My father died. I took a couple of weeks off. I've been up in Moruya with Mum and Kathy.' He motioned to the spare chair. 'Don't stand there like that.' He gave a short laugh. 'I wasn't hiding from you. I've given up smoking. We don't have to sit outside anymore.'

I pulled out the chair and sat. 'I'm very sorry about your father,' I said.

'It's okay.'

'I know you loved your father.' I was feeling the helpless stupidity of confronting a friend's bereavement. A friend? Well, yes, I suppose he was becoming a friend. He was making light of his father's death but I felt he was deeply affected by it. When my own father died I was John's age. I wept after I got the phone call, surprised by the force of my grief. A week later I'd forgiven him everything. It was a relief. A surprise bonus. And within a month I was repacking him in my memory according to my own version of our story. My father was a gentler man for me once he was dead. I was freer to love him than I had been when he was alive and had felt himself called on to compete with me and to deny my successes.

The waitress came over and I ordered a skinny latte.

John and I sat without speaking for a good minute after the waitress had gone. The café was busy, noisy with clatter and loud talk. Mostly young people. I often seem to be the only old person in these places. I reached for John's book and turned it to see the title. It was an old Penguin Classics edition of Homer's *The Iliad*. The E.V. Rieu translation that my generation had been familiar with. I hadn't read it for forty years—more, probably. There were yellow post-it notes sticking out of it.

John said, 'I'm doing it with the kids.' He pushed at the book. 'Not the whole thing. Just sections. They like the bloodshed.'

The waitress brought my coffee and I thanked her.

I stirred sugar into my coffee. 'I've missed our sessions,' I said.

He nodded.

'No school today?'

'Curriculum day.'

We fell silent again. It was not an uncomfortable silence exactly, but I did begin to realise how little I knew him, despite his private disclosures. I felt I knew his wife better than I knew him. He'd been giving me all these intimate details of their married life and in the process had revealed very little about himself. I could not have imagined right at that moment, for example, what he was thinking. Was he thinking about teaching Homer's *Iliad* to his second-language students? Or was he thinking about his dead father? He hadn't exactly given himself the starring role in his story. In many ways he had done a pretty good job of effacing himself. I watched him sitting there slumped back in his chair, the fingers of his left hand playing with the book, and I could not begin to imagine what he was going to say next. Perhaps he was just trying not to think about having a cigarette.

I said, 'You left me hanging with your promise to Sabiha never again to ask her to come to Australia.'

He smiled and nodded and said nothing.

I thought about the gulf of years between that day in their bedroom at Chez Dom when he promised Sabiha he would not ask her to go to Australia until her father had seen their child, and this day here now sitting with me in the back of the Paradiso in Carlton. I said, 'Did you keep your promise?'

He looked up at me slowly, as if he had been making an assessment of something miles away from what I was trying to talk about. Then he met my gaze directly. He said, 'Houria died, you know.'

I felt the shock of it. That sudden empty space of disbelief death makes where someone has been present, with a life still to be lived.

'She was a good mate to me through it all.'

I wondered what *through it all* referred to.

His eyes stayed on mine, holding my gaze but looking into me, looking through me, beyond me and into his own past and the death of that fine woman Houria Pakos, who it seemed I was not going to get the chance to mourn. Her death already so long ago. The end of Houria seemed terribly unfair to me. I had been looking forward to knowing her for a long while yet. So that's what he'd been thinking of: death; his father's and Houria's. One death leading to thoughts of another. I had plenty of deaths of my own to think about if I cared to. There were a lot of them out there, dead friends and intimates. My own ghosts. Easy to love now. I have more dead friends than living ones these days.

'It took us a while, a month or so I suppose it was, to realise that without Houria the café wasn't really Chez Dom anymore. The connection with Dom Pakos and their early days had been broken. It wasn't long after we buried Houria that Sabiha began singing her old songs to the men on Saturday nights. She said she wanted to give them something to remind them of their homes and their wives and children. But in a way, I knew she was really singing for Houria, for that lost connection with her father's sister, with her own past in El Djem. Like all deaths, Houria's brought about the end of more than just one life. Houria didn't have a lot of time for the old songs when she was alive, but somehow being dead made it seem as if she might be able to appreciate them after all.' He looked at me. 'All temporal prejudices set aside,' he said. 'If you see what I mean.'

I thought I had some idea of what he might mean and said so.

'Things changed for Sabiha and me after Houria died. It wasn't just her death. Vaugirard changed too. Even the smells in our lives changed. It all seemed to happen at once. The abattoirs closed, then they started building a park where the slaughterhouse had been. A year or two later the second-hand book market opened and we began to get the occasional tourist discovering us. After Houria died it seemed as if nothing quite stayed in place. Suddenly she was gone and we were in charge of everything, *forever*. We kept going. Perhaps we shouldn't have. Perhaps we should have called it a day and come home to Australia then. But we stayed open. It was our only income. And, yes, I'd made my promise, and yes, I kept it. Sabiha didn't fall pregnant and we stood still, while one year followed another. It was probably my fault. We stopped talking about it. We stopped going to doctors and having tests. We stopped talking about having a child. I thought I was going to end my days in Chez Dom. I probably got a bit depressed and started drinking more than I used to. And I read too much. I hid in my reading. I still do that.' He laughed. 'When I climbed into bed beside Sabiha one night after I'd been drinking she told me my smell made me unattractive to her. It was a shock. We were both under a lot of pressure. I felt disgusted with myself for drinking but I was angry with her for saying it to me. I was hurt.' He looked at me to see if I was listening. He didn't say anything for a while but sat looking at me, an apologetic smile in his eyes. 'I didn't understand Sabiha then. I had no idea really. But that was me *then*,' he said. 'It's not me *now*.'

'No,' I said. 'Of course it's not.'

'The next day I said something really stupid and hurtful to her. And that one stupid remark seemed to determine the rest of our lives.' He searched my eyes. 'Do you know what I mean? Has that ever happened to you? Something like that?'

'What did you say to her?' I asked.

My question seemed to make him anxious and he didn't speak for a while. Then he drew a deep breath. 'I suppose we'd both reached a point of crisis without realising it. I felt as if I was never going to get home to Australia. I resented her insistence that she had to present her child to her father before we could move on. I didn't say it to get my own back. I wasn't trying to hurt her. The pressures on us were all under the surface. We'd stopped talking about what was important to us. Everything had become subterranean and unspoken. It didn't seem like that to us at the time, of course. It just seemed like one day was following another. But looking back now I can see that's what happened to us. We still loved each other. We've never stopped loving each other. We continued to be gentle and kind to each other. We still wanted to make each other happy.'

He stopped talking suddenly and looked down at his hands, which he spread on the table in front of him, palms down. They were youthful hands. Strong and well shaped and without blemishes. The hands of a younger man. He sat examining them, as if he was proud of his hands. I didn't prompt him in case he decided to say no more. Confession, after all, even to a relative stranger, such as I was to John, is not always the easiest strategy for absolving ourselves.

He said, 'It was one of those things we just blurt out without thinking.' He looked up at me. 'Sometimes you shift just one small rock and the whole mountain falls on you.'

Three

One Tuesday, a few moments after the last lunchtime customer had left the café, Sabiha came into the dining room from the kitchen carrying her own and John's lunches. So far there was nothing to distinguish this Tuesday from any other Tuesday in the routine of their lives. Sabiha backed through the bead curtain, pausing to let it slide over her shoulders, then turned and walked across to the table by the window, where John was sitting reading a book. Sabiha stood a moment while John set aside his book, then she put his midday meal on the table in front of him.

John pulled his chair in closer to the table. He looked up. 'Thank you, darling,' he said. 'It smells great.'

She sat across from him, her own meal in front of her.

They began to eat the seared lamb and vegetables, taking a sip of the red wine and reaching for a piece of bread from the bowl in the centre of the table. The delicious smell of a subtle blending of spices rose from the food. Under Houria's tuition Sabiha had long ago mastered the art of spices. Seated at their usual table by the window, she and John were able to enjoy the distraction of the passing traffic and pedestrians along the narrow confines of rue des Esclaves.

Outside, the autumn day was fine and warm, the street noisy and busy at this time of the day. Across the road, ancient Arnoul Fort was standing in the sunlight in the doorway of his shop as he often did, smoking a cigarette and watching the comings and goings. In their youth Arnoul and his wife Monique had known by name everyone in the district. Now the old man knew scarcely anyone who passed his door. It was to Arnoul that Houria had sent Sabiha long ago to find a matching thread with which to repair the leather patch on the sleeve of John's jacket. Sabiha had wanted her repairs to be perfect. Although he had not worn the old brown jacket for many years, John had not thrown it away and it still hung on his side of the wardrobe upstairs in their bedroom; the bedroom that had once been Dom and Houria's, and then Houria's alone.

For the past three years Bruno Fiorentino had been delivering a box of his hothouse tomatoes to Chez Dom regularly every Tuesday. After he delivered the tomatoes Bruno stayed for the midday meal, which John insisted was on the house. On Tuesdays Bruno was invariably the last customer to leave the café. Today, as usual, just after John and Sabiha began their own meal, Bruno drove past the window in his van hooting his horn and waving his arm to them.

As Bruno's familiar green and orange van swept past the café, its horn blaring, John looked up from his plate and gestured with his fork out the window. 'Did you know Bruno's got eleven kids?' he said.

Even as he said it, John couldn't understand why he didn't resist the impulse to utter these words. How could he be so insensitive? Dismayed, he reached across the table and put his hand over Sabiha's, apologising to her and expecting to see tears gathering in her beautiful dark eyes.

But instead of weeping, Sabiha withdrew her hand and laughed. It was a loud laugh, more like a cry of dismay and anger than a laugh.

John flinched and stared at her in astonishment.

His timing could hardly have been worse. Since celebrating her thirty-seventh birthday in June, Sabiha had been finding it difficult to accept that she was a woman nearing forty. It was late September now and another year was already nearly gone. Last Friday morning when she was at the market, she found herself standing stock still murmuring incredulously, *Can this really be me?* She had felt, suddenly, that she was trapped inside the body of an older woman. Inside, where it really mattered, Sabiha knew herself to be the young woman who had fallen in love with John all those years ago. Standing there in the market on Friday, a gust of panic had swept over her and she had seen herself—the young woman, that is—running wildly among the stalls, knocking people aside and tipping over piles of apples and cabbages and . . . And *what?* There was nothing to be done. Nothing.

Her panic lasted only a moment, but the question remained with her: where had the years gone? For some time she had been feeling haunted by the passing years. She was nearing forty and had only a few years left before the onset of that time that is known, with good reason, as the change of life. What then? It would be the end of her hopes of motherhood. It brought tears to her eyes whenever she thought of the night when she and John first made love. Since then she had learned to live with constant doubt.

When her childlessness persisted, and no cause for it could be found, Sabiha had begun to feel as if a wall of indifference was being erected around her, cruelly cutting her off from the purpose of her existence, and she asked herself if she was being punished for a crime she had not committed. The injustice of her childlessness burned in her every day. What had she done to deserve it? Her life had surely been blameless. Eventually they had stopped talking with each other about their childlessness. It was too painful. But although she never spoke of it, Sabiha's determination to bring her little girl into the world had remained as strong as ever. She had never lost hope. One day, she was sure, she would hold her little daughter in her arms. The same child whose existence she had felt fluttering in her belly that summer day as she lay in John's arms on the bank of the river Eure in Chartres. It was the only child she cared about. It was her little daughter she dreamed of.

When John asked her if she knew Bruno had eleven children, Sabiha had been thinking about her moment of panic in the market on Friday, an image in her mind of the young woman running away from the ageing woman. She stopped eating and looked at him in astonishment. When he placed his hand over hers and said, 'I'm sorry, darling, that was a really stupid thing to say,' she wanted to hit him in the face with her plate of food.

She withdrew her hand from his and, instead of hitting him, she laughed. It was the laugh of decades of frustration, injustice and anger. Then she reached for her tumbler of wine.

'Yes!' she said. 'He has given her one child for each year of their marriage!' And she laughed again, the same loud, coarse laugh that was not her laugh but was the laugh of some other, fiercer woman than she. She drank all the wine in her glass and set the empty tumbler on the table. She sat a moment, her fingers gripping the empty glass as if it were a grenade and she was considering tossing it through the window, or at John's head. Then she looked at him and smiled.

'I'm sorry,' he said. He was unnerved by the peculiar smile on her face.

She said, 'Bruno's is a perfect score, John!'

It seemed to him that Sabiha said this with a malicious emphasis. It was so unlike her he didn't know what to say. Perhaps it *was* his fault. They would probably never know. Sabiha was waiting for him to say something. 'Well?' she said. 'Is it, or isn't it?'

'Bruno and Angela have been married a good few years longer than we have, darling,' he said, trying to make it sound as if everything was normal between them. 'Eleven is not nearly one child for each year of their marriage. It's a lot of kids, but it's not a perfect score.'

'You can be so pedantic,' she said, as if the thought fatigued her.

His mind had gone blank when she gave that dreadful laugh. The laugh had made him feel lonely.

'Eleven! Fifteen! Twenty!' Sabiha said, as if she might howl or burst into tears or strike him in the face if he said another word, her patience exhausted. 'What difference does it make? Bruno's is *a perfect score*, John! Face it!'

She reached for the jug and refilled her tumbler with the red wine. She lifted it to her lips and took a long drink, then set the glass back on the table with exaggerated care. *Now* there were tears in her eyes. A pin had come loose and Sabiha's hair had fallen forward over her face. She raised her hand and pushed it back.

John wanted to take her in his arms and tell her: *Somehow, one day, my darling, you will have your child. I promise you, with my life, with all I am and all I have, I promise you, you will have your child.* But of course he could promise her nothing of the sort.

'You're right,' he said meekly. 'Yes, you're right.' He sat gazing unhappily at the food on his plate, unable to look up and meet her eyes. He felt guilty, wronged, unhappy and alone. He could think of nothing to say.

With exacting deliberation he cut a small piece of lamb and speared it on his fork, lifted the fork to his mouth and put the meat in his mouth and chewed it. Sabiha was still looking at him. His mouth was dry and he realised he was not going to be able to swallow the lump of meat. He chewed on the thing and looked out at the street. The afternoon sun was reflected in the window of the Kavi boys' grocery store on the corner, the mean building opposite transformed into a golden temple. Sabiha had never called him John before. Not even in the earliest days of their life together. He had always been dearest, or darling, or my love, or my Hercules. My hero. Even my lovely Aussie man. Never John. Despite everything, he felt he was in the right.

He reached for his glass and washed down the dreadful thing in his mouth. He felt it go down his gullet and thought of his old dog, Tip, golloping a piece of raw meat, the gulping sound of it going down her throat. The wine was hard and cold and acid on his palate. His usual supplier was taking him for granted. He had known it for some time, but had preferred not to make a fuss. He knew they called him the quiet Australian. And he was. He prided himself on being easy to get along with. He liked to be liked. He decided to put up with the poor quality of the wine no longer. He would have it out with the wine merchant this afternoon.

When John said nothing, Sabiha gave a small exasperated laugh and took up her knife and fork and went on with her meal.

Minutes passed, the silence broken only by the click and scrape of cutlery against their plates. Behind them the empty tables of the dining room. Beside them the familiar faded green of the timber trim around the window and door, last painted by John almost ten years ago, when Houria was still alive.

The telephone began to ring.

Sabiha put down her knife and fork and got up from the table, and went behind the bar and lifted the receiver. 'Hello,' she said. 'Sabiha speaking.'

In a voice she scarcely recognised, so hollow and faded was it from its former confident manliness, her father said, 'It's what you've been expecting, my dearest child. I have cancer.' He laughed. It was a throaty, subdued laugh that remained in his chest.

Sabiha understood from her father's laugh that it amused him to greet the cancer as a messenger come at last to deliver him from the burden of his life, and that he did not resent too greatly the knowledge that he was soon to die. She was swept by a gust of grief and anger.

He told her he loved her and said he hoped she would be able to visit him soon. He added, 'But only if you and John are not too busy.' She replied that of course she would come over and spend some time with him. She did not say, *To wait for the end with you.* But they both understood this was what she meant. There was a silence. She heard the roar of a motor in the background and asked, 'Is that the Tunis bus?'

Yes, he told her, the bus had just pulled away.

She saw the old green and yellow bus driving away from the front of the post office, its exhaust belching black smoke, her own face pressed to the window, leaving her home for Paris, her hand raised in farewell to her mother and sister and to her beloved father. She could smell the exhaust in the muggy heat of an autumn morning at home.

'Did you walk up to the post office on your own?'

He told her he had done so.

She asked after her sister, Zahira.

He told her, 'Zahira is well and is taking good care of me. It will be hard for her here on her own when I'm gone.'

After she had spoken with her father, Sabiha came back to the table and sat down. She did not go on with her meal but sat looking out at the sunny street. The lamb and baked aubergine and spicy stuffed tomatoes on her plate had gone cold. She was seeing her father returning from making his telephone call along the dusty road to their old home in El Djem. In her imagination she watched him struggle with the hasp of the iron gate, as he had always struggled with the troublesome thing. When he had the gate open, she watched him cross the narrow courtyard to the house, knowing his every faltering step, seeing him duck his head and put out his hand to steady himself as he passed under the low branches of the pomegranate tree, where his chickens roosted at night, beside his patch of vegetables. The door to the house opened before he reached it. Zahira was waiting for him in the cool interior. Sabiha watched her father sit in his chair and take in his hand the glass of mint tea Zahira offered him. Sabiha thought of her father's name for her, The Difficult One, as if that person was her truest self. His boast that she was the one who had married a foreigner and escaped the poverty of El Djem to live in Paris. He had always been her champion. He was proud of her. He was her hero. The last time he had telephoned her had been almost five years ago to tell her of her mother's sudden death. How quickly those five years had gone by.

She straightened and looked out the window at the street, where Bruno of the perfect score had passed a moment earlier. And she knew, with sudden understanding that made her draw in her breath sharply—so that John looked at her quickly—how fragile and brief the span of a person's life was. Her father, who had always been there, was soon to be there no more. The *forever* of her childhood was no longer forever.

She turned to John. She had spoken to her father in Arabic. 'It was my father,' she said. There was anger as well as sorrow in her voice. 'He's managed to give himself lung cancer at last.'

'I'm sorry,' he said. 'Is there anything they can do for him?'

She got up and collected their plates and the cutlery.

'Are you all right, darling?' he asked.

She stood a moment looking down at John. She wanted to say, Of course I'm not all right! What do you think? All you're thinking about now is going home to Australia the minute my father dies. I know that. His death will be a relief for you. Well I'm not going to be defeated. I'm not giving up. I will still place my little daughter in my father's arms before he dies. You'll see!

'They've offered him an operation,' she said, 'to remove one of his lungs, and then chemotherapy. But he's not going to have any treatment. He's going to leave on his own terms. That's my father. He's right.'

She went out to the kitchen and began washing up the piles of dirty dishes and pots and the cutlery from the men's midday meal. She would tell her father to wait for her. He was a man of courage. He would find the courage to wait.

While she worked, Sabiha sang a song. It was a song of a woman's dream that her grandmother used to sing to them when Sabiha and her sister were children. In the dream the woman goes out alone into the desert one night and kills a lion. The lion has been threatening the children of the village for years and the men have failed to kill it. Today, as she worked at the sink and sang the old song, the meaning of the woman's dream was clear to Sabiha, and she felt her spirits lift. The time had come for her to take matters into her own hands, just as the woman in her grandmother's old song had done. She could wait no longer but would go and kill her lion. No one else was ever going to do it for her. If she did nothing, soon it would be too late. Her change would come and all the children would be dead.

Zahira would soon be alone in their old home, where they had been happy children together, with no one to care for but herself and nothing to do but bear the shame of her spinsterhood with courage. How did one kill such a lion as that? Sabiha did not think it would be possible. For Zahira, the moment of opportunity had passed many years ago. What choice did her sister have now but to submit to her fate with dignity?

She cried as she stood at the sink, thinking of her father. It gave her strength and reassured her in her faith to realise that her grandmother's song of the woman's dream had come back to her when she needed it. She had begun to sing the song without thinking what it was she was singing, the words of the song coming into her head and asking to be sung. How little she and her sister had understood the words of the song when they were children, but had been entranced by the thought of the woman walking alone into the desert under the stars, the old lion watching her approach his lair with an air of bored indifference, his eyes drooping sleepily, never suspecting the woman was coming to kill him. It was a good song. It was a great song. She had always loved it. She was thankful it had belonged to her grandmother and her grandmother's mother before that, linking her back through the generations to the old days of the women of the tribes, until at some distant point the origin of the song's poetry was touched with the inspiration of the gods. It was a song that had grown from the soil of her past. A song of her belonging. Now, when she needed it, it had yielded up its strength to her.

*T*he following morning Sabiha was at the bench in the kitchen preparing a batch of filo dough. It was another fine day, a shaft of sunlight shining through the open door onto the old tiles of the floor. She could smell the warmth of the day. She was measuring onto the marble two even mounds of the flours she was to mix, when she was suddenly struck by the conviction that there was no real hope of her ever having her child. It came at her like a hawk out of the sun, the certainty that the child was nothing but her own foolish dream. Her heart thumped once as if it would cease to beat forever, then began to race, its stately rhythm abandoned. She clutched the edge of the cold marble bench, her eyes closed, her lips parted, her heart thundering in her chest. 'God help me!' she whispered, the world plunging around her.

John came into the kitchen from the lane. He was carrying a sack of onions over his shoulder. He stopped and looked at Sabiha in alarm. She was hanging onto the edge of the bench, her legs parted, her stomach thrust against the marble, her head thrown back and her eyes closed, her lips parted and her breath coming in short gasps, a low moan or murmured word escaping her at each urgent breath.

John dropped the sack of onions on the floor and stepped across to her. 'What's wrong, darling?'

She pushed his hands away and stepped back from the bench, bringing her floured fingers to her throat. 'It's all right,' she said. 'It's all right!' She even managed an odd little cackling laugh. 'I ate a sesame biscuit and a piece went down the wrong way.' She cleared her throat theatrically. The seismic tremor in her body was subsiding. It was all right. It was nothing to do with John. It wasn't going to bring the house down. It was as if she had been slapped hard across the face by her sudden doubt and woken up. Of course she would have her child! Of course she would. 'I thought I was going to choke for a minute.'

John stood looking at her. He didn't believe her. There was a wild kind of innocence in her eyes, as if she had been highly excited by something. 'What happened? What have you been doing?'

'I haven't been *doing* anything. I told you, I ate a biscuit.' She was defensive, staring at him wide-eyed, daring him to disbelieve her. 'I ate it too quickly. That's all. Don't make a fuss.' Her fingers kneaded her throat, dusting her dark skin with the white flour. She wanted to laugh. 'I'm okay.' She did laugh then, a wild snort of laughter that bordered on something a little hysterical, something a little out of control, emotion blooming in her helplessly. She was smiling. She couldn't help it. *Things are no longer as they were.* The thought excited her. Her terrible doubt had not succeeded, but something *had* given. She was no longer standing still. The years of meek, silent inward desperation, the waiting in an agony of uncertainty for something to happen, it was done with. It occurred to her that perhaps John would be left behind. That perhaps, in a way, she had already left him behind. She watched him go to the sink and fill a glass with water. She felt sorry for him. He handed the glass of water to her and stood and watched while she drank it obediently, as if he were her parent. She held out the empty glass and he took it from her and set it on the bench beside the two mounds of flour. He stood close to her, his gaze going over her, lingering on the swelling of her breasts beneath her white blouse. She put her hand to her breast.

'What's up?' he said. 'What's the matter with you?'

'Nothing. I don't know.' The laughter refused to be held. 'I'm sorry,' she said, laughing.

He would have kissed her on the lips, but she drew away from him. Suddenly he wanted her. He searched her eyes. 'Let's go up to bed,' he said. He reached for her hand. 'Come on!'

She pulled away. 'Don't be silly!' She pushed at his chest, flouring his blue shirt. 'I've got to make the filo.'

'Let the filo wait!' He took her in his arms.

She struggled free. She was strong, determined. 'Please!' She was remembering, with intense remorse and regret, the times they had been unable to wait another minute to have sex and had run upstairs the second Houria was out of the house, laughing with excitement in the middle of the day, making love in the sunlight on their bed. 'Let me go, John! I've got to make the filo.' She saw how he was rebuked by her use of his Christian name.

He stepped away from her, dismayed, angered.

'I'm sorry,' she said. But she wasn't sorry. She was glad.

He turned away.

She watched him carry the heavy cutlery drawer out to the dining room. It pained her to see the puzzlement and hurt in his eyes. She knew him to be the most loyal husband any woman could hope for, and knew also he had sacrificed his career and his dreams to marry her and remain with her in the café all these years. And she loved him and loathed the thought of hurting him. She listened to the clatter of knives and forks from the dining room where he was setting the tables for lunch, and she wondered if she should take off her apron and go out to him and invite him up to bed. She stood a moment, listening, then turned back to the bench and went on with the pastry.

Into the words of the old songs the sufferings and hopes of women had been gathered over the centuries. Only her grandmother and the silent Berber women in their camps would not doubt her sanity for believing in the existence of her child. She began to sing softly. The songs were her grandmother's legacy to her. John and their customers might enjoy the melancholy of her singing on Saturday nights, and even be moved to tears on occasion by their own nostalgia, but they would never be the familiars of her songs. She stood at the marble bench kneading the filo dough. She formed it into a ball and stroked the soft silky pastry with her fingers. The shiny ball of pastry might have been the shaved and featureless head of a man, an unfinished man who had yet to be given eyes and a voice. She sang softly as she wrapped the pastry in muslin and placed it on the cold slate shelf in the larder. She asked herself, Is the rhythm of my heart changed forever?

She stood gazing into the darkness of the larder.

A firm resolve to act had formed itself, emerging out of the shadows, a boat coming silently into harbour with its strange cargo. It was simple enough. She knew it already; she would wait no longer for her child but would go and fetch the child herself.

She closed the larder door and turned to the refrigerator and took out the shoulder of lamb. She unwrapped the joint and laid it on the board and stood honing the blade of the short boning knife on the steel, looking down at the blue and purple flesh of the slaughtered lamb, the fine sinews and membranes, the intimacy of its splendid flesh. There would be emotions she had never dreamed of. She could *feel* her grandmother's approval. She was sure of it. Her grandmother's strength was in her resolve. Without her grandmother she would not have been able to make such a decision. She would not have had the courage for it, nor the imagination.

She set the steel aside on the bench and took a grip with her strong fingers on the rounding of the shoulder. She slipped the narrow blade along the flesh, parting the muscle from the white bone, glistening with the colours of the rainbow and never until this moment touched by the light of day. It astonished her, this hidden work of nature. That bones could be so hard, so set among the yielding flesh of the lamb. Why was this hidden world of bone so terrible and so beautiful? Why did the sight of it fill her today with such unsettling wonder at the strangeness of her own life? She filleted the meat and chopped it into pieces, then put the bone in the stockpot to simmer with the herbs.

•

John laid out the knives and forks, four sets to some tables, two to others. The men all had their customary places. He dropped a knife and it clattered to the boards. He swore and stood looking down at the knife. What was the matter with her? He took a deep breath and bent and picked up the knife. He stood weighing the knife in his hand, feeling a sudden violent urge to hurl the heavy thing through the window, to watch the glass shatter into the street and see the passersby shrink back in fear. He breathed on the blade and wiped it on his black apron then set the knife carefully in place on the table.

He made his way around the small dining room, going from table to table, setting each place for their customers. André went by the window, returning from walking Tolstoy number four—or was it number five? André himself didn't seem to know. André rapped a greeting on the glass with his ring and waved.

John had never known Sabiha in such a mood before. 'John!' he said with disgust, and felt a little touch of despair. Sabiha would be thirty-eight next June. If she was ever going to have a child it would have to be in the next few years. They didn't talk about it anymore. She got so upset, it just wasn't worth it. But perhaps they *should* talk about it. Perhaps he should insist. She must feel terribly alone with her dread that she was never going to have her little daughter. But how could he bring up the subject now, in this atmosphere? He would have willingly given a year of his life to have been able to take back that stupid remark he'd made at lunch yesterday. But it wasn't just that. It was *everything*. It had been building between them for years. It was the time of their lives as well as everything else. The old people getting older and passing on, the sudden feeling of being next in line. Change being forced on them even as they stood still. The old dreams diminished. All that.

He finished laying the tables and went behind the bar and poured a glass of brandy. He drank the brandy in one swift gulp, closed his eyes, then poured another. He lit a cigarette and took a drag and drank the second brandy. He stood looking at the telephone on the wall beside the bar, the empty glass in his hand, smoke trailing from his parted lips. Her father dying, her change of life coming on like a beast stalking her from inside her own body, and the dreadful strain of not becoming a mother. It might all be getting to be too much for her. He made a vow not to be selfish, to stop thinking about himself and to do his utmost to support her in every possible way. Life without Sabiha would not be worth living.

He stubbed his cigarette out in the ashtray on the bar and rinsed the glass at the small sink. He stood drying the glass on a tea towel. Perhaps it was too late to go home. He might have left it too long. This possibility had not occurred to him before. He was a young man of twenty-seven when he first walked through that door. This coming December he would be forty-two, a middle-aged man, a few swift years from fifty. His future was no longer filled with romantic possibilities. He was *living* in his future. This was *it*. He had achieved nothing. The world and his peers had moved on without him. He'd kept up none of his old connections. He hadn't even written to his sister Kathy for years. Except for writing to his mother and father fairly regularly he had neglected his Australian connections. And his mother and father lived in the past. Since they had moved to their retirement unit in Moruya it was all his mother ever talked about: her past, the golden years of her life with his father and the children growing up on the farm.

John hung the tea towel on the nail and looked at his watch. He should go and see his wine merchant and have it out with the man. He didn't move, however, but stood with one hand resting on the worn surface of the bar, looking out through the open door at the familiar scene in the street. He would miss this place. Chez Dom and the people on rue des Esclaves. His friends: André, old Arnoul even, Bruno, in a way, Nejib and his soulful oud on Saturday nights accompanying Sabiha's singing. And one or two of the other men. No great friendships, to be sure. No deep, intimate, sharing, comforting friendships with someone of a like mind to his own. No one who read books. But still, he would miss them. He would miss his *place* here.

He had been dreaming for so long of going home he could no longer think clearly about the reality of it. The telephone call from her father yesterday had handed him his dream of a return, but did he really want to return? He stood looking out the door at the street, the smell of Sabiha's cooking, the sun on Arnoul's faded bolts of cloth, the Kavi boys in their corner grocery shop. Did he really want to leave this behind and start again in an Australia that he would not know, a place where he would not be known? He didn't know what he wanted. The windows were grimy, he could see that much. Instead of calling his wine merchant, he would clean the windows. He was at a disadvantage whenever it came to arguing with the French. One great blessing of being at home would be to have access to the vernacular of his own mother tongue once again. How out of touch had he become? he wondered. His own language was a large dimension of his life that was missing here, and would always be missing so long as he lived in France. Sabiha's English had remained rudimentary despite his efforts to teach her over the years. So where would that leave her in Australia?

He went out the back and fetched a bucket and cloths and started cleaning the windows. Maybe they would just keep going here, make no dramatic change in their lives, just keep at it till they began to look like André and Simone and old Arnoul Fort, dealing with each day as it came until there was no longer any need to think about making changes. Until there was no more future to worry about.

*A*t five minutes after midday the following Tuesday Bruno Fiorentino came into the kitchen of Chez Dom from the back lane. Against his stomach he was carrying a case of semi-to-coloured Grosse Lisse tomatoes from his hothouse. He stopped just inside the door and set the box of tomatoes on the floor, then straightened, took off his cap and wiped his forehead with the back of his hand, and stood looking down at his tomatoes. He was proud of them. They were the pick of the crop. Each one perfectly matched with its neighbour. He looked across at Sabiha. She was busy at the stove and had her back to him. When she didn't turn around he cleared his throat and said, 'Good morning, Madame Patterner.' He always used this form of respectful address when he spoke to John's wife. 'The stew smells wonderful today.'

Bruno said pretty much the same thing every Tuesday when he came into the kitchen of the café. And whenever Sabiha paused at his stand at the market early on Friday mornings to exchange a greeting with him, as she invariably did, he was just as formal and always remarked that the day was sure to be fine or, if it was raining, that the rain would clear by lunchtime. And Sabiha always dutifully asked if his wife, Angela, was well, and he in his turn assured her that his wife was in fine health. This exchange, or some variant of it, had for three years been the extent of conversation between Bruno and Sabiha.

Bruno had arrived at the café one day three years ago peddling his hothouse tomatoes. He was accompanied that day by a teenage boy of startling beauty, almost a young man. Bruno had introduced the boy to John with pride as his eldest son. Bruno the second, as if father and son were the heirs of an ancient family. From time to time the son was with Bruno at the market, but on Tuesdays Bruno always came to the café alone.

This Tuesday there was something a little different, something a little unexpected, in Sabiha's response to his greeting. She turned from the stove and considered him a moment before saying, 'Good morning, Bruno.' She seemed to examine him critically, almost as if she was going to question him. 'The *harira* will be ready in two minutes. The tomatoes look beautiful.' Before she turned back to her work at the stove, Sabiha's gaze rested on Bruno a little longer than was customary.

Bruno wondered if there might be something amiss with his clothing and checked himself. He was a fraction under six feet tall, a man in his middle forties, a sturdy countryman with alert blue eyes, a slightly flattened nose, and the well-muscled arms and shoulders of a wrestler. He had boxed in his twenties as a cruiser weight, and had about him the calm self-confidence of all such men who have tested their physical strength and courage against their peers in their youth.

As he stepped past Sabiha on his way through the kitchen to the dining room a tangy waft of tomato smell hit her. 'You bring the smell of the countryside to town with you every Tuesday, Bruno,' she said, and she turned and looked directly into his mild blue eyes and smiled.

With one hand already raised to push aside the bead curtain, Bruno paused and returned her look gravely. He did not quite know how he might respond to this unusual comment. There was a silence between them, which could have extended into awkwardness if he had not said, 'Thank you,' and continued on through into the dining room, letting the dangling tails of the bead curtain fall behind him.

The men all looked up from their meals as Bruno came clattering through the bead curtain. It was Tuesday. The big Italian was here. They shrugged and went back to their conversations. Their voices, however, were a shade lower than before Bruno came into the dining room, the atmosphere now no longer quite as homey and relaxed as it had been before his arrival. They resented his presence among them, but he was John's guest, so they tolerated him.

Bruno paused by his table, a hand on the back of the chair, and surveyed the room and its occupants, a smile in his eyes, an arrogance in his manner, looking them over as if they were a yard of cattle. He drew out the chair and sat. It was a position from which he was able to command the room. None of these men had ever been invited beyond the curtain.

John came out from behind the bar and greeted Bruno. He set a half-litre jug of red wine and a small basket of freshly cut bread on the table before him.

'So is the price of tomatoes still up this week?' he asked. 'Are you still celebrating?'

Bruno broke off a piece of bread and put the portion in his mouth and chewed it. He did not look at John while he chewed, his gaze resting instead on the man at the nearest table. The man returned his look steadily.

'They've slipped a bit this week,' Bruno said, and laughed. 'It's the bloody Italians again. It's always the same in the autumn.'

The tall man at the next table was Nejib, the oud player who accompanied Sabiha on Saturday nights. Nejib said, 'They're your own countrymen. So why do you complain about them?'

Nejib's companion was looking at Bruno and listening to the exchange with interest. He lifted a hand and fingered his moustache. Something frantic danced in this man's eyes. They were often together, these two, Nejib and the silent man with the exquisitely groomed moustache.

One or two of the other customers laughed and looked at Nejib and then at Bruno.

John stood by Bruno's table.

Bruno reached and grasped the handle of the wine jug and he lifted it and poured wine into his glass, watching the ruby liquid run from the spout, his head on one side, admiring the light through the wine. When the tumbler was full he set the small brown jug aside and reached for the glass. He lifted it to his lips and drank a little of the wine, as if appraising its qualities.

'Your wine's not improving, John,' he said regretfully. 'I can get you a good deal with one of my countrymen for something superior.' He smiled at Nejib. 'My countrymen don't only cultivate tomatoes.' He raised his glass, saluting the other man with the wine, then with irony in his tone he said quietly, 'Cursed by the Prophet, hey, Nejib?'

John left them to their veiled rivalries and went out to the kitchen. He said to Sabiha, 'One of these days those two are going to find an excuse to settle whatever it is between them and Bruno. I just hope it doesn't happen here. I wish Bruno would drop it.'

In the dining room Bruno drank deeply of the wine he had just that moment disparaged, and while he drank he did not take his eyes from the eyes of the other man. In the end it was Nejib who looked away. At this, Bruno said something. Perhaps it was not a word but was a sound denoting satisfaction, a kind of insolence in the tone of it. He set the glass on the table and wiped his lips with his fingers and spread his napkin in his lap.

He looked up as John approached his table, three deep bowls of steaming *harira* balanced expertly along the length of one arm, another in his free hand. John set the bowl of chickpea and lamb stew in front of Bruno, wishing him a good appetite, and moved to the next table and served Nejib and his silent companion.

Bruno leaned over the bowl and breathed the spicy smell of the stew, his eyes narrowed with pleasure. He crossed himself and took a piece of bread in one hand and his fork in the other and settled to the enjoyment of his Tuesday lunch. He might have been alone in his own kitchen at home, Nejib and his companion not so much ignored as dismissed.

An hour later Bruno was the only customer left. He sat with his legs stretched out under the table, his boots crossed at the ankles, alternately picking his teeth with a toothpick and sipping from his glass of wine. He belched and might have been the steward of some great estate in a former age, taking his ease, permitting himself a bonus of leisure while lesser men had been required by their masters to return to their labours. There was something complacent, and even a little timeless about Bruno Fiorentino's fine figure as he sat alone in the modest dining room of Chez Dom, gazing vacantly before him, aware only of his daydreams, a quality of calm and inner wellbeing about him that other, less contented men might well have envied. That he might himself be vulnerable did not occur to Bruno.

He cleared his throat and set the toothpick in the ashtray, drank the last of the wine and pushed back his chair. He was about to get up from the table when

Sabiha came out from behind the bead curtain. At the clattering of the beads Bruno turned. It was unusual to see Sabiha out of her kitchen at this hour on a Tuesday. In fact he could not remember *ever* having seen her come into the dining room. It was with a nervous anticipation of something novel that he settled his weight in the chair again and waited.

Despite their three-year acquaintance, Sabiha was unknown to him. She was a woman to be admired in secret. He was a little in awe of her and had often wondered how it must be for John to live with such a woman. What is marriage, what is a man's life, Bruno had often asked himself, without a family to delight him at the end of his day's work and to carry on his name after he is finished with this world? Bruno did not expect Sabiha to be as other women were, but saw her as the representative almost of another species, the object of men's fantasies rather than a modest wife and mother. And, of course, she was not a Christian. For Bruno, the devout Catholic, Sabiha was a woman apart; exotic, haughty, beautiful, deeply private and the cause of much conjecture and wonder to him over the years.

Sabiha came up to his table now and set a small blue and white dish in front of him. On the dish were two fragrant honey-dipped briouats. As she paused beside him her hip brushed lightly against his shoulder and she spoke softly. 'Here is something sweet from Sabiha to Bruno,' she said. After making this astonishing announcement she turned and walked away.

Bruno swung around in his chair, startled by her words, by the warm pressure of her hip against his shoulder. He could feel the glow of her touch coming into his cheeks. He was glad he was alone in the café and that Nejib and his sinister companion were not there to witness his confusion. He watched as Sabiha let the bead curtain fall behind her. He remained turned in his seat, watching the curtain settle, the clicking of the beads in the silence, half expecting to see her come out again, to laugh at his confusion. After a minute he turned back to the table and looked at the sweet pastries on the dish in front of him.

A blade of pain flashed across his groin. 'Ah!' he exclaimed, and drew in his breath sharply. He stretched his arms and shoulders to ease the tension that was in him. He could smell the briouats, as if he smelled Sabiha herself. Layers of her golden filo wrapped around sweet almond paste and orange flower water, dipped in boiling honey while still hot from the oven. They lay before him on the dish. Her offering. The silence beat against his ears. He looked about him. There was no one to see him. He reached and took one of the pastries delicately between the first finger and thumb of his right hand, hearing in his agitated thoughts her softly spoken *Something sweet from Sabiha to Bruno*. He lifted the pastry to his mouth and bit into it. The pastry was still warm. Who could resist Sabiha's sweets! He closed his eyes. It was the food of the gods.

Bruno ate both pastries, savouring each mouthful, closing his eyes, feeling the warm touch of Sabiha's hip where she had leaned against him. There was a vivid tension in his thighs of a kind he had not felt since he and Angela were first married. He permitted himself a small groan. He did not know what to think. He licked the honey from his fingers and with one extended finger delicately pushed the empty dish away across the table, his lips compressed. Now he began to feel afraid . . .

He knew he was not going to mention this incident to Angela when they were sitting by the stove together this evening, but was going to keep it to himself. Knowing this made him feel guilty. Would he seem guarded, he wondered, as if he was holding something back from her? Neither ever kept anything from the other, but each delighted in sharing every incident of their day when they met in the evening. Would he mention the briouats to her inadvertently, perhaps later, when he had forgotten to worry about it? It was a troubling possibility. But how was he to explain himself to his wife innocently and calmly when there was nothing *to* explain? What troubled him was not what he had *done*, but that Sabiha's touch and the confiding tone of her softly spoken words had aroused him. He was certain that if he as much as mentioned the briouats to her, Angela would know this at once. He could feel her certainty of his betrayal flash into her mind. The thought terrified him.

He got up and brushed at the sticky crumbs of pastry clinging to his trousers. He stood looking at the blue and white dish, hesitating, feeling with his tongue for the remnants of the filo, brushing at his lips with his fingers. He made up his mind then and leaned and picked up the dish and stepped across to the bead curtain. He pulled the curtain aside and looked into the kitchen. His mouth was suddenly dry.

'Madame Patterner?' he called. He did not know what he was going to say if she came into the kitchen and asked him what he wanted.

His box of Grosse Lisse was still sitting by the open doorway. Tolstoy was looking in at the tomatoes from the laneway, as if he was waiting for a mouse to jump out of the box. The dog looked up at him and gave a short warning bark.

'It's okay, Tolstoy,' Bruno said. He felt like a thief. Tolstoy gave a low growl. There was no sign of Sabiha or John. A pot was steaming on the stove, the lid rattling. Bruno let the curtain fall and turned back into the dining room and set the dish on the table again. He nudged the dish with his finger, as if he still considered doing something with it and was reluctant to leave it. Then he turned away and walked over to the front door and let himself out into the street.

Bruno stood on the narrow footpath outside the café. Something had happened between himself and John Patterner's wife. He was not sure what it was. But he was sure it was not *nothing*. He walked around the corner to where he had parked his van and opened the door and climbed into the cabin. To think such thoughts as were in his mind at this moment in the bright day was madness. He reached into the glove box and took out a tin of throat lozenges. They were blackberry flavoured. Angela always made sure he had some with him. He put one of the purple lozenges in his mouth and sucked it, the sweet blackberry flavour filling his mouth. He leaned on the wheel and looked along the alleyway, sucking fiercely on the lozenge and trying his best not to think of Sabiha's hip. But the softly encouraging sound of her voice was in his head like a song, and he could not silence it. He did not

want to silence it. He sucked hard and closed his eyes
and thought of her hip against his shoulder.

He opened his eyes and swallowed the last sliver
of lozenge. What had he done, he asked himself, to
make John's wife do this to him? He was certain he
had never done or said anything that could have been
taken by Sabiha as suggestive or improper. He had
never given her any kind of secret sign. None at all.
The very thought of it shocked him. Suppose Angela
were to hear of this? It was unthinkable. Or was it all
his own imagination? His own stupidity? Had Sabiha
not meant anything at all by it? Had she been thinking
of him sitting on his own in the dining room and
just decided to give him a treat? Her hip touching his
shoulder might have been an innocent accident. But
she had not just *let* her hip touch his shoulder! No, he
could feel it now; she had *leaned* her hip against him!
There had been pressure there, a light pressure but
real. She had *known* what she was doing. It had not
been an accident. It had been a *sign* to him. A strong
sign. But a sign of *what*, for God's sake? The touch of
her warm hip through the cotton fabric of his shirt
had seduced him utterly. 'Mary, Mother of God!' he
said and crossed himself. He reached for the key and
started the motor.

He drove out of the alley and turned left. Passing the front of Chez Dom he ducked his head and looked in. John and Sabiha were not at their table. The dining room was empty. He did not toot his horn but drove on. Above the roaring of the van's motor he shouted angrily, 'She *pressed* her hip against me!' Why had she done it? If not for *that*?

As Bruno made his way through the traffic, despite his resolve and his fear he found himself imagining Sabiha's bare skin under her skirt where she had leaned against his shoulder. There was madness in this, to be sure, and his heart beat faster with it, but once he had begun to think of it he could not resist the thought of her nakedness and her intention. He parked the van and got out and walked around to the back and opened the doors. He stepped into the back of the van and walked down the front and pulled out a box of Black Russian and another of Father Tom. He set the Black Russian on top of the Father Tom and lifted the boxes in his arms, cradling them against the strong muscles of his stomach. He stepped down from the van and stood outside the grocery store with the two boxes of tomatoes in his arms. He had seen, suddenly, how difficult it was going to be for him when he walked into the kitchen this evening and kissed Angela. He could hear her saying, So, my darling, did

anything interesting happen to you today in the big
world out there? Would he be able to answer her
confidently, No, my love. Nothing special. And how
about you? Have the children been behaving
themselves?

For the first time in their married life he was going
to lie to Angela! But that wasn't all. Later, when they
were lying in bed together and the children were asleep,
she would turn to him and put her hand in his and say,
What is it, my dearest man? Tell me! What happened
today? What is troubling you? For she would know. Oh
yes, Angela would know that *something* had happened.
She would sense it in his voice, see it in his eyes, know
it from the way of him. It was impossible to keep
anything from Angela. She knew everything. He was
sweating.

Bruno's thoughts swerved about wildly and he
stepped across the footpath and went through the open
door of the shop. He hailed the owner of the store in a
voice that was scarcely recognisable to him as his own.
The shop was crowded and smelled strongly of oranges.
He found a space and set the boxes of tomatoes down
and straightened. He lifted his cap and wiped the sweat
from his face with his sleeve. The strange way Sabiha
had looked at him when he arrived at the café that
morning. Her unusual remark. The way she stood and

looked directly into his eyes, as if she was going to ask him something. It was not an accident. It was not just his own imagination. It had happened. It was real!

He went back out into the street and stood with his hand to the handle of the van door. What was he to think? He knew what he *felt*, what his body *felt*. He could not mistake such a reaction as *this*. But what was he to *think*? What was he to *do*? He jerked the van door open and jumped in and slammed it behind him. He cursed and started the motor. He wanted to be safely at home having his dinner with Angela, the kids hanging off his shoulders and yelling at him.

*A*s usual on Friday at a little after five in the morning, being careful not to disturb John, Sabiha slipped out of their bed and pulled her dressing-gown on over her nightdress. It was still dark, the only light a yellow glow around the edges of the curtains from the streetlight on the corner outside the grocery store. She steadied herself with a hand to the bedhead while she felt around with her toes for her slippers. She walked over to the door and went downstairs and out the back to the toilet. Sitting on the toilet, she rested her elbows on her knees and put her chin in her hands and stared at the back of the door. She had counted the days, had calculated her move. This Friday was her fourteenth day. There was no need for her to vary her customary routine.

She had left the toilet door half-open and could see a thin edge of the laneway. It was silent and deserted at this time of the morning. She shivered in the chill. She had dreamed her baby cried out for her, the heartbreaking wailing of her child drifting in her mind like an old sickness. The dream had woken her and she had whispered, 'Don't weep, little one. You will soon be in your mother's arms.'

She made the coffee as if the routine of her life was securely in place, and their world was not falling into the sun. She warmed her hands over the gas flame, then heated the milk in the little copper pan that Houria had kept for this purpose, and maybe Dom too before Houria. When the coffee was ready she sat with her elbows on the kitchen table, cupping the warm bowl in both her hands and gazing at the stove, not seeing the stove but seeing some thought that had no shape, only the dread of it. The unmediated moment itself. Soon it would be upon her.

She drank a little of the coffee then set the bowl on the table and broke a piece from one of yesterday's sesame biscuits and dipped it in the coffee and ate it. She thought of her father sitting in his wooden armchair with the blue cushions at his back. He was waiting for the moment when his favourite daughter would come home and place her child in his arms. Then death could carry him off peacefully. And when he was dead her uncles would come and bury him. Her father had no religion, but the uncles would insist on a religious burial. Her father had always been different from the rest of his family. She remembered with pride how he had stood up to the soldiers when their neighbour's house was ransacked in a search for weapons. He had stood in the midst of the soldiers that day and ignored their curses and their guns. He had challenged death that day and not flinched. Surely he was that same man now? She was confident he would challenge the cancer in the same way he had challenged the authority of the soldiers; would calmly ask the cancer to wait until he held his grandchild in his arms.

She carried a bowl of coffee and two sesame biscuits upstairs. In the bedroom she switched on the bedside light and moved John's book aside and set the coffee and the biscuits on the chair beside the bed. John raised himself on his elbow and thanked her. He watched her getting dressed.

'Are you all right?' he asked her gently. 'Did you sleep okay?'

She slipped the dress over her head and stood with her head bent doing up the buttons. She did not look at him.

'I hope you're going to wear your overcoat,' he said. 'That dress isn't going to keep you warm.' He watched her. He searched for something to say to her that would lighten the mood between them. 'Last week you forgot the saffron,' he said, and laughed. 'Remember?' It wasn't a very convincing laugh.

'It's on my list,' she said softly, struggling with the last button. The world had split in two as it hurtled on its way into the cauldron of the sun. Nothing like it had ever been imagined.

John said, 'Darling, why are you crying? Please tell me. Come over here and tell me.'

She looked at him. 'I'm not crying,' she said, and smiled. 'Is there anything special you want this week?'

'I'm sorry,' he said. 'Whatever I've done or not done, darling, I'm sorry.' He sat up and held out his arms to her. 'Come on!'

She came over and leaned down and touched her lips to his.

He would have held her but she straightened.

She stood looking at him. 'I was just thinking of my father.' She shrugged and smiled. 'I'd better go.' It seemed to her in that moment that the two of them must be the loneliest people in the world. Why? she asked herself in despair. Why are we so alone? What have we done to deserve it?

John reached for the bowl of coffee and drank from it. He made a slurping sound when he drank. He set the bowl on the chair again and wiped his lips with the back of his hand then dipped a sesame biscuit into the coffee and bit into it.

She looked at him. Biscuit crumbs clung to his lips, a sesame seed glinting like a baby's tooth on his unshaved chin. She might have leaned and tenderly brushed away the crumbs and the seed with her fingers and kissed him. She buttoned her overcoat and stood at the end of the bed.

A dread of something terrible touched him; the way she stood there looking at him, her face a mask weirdly uplit by the bedside lamp, her eyes so still, so sad, so determined. As if she was not here with him but was in some other place. At the door she turned and lifted her hand to her lips and kissed her fingers and blew the kiss to him. Then she was gone.

*I*t was still dark when Sabiha left the café by the back door. She closed the door behind her but she did not lock it. She stood a moment in the dark looking along the lane, her back to the door, the air cold and smelling of the night. The city was only just waking. André's cat sat on the roof of the van watching her, a gleam of light reflecting in its eyes. She walked to the end of the lane and turned right into rue des Esclaves towards the *métro*. A street-cleaning machine was crawling along the gutter spraying water, its brooms swishing around, gathering up last night's rubbish.

She waited on the platform. There were few other people waiting with her. She did not look at them and they did not look at her. She would remember later, though imperfectly, the inward-curving advertisement on the wall of the tunnel opposite her proclaiming in gold cursive lettering overlaying a grand old building the words *Stolichnaya Vodka*. These two foreign words would recur to her again and again in an emphatic voice, the key to a tormenting riddle. The train pulled in and she got on and sat by the door, her bag on her knees, her hands folded over her bag. She closed her eyes and bent her head.

The train speeding her through the blackness of the tunnels, pursuing a howling fugitive from the underworld. In the screeching of the rails along the curve she heard the screams of the hunted woman. Then, suddenly, by a kind of miracle that is not to be understood, the speed of the train and her solitariness calmed her. Soon enough the sun would rise and the night would be over. A moment of happiness swept through her like a cool reviving breeze on a stifling summer evening at home—that moment when her father looked up from reading in his chair by the back door and smiled with pleasure to see her there. She could not say why she was happy in that moment.

The train came to a halt and she stood up. When the doors opened she stepped out onto the platform. The escalators were crowded now with people riding down to meet the trains. She rose through the spent night to the day. I am Sabiha, she said, rising towards the surface. This is who I am. This is the name my mother and my father blessed me with when I was born. I love my name, and I cherish the memory of my mother and father.

•

She walked down the aisle towards the back of the market as always, the men watching her as she walked by. She went into the women's toilet. In the booth she removed her underpants and put them in the left-hand pocket of her overcoat, then she took a pad from her bag and put it in the right-hand coat pocket. She reassured herself that she was preparing to undergo a clinical procedure. There must be no suggestion of disgust or guilt or shame in this. This was no more than a resumption, she told herself, of the endless procedures she and John had been required to submit to during the early years of their marriage. Nothing more than that. A means to the same end. Some of those procedures had been humiliating. Some had been enough to chill the soul forever. The only difference today was that *this* particular procedure had not been officially sanctioned. She had filled in no form, had signed no indemnity against the unforeseen. This was not part of the elaborately efficient world of the French medical bureaucracy. She was here to fulfil a practical purpose. She would be detached, therefore, and unemotional. She would *undergo* the procedure. Would submit to its necessities without complaint just as she had in the hospitals.

She gloved her forefinger and thumb with toilet paper and gripped the seat by its edge and lifted it. She held up her skirt and crouched above the bowl and emptied her bladder. The back of the cubicle door was painted a dark glossy green. It reminded her of waiting for her mother with her sister in the hospital in Tunis when she was fourteen, staring at the shiny green door through which they had been told her mother was to return to them with a new baby brother or sister. Only there had been no new brother or sister. Her father's patient explanation had not convinced her. She and her sister looking at her mother in the bed as if their mother had been placed under some strange enchantment and was no longer herself. Her mother's sad smile from the remote place to which she had gone with her dead child. The cubicle door was just the green of that old hospital door. She would not let the memory overwhelm her. She would not be cowed by such signs as these.

When she had finished, she stood and buttoned her overcoat and stepped out of the toilet block into the noise and blaze of the powerful overhead lights, the acres of boxes of fresh fruit and vegetables illuminated brighter than daylight, the yellow and blue forklifts, like enormous plumed insects snorting and foraging among the diminutive men and the gorgeous produce, selecting this and that and carrying it off. She realised she was clutching her bag to her chest. She breathed slowly and let the bag hang loosely from her hand, and she lifted her free hand and brushed her hair back from her face with her fingers and stood straighter, stepping out with her accustomed poise, her head held high, looking neither right nor left, walking as if she walked in a place where she could not be seen—in the desert at night under the stars, where solitariness is a gift to the grieving soul, journeying towards the dreaming lion in his lair. She was afraid, but now she knew she was going to go through with it.

As she walked between the aisles of produce, Sabiha scarcely heard the cries of the men or saw the spectacle of it that morning. She was remembering, with sorrow and shame, the days when, at her insistence, John had been repeatedly required to give specimens of his semen to be tested. It had been as if they tested him for the quality of his manhood, as if he himself were being brought into question. She had witnessed the humiliation of it in his eyes, in the apology of his gentle smile. They had not talked about it. It was she who had seen that these tests and questions had begun to define them and to defile them, and she had brought the dreadful inquiry to an end. 'We will do no more of these tests,' she said one day. They had scarcely talked about it since.

They had not been eligible for the more advanced therapies, the new technologies of human reproduction. There was nothing *wrong* with them. They had no *condition*, and the doctors did not deal in matters of the human soul. It was suggested they consult a psychologist. John would have done so but she declined. They would abase themselves no further. Their love had survived changed. Something thereafter remained incomplete. The silence between them announced it every day. Then John had suddenly taunted her with the number of Bruno's children, and something in her had given way. The waiting had come to an end. Perhaps it was for the best.

As she approached Bruno's stall, Sabiha's skin felt chilled and she was trembling. She reminded herself that she had always been nervous whenever she had had to submit to a physical examination and had never overcome those feverish bouts of nerves that had made her shiver when she took off her clothes for them, her skin breaking out in goose bumps as she stood in the cubicle and waited. She had always had to steel herself to go through with it. To smile at the nurse and the doctor while inside she cringed and protested.

As she drew closer to the stall she repeated to herself, It is just a clinical procedure. Trusting the lie to provide her with a modest private model of universal morality; a key to something good and true, to stand between her and her despair; a charm with which to enchant the forces of her disbelief. But the words that spun in her head, contradicting her meek insistence, were Stolichnaya Vodka. Something in her was not convinced. Something protested. Something in her resisted and cried out against this. Something *old* in her, it was. An archaic belief that refused and stood its ground and would not yield to her semantic play. A belief more ancient and more durable than clinical procedures. She recognised in this resistance the sentiment of her grandmother's songs; the wisdom of the old women. It was this that refused to submit to her dissembling. An echo of her fabled Berber ancestors roused to voice its protest. Tell the truth, her grandmother had always said. Speak it, whatever it is. Do what you must do but do not lie about what it is that you do. Do not call it something else. Call it what it is.

There it was, displayed to her openly by the simplicity of her grandmother's truth: the realisation that she was not the first woman to have ventured this solution to her childlessness. She stopped abruptly and stood still, clutching her bag to her chest once again, knowing suddenly that this thing she proposed was as old as motherhood itself. As old as woman. She was not alone. Her grandmother was with her.

She saw Bruno then. He was unloading his van, the broad back of his red and blue striped shirt. She might have been watching him through the wrong end of a spyglass, or seeing him at the end of a tunnel, the fruit stalls and their people to either side of him blurred and out of focus. He was so real, so physically there, she held her breath. He swung around from the open doors at the rear of his van, three boxes of tomatoes embraced against his chest, his shirt sleeves rolled to the elbows, his jeans faded almost to white at the knees, his long black hair loose and glossy. In front of him the elaborate display of his beloved varieties, Costoluto Genovese, Caspian Pink, Dorothea de Brandis. They might have been delicate varieties of roses, or ladies of the theatre whom it was his delight to serve.

Her stomach lurched and a fine sweat came to her skin as she stood waiting for him to see her.

How beautiful he was. She was surprised. She had not seen his beauty until this moment. His muscled arms and shoulders. His calm. The ease and grace of his movements. The perfect manliness of his world. The threat of his beauty touched her, and if she had witnessed his death this minute she would have felt not regret but relief. How could she do this? She knew now there was no going back. She was already in that other place. The old reality had no meaning.

He saw her then and stopped, standing so still he might have been a figure of stone, his black hair fallen across his face, his lips parted.

Without taking his eyes from her, Bruno slowly bent his knees and set the boxes of tomatoes on the concrete, then he straightened and stood with his hands hanging by his sides. He might have been a man who had detected the stealthy approach of his enemy and was stilled by fear, nerving himself to the contest ahead of him.

It was Sabiha who moved.

She walked along the last few yards of the aisle and went up to him. She stood so close to him she smelled the familiar tang of tomatoes on him. She offered him no greeting, but looked into his eyes and waited for him to understand her purpose there this morning. She saw that something in his gaze was stricken by what she offered him, and she understood that he was mastered by his lust for her. Without a word he turned and walked around his display to the back of his van and she knew herself invited to follow him. At the rear of the van, where the doors stood wide open, he stopped and held out his hand to her. She took his hand, as if it was an act of common chivalry from him, and he helped her up into the back of the van. The touch of his fingers sent a shock through her and she drew in her breath, a small sound of distress escaping from her throat.

Inside the tall van she set her bag down and rested her back against the side wall and closed her eyes. She could not steady her breathing. The van dipped and rose as Bruno climbed in. She heard him closing the doors. Blackness pressed on her eyelids. She felt him move around her now. He was close, his smell strong, his breathing hard, his fingers finding the buttons of her overcoat, opening her coat then reaching and lifting the skirt of her dress. His hands on her bare thighs, a low moan from him as his fingers found her nakedness. Then he was easing himself into her, gasping, gripping her buttocks and pressing her to him. She opened her thighs and lifted one leg onto a stack of tomato boxes, crouching and taking him deep. He groaned, his body shivering, his voice a scattering of broken syllables, pleading or sorrowing, 'Aah! Aah!', and might have been taking a knife in his flesh.

The exquisite pleasure was unexpected. It shocked her. She fought against it and cried out. She thought she would go to her knees with it and she gripped his arms and cried out to him, 'Bruno! For God's sake, Bruno!'

His wordless howl as he came inside her was of a man struck to the soul.

And those cries of ecstasy were her own.

The sheetmetal side of the van buckled at her back and boomed.

They stood astonished, their bodies locked together.

She gasped and drew away from him. Retrieving her underpants from her overcoat pocket she put in the pad and stepped into them. She smoothed her dress and buttoned her overcoat and felt in the darkness for her bag. Her body was trembling. Her head pounding. She was reaching for the door handle when she was stilled by a strange sound. Bruno was sobbing in the darkness. A chill went through her. He was crouched at her feet weeping.

She found the handle and opened the doors and stepped down from the van. She walked along the aisle towards the front of the market, the doors of Bruno's van swinging and screeching behind her. She closed her mind to him. Wasn't he a man? Why did he kneel and weep? She would not be able to make her careful purchase of spices from her friend Sonja. She just couldn't do it. She had to go home at once.

As she walked through the market Sabiha's emotions veered this way and that, then stopped dead. Then gusted, exultant, racing into the future. She was certain Bruno had opened the way of the child within her. But she was no longer herself. His tears terrified her; the unforeseen looming at her, suddenly, out of her act, out of his torment, out of the strange place she had entered with him. She had not counted on that. Men were free with their seed and boasted of it. Men betrayed their wives and laughed. Why did this man fall to his knees and weep? She was shaken by Bruno's grief.

As she walked to the *métro* Sabiha's mood was of a strange elation. But for the pressure of the pad between her legs she might have dreamed it. But it was true. She had done it. And she was not the first. As old as woman herself, she repeated. The drift of her child into the infinite dark had been arrested at last. Now the little baby had begun slowly to move towards its mother. Her passion was to be the mother of her child; to bring it life, to succour it, to comfort it, to give it her own life if necessary. And if she were to be condemned for the means by which she had satisfied this passion, then she would stand up and look her judges in the eye and freely admit her guilt. *Yes, I did it. I did it for my child*, she would tell them. And who would condemn her for that? A woman with a child growing in her womb is not alone.

*J*ohn was sitting up in bed listening to her footsteps as she went down the stairs. He didn't hear the door close and waited a moment, unsure whether she had gone or not. He called out, but there was no reply. The house was silent now with the silence of emptiness. He stuffed her pillow as well as his own at his back and reached for his book. He took a sip of coffee and opened the book on his lap. He loved the peace and quiet of this hour. After Sabiha had gone to the market on Friday he usually stayed in bed and read. This morning he stared at the open book in his lap and thought of her tormented expression as she blew him the kiss when she was leaving; as if she was departing from his life forever. His throat tightened at the thought of it.

He put on his clothes and opened the curtain and stood at the window. The blossoming clouds were still pink with the dawn. Customers were already coming and going at the Kavi boys' corner store. Life was going on out there as usual. He picked up his bowl and went downstairs. He set the bowl on the sink in the kitchen and went through into the dining room. He picked up the mail from the floor and opened the street door and looked up and down the street. André was already coming back from walking Tolstoy, the great shaggy beast loping by his side as if it was moving in slow motion, its grey eyes fixed on the bloody deeds of ancestors who had ripped wolves apart on the wintry steppes of Siberia. John waved to André and went back inside and closed the door. He put the mail on the bench in the kitchen and went into the bathroom and took off his shirt. While he shaved there were the voices of the workers arriving at the laundry down the laneway.

He ate breakfast then picked up the mail and went into the sitting room. He put the light on. A stillness in here, the smell of their evenings. The television in the corner on an upended half barrel, a red cloth draped over the barrel like a skirt over the hips of a woman. Houria and Dom's old green two-seater couch facing the television. A small square wooden table and an upright chair behind the couch. In the corner beside the table his own pile of books, collected from the second-hand book market.

He put the mail on the table beside the pile of unpaid bills and drew out the chair and sat down. He lit a cigarette and looked through the mail. There was a letter from his mother, his name in her familiar handwriting and the Australian stamp. He opened the envelope and drew out the two closely written sheets. There was also a postcard. The postcard was a photograph of the new road bridge at Moruya. He sat looking at the picture, smoking, and remembering the trestles of the old timber bridge, the rumble of his dad's Ford going over on their way into town. The timber bridge had been washed away in a record flood and the town had been without a bridge for more than two years. He sat smoking and reading his mother's neat handwriting. There was nothing much wrong with her eyes.

My Dearest Son,
Things are much the same with me and your father. The doctor put him on a bit of oxygen last week, that's all. But he's fine. There's no need to worry. He says to give you his love. Did I tell you? Uncle Martin died. I think I might have

told you last time. Martin was eighteen months younger than me. So it makes you think, doesn't it? There but for the grace of you know who. Martin always asked after you. He expected great things from you. It was a lovely funeral. There must have been two hundred people. I didn't know he had so many friends. It was a cremation of course. Our boy in Paris, he used to call you. We've still had no rain. Aunty Esme told me Chinaman's Hole is dry for the first time ever. I think of you and Kathy and your mates down there carrying on till all hours of the night. You used to have such a lovely time, the whole gang of you. I used to love it when you were all down there at Chinaman's in the summer. Which reminds me, I hate to ask, but have you made those plans yet for coming home for a visit? I'm always asking, aren't I? One of these days you'll surprise the pair of us. I see you coming through the front door here sometimes and my heart gives me such a kick. Kathy's talking about getting married! Can you believe it? They came to see us in August. They were on holidays. Touring, he called it. He's English. They were staying a day here and a day there, stopping at the smart B&Bs that have sprung up everywhere along the coast. I worry how they can all make a living. You wouldn't know us these days. He's very nice, but I don't know if he's going to be a match for our Kath when she gets going. A bit too nice for his own good if you ask me. Kath needs someone definite. Dad just called out to give you his love. I said I had already. He said, well give it to him again. He's just the same. He'd love to see you. He really would. And you know I would too darling. It's a beautiful day. There's a pair of rosellas comes every morning to the seed I've hung in the apricot tree. We've only got the one tree here. Think of how many trees we had once! They've just come in now.

With all our love, my dearest boy,
Mum.
PS Please give our love to your wife.

John folded the letter and put it back into the envelope.

Swimming at Chinaman's all summer holidays with his friend Gibbo and Kathy and her mates. He could see the casuarinas on the bank screening them from the house and the beach of smooth river stones. Mucking around down there until the middle of the night. Loretta letting his fingers explore the inside of her thigh in the moonlight, her skin chilled and wet and goose-bumped and exquisitely soft. The softest skin he had ever touched. He could smell Chinaman's now, the sour leaf rot of the churned water on their skin. He could not imagine Chinaman's dry. Where had the green water dragons gone and the black eels if the pool was dry? He felt a deep regret that his old home was no longer as it had been when he was a boy and he longed to know it again, to smell the river and the bush and to see his old friends still young, laughing at him for his shyness and calling to him. He wondered what had happened to Gibbo and Loretta and the rest of them. They must all be out there somewhere.

After he'd finished dealing with the bills he went out and started cleaning up the kitchen. He would have the place tidy for her when she got home.

When Sabiha came into the kitchen from the lane John's music was on very loud. He stepped across to meet her and kissed her on the cheek. He yelled over Carole King singing, 'So you've been seeing our Bruno!'

She drew back from him, lifting her hand and touching her cheek with her fingers as if he had slapped her.

'Sorry!' He raised his hands in mock self-defence. 'You smell of tomatoes, darling.'

She turned the music off and put her empty shopping bag down by the stove. She took off her overcoat and hung it in the alcove by the stairs. She was trembling. Tolstoy was barking in the lane, as if he'd caught something of her fear and anxiety.

John was watching her.

She struggled to hold his gaze. She didn't know what to say and murmured helplessly, 'Bruno's not the only person we know who sells tomatoes.'

He couldn't help smiling at this. 'Oh, come on, darling! Don't take me so seriously.' He tried to keep his tone light and neutral. 'It was just something to say. Where's the shopping?' She seemed so down and grim. 'Bruno's still our tomato man, isn't he?' He reversed the broom and went on sweeping the kitchen floor, bending to get the head of the broom under the front of the stove. 'Anyway, I *like* the smell of tomatoes.'

It wasn't shame she felt. She had sat in the *métro* this morning with her head bowed and a sense of doom hanging over her, expecting nothing less than the death penalty for what she contemplated. But no shrieking fireball had shattered the walls and brought the roof down on them. They were not buried, after all, in the smoking ruins of their lives. It all stood in place still, quiet and at peace—now that Carole King was no longer wailing at them. The dailiness of their routine was undisturbed. John sweeping the floor.

She said, 'I'm going to have a lie-down for a few minutes.'

John straightened and looked at her.

She felt sorry for him. 'I just need a few minutes to myself.' She smiled. She had betrayed him. Or what *is* betrayal? What jury of wives would not condemn her? What she felt, she decided, was guilt and fear. But she did not feel shame. The distinction was important to her. She would plead guilty: Yes, I did it. But there would be no remorse or regret for what she had done. I would do it again. If I need to I *shall* do it again. She was thinking of him now. She could *smell* him on her clothes. It wasn't *just* the smell of tomatoes, it was the smell of Bruno, his man smell. It was a wonder John hadn't smelled it. When Bruno's hands touched her naked thighs the pleasure had been searching, sudden, imperious, driving a shot of electricity into her. At the first touch of his hands a wave of exquisite dizziness had swept through her and she thought she was going to faint. She closed her eyes now and turned away from her husband's puzzled gaze.

John leaned lightly on the broom as if he were a boatman about to delve for the bottom with his punt pole. She was unreachable.

'You'd better go and lie down then,' he said.

When she had come through the door a moment ago there was some fine and heightened preoccupation in her dark eyes. It had claimed his attention at once; the flame of an extraordinary excitement. Something fleeting—the last of her youth, was it? She was more beautiful and more sad than he had ever seen her. But at this moment she was no longer his woman. She was too deep and too alone. He thought of the girl who had lain in his arms on the bank of the Eure that summer day in Chartres, and for an instant the transformation of the years bewildered him.

'I just need a moment to myself,' she said again, and turned and went out.

He listened to her footsteps on the stairs, waiting for the creaking of the boards as she crossed the bedroom overhead, imagining her sitting on the side of their bed, her head in her hands. Was there in her sadness, in this change, a sense of their eventual end? To age, and then to die. The futility of it all. It was there in her songs on Saturday nights, the knowledge of death and nostalgia. He had seen men weep for her singing, reminded of their exile and their mortality. He had seen a tear slide down Nejib's dark cheek more than once as he plucked the sweet strings of his beautiful oud in accompaniment to her melancholy songs.

John was still listening for her footsteps but the boards had not creaked. She must be sitting at the dressing-table looking at herself in the mirror, taking her hair down and looking into her own eyes. His beautiful wife, Sabiha. What strangers they really were to each other. Strangers to each other's language. To each other's childhood. Strangers to each other's tribe. He loved her helplessly.

He went on sweeping the kitchen floor. He gathered the dirt in front of the broom, turning the head of the broom sharp-edged to get the bristles into the wide cracks between the old tiles. He swept the dirt out the back door into the laneway, pushing it to the side over the top of the drain, scrubbing the broom head back and forth until he had forced the last of it through the grille. It was raining, the cobbles black in the cold grey light. He stood at the open door breathing the smell of the rain, remembering the vivid smell of rain when the first drops splashed onto the dry leaf litter of the stringybark forest in summer and the wonderful scents stored there throughout the dry were released into the humid air, rich and heady for the first minutes of rain. He longed to smell that smell again. It was the smell of everything that had once made him hopeful about his life. He and his father dancing around stupidly in the rain, yelling, *It's rain-ing, it's pour-ing, the old man is snor-ing* . . . His father telling them, *It's raining money*. So they all jumped in the car and drove down to Moruya and went shopping and then to the pictures. That rain in summer, it was the smell of happiness.

•

She lay on her back on the bed, her blue woollen blanket covering her, shaping her, the rain pattering softly against the window. She was calmer now, listening to the familiar sounds of the street, the comforting rain tapping on the window. She was not sorry for what she had done. She was glad she had found the courage to do it. But she was a changed woman. She had become the woman who had walked alone into the desert night under the stars and killed the lion.

She was going to be a mother.

She was going to hold her child in her arms. The little baby would look up at her here on this bed. It would sleep and cry and be joined to her breast. Its little body would be warm and vulnerable, delicate, soft as clouds and yearning for its mother's touch. She put her hand under the blanket and placed her open palm over the pad and she thought of the potent abundance of Bruno's astonishing seed. She cupped her mound with her hand and the tears ran down her cheeks. She was exhausted.

She woke from the dream with a start.

The room was cold.

It was a dream of the smooth sweet pleasure of sex. She still *felt* it. She had woken thinking not of her child but of her regret that if she really were pregnant then she would have no reason to go and see him ever again. She was awed by her response to him. She sat up, waking from the feeling of the dream. Had she destroyed him? Bruno, the loyal father and husband. The image of him kneeling on the floor of his van weeping frightened her. She wanted him to stand up and smile at the great pleasure of what he had done. Not cringe on the floor weeping!

She wrapped the blanket tightly around her shoulders and lay down again. The woman who killed the lion had not feared the living lion, but had feared the lion only after it was dead. It was her defeated victim the woman had feared, when the beast's nobility had become the carrion of the scavengers, the yellow-eyed hyenas and the ragged vultures that dropped from the sky like evil dreams. It was only then the woman had begun to see that she had brought herself to the notice of these shifty-eyed gods.

How could the modest routine of their lives at Chez Dom survive what she had done? She still *felt* him inside her. She still heard his moans. What of his wife, Angela, and his eleven children . . .

She lifted the blanket aside and got off the bed and put on her shoes. She was going to be late with the men's midday meal. John had turned his music on again. She had never learned to like his music. She would not think of him. Not yet. The time would come for thinking of Bruno and for thinking of John. She would deal with the need for thinking when it was time for her to settle with them both. Now she must prepare the meal or the men would go hungry and then they would go to another café for their midday meal and she and John would go broke. Then what would they do? Without Chez Dom they would have nothing.

She went downstairs into the kitchen and turned off the music. She took her apron from the hook beside the stove and wrapped it around her waist and tied the strings in a bow at her back. She called, 'Are you there, darling?'

Her kitchen! For the moment she was safe.

She called, 'Did you get Saturday's meat?' There was no answer.

She stood at the bench, sharpening the big vegetable knife with the stone.

André's cat came in from the lane and sat inside the open doorway and watched her. She saw its shadow and said coldly, 'I've got nothing for you.' She turned and looked at the cat. It blinked. Would her grandmother have recognised in this cat one of the old scavenger gods? The masked gods of her old people? Sabiha herself knew only the most faded remnants of her grandmother's ways. Tones of suggestion so weathered, so neglected, so distant they held only shreds of meaning. Their richness lost even to someone like herself, instructed as a child where she must look for them; in the yellow eye of the hyena at evening, in the black rags of the vulture in the morning. Sabiha had never seen a hyena or a vulture in real life. Waiting was what cats did best. Waiting and watching. Growing invisible in their stillness. Until the moment came for them to pounce. Yes, she decided, and she turned back to the bench and got on with her work, cats are of the family of the old gods.

Twenty minutes later she heard the van coming down the lane. She had not noticed it was missing. John must have gone out while she was asleep upstairs.

He came into the kitchen and heaved two heavy bags of meat onto the bench, then stood back easing his shoulders and rubbing his arms.

'It's getting heavier,' he said. 'Or I'm getting weaker.'

She was glad to have him home with her. She smiled at him. 'I was wondering where you'd got to,' she said. 'You left your music playing.'

They looked at each other.

He stepped forward and held her against him.

She relaxed into his arms and rested her head on his shoulder and whispered, 'I love you so very much, my John Patterner.'

'And I love you too,' he said. 'You smell wonderful.'

'So do you,' she whispered. 'You smell like home.'

He was moved and he laughed and held her away and looked at her. 'You're crying again.'

'I'm sorry.'

He held her close, his voice muffled by her hair. 'As long as we can hold each other like this, my darling, you can cry as much as you like.'

They remained in each other's arms for a long time. John closed his eyes and breathed in the smell of her hair and her neck.

•

The tears ran down her cheeks as she sliced the onions. She wiped her tears with a corner of her apron. John was singing the Carole King song in the dining room while he set the tables. How would she ever be able to tell him what she had done? She picked up the board and with the thick edge of the broad knife she swept the chopped onions into the pan—it was exactly the action Houria had used. Sometimes she felt as if she *was* Houria. She gave the onions a stir then leaned and took a stick of celery from the basket under the bench and broke it apart and washed the earth from it under the tap. The lovely smell of the wet earth on her fingers. She remembered her surprise when she first discovered that French earth did not smell the same as her father's earth. Her surprise that *all* earth did not smell as the earth of her home. No matter how long she lived in France, she would always be a stranger here; she and John, strangers both of them. Yet Houria had not been a stranger here. Why was that? How was it, she wondered, that Houria had made Paris her home? She had begun to realise that once this child was born she and John would no longer be able to go on living in Paris. And for John, Tunisia was an impossibility. For *herself* Tunisia was an impossibility. For the first time in her life Sabiha admitted that she no longer expected to go home one day to live. It had always been in her mind, this idea that Paris was not her permanent destination and that one day she would return and go on with her life in El Djem. But of course she wouldn't! How could she? Once her father had seen the child she would be free and her time at Chez Dom finished. She had not *emigrated* to France, after all, but had come over to help while her aunt recovered from her grief.

Chez Dom had never really belonged to her and John. The café had never become theirs. John, especially, had not believed in Chez Dom as his life. The café should have quietly died with Houria's death, and she and John should have closed the doors and gone away and made their own lives. They had made nothing of their own. It was clear to her suddenly, *today*, that after this child was born she and John must go to Australia and make a new life there, the three of them. In Australia they would be a family. The muscles of her forearm were aching with grinding the spices in Dom's old mortar. She straightened and eased her forearm, flexing her fingers. Before today I knew myself to be a good woman, she thought. Now what can I say of myself?

Four

Clare and I were having our usual coffee yesterday morning at the kitchen table, she reading the newspaper and me staring out the back door at our forlorn garden wondering how I was going to fill my day. Stubby was resting his head against my legs under the table. Every now and then Clare read out some snippet of news, then fell silent again. Out of one of these silences, and without looking up from the newspaper, as if she was reading something, she said, 'He's probably working up the courage to ask you to read his novel.'

This is the way we conduct our conversations. It took me a moment to wake up to the fact that she was talking about John. 'A novel about what?' I said. 'John's not a writer.'

'Has he told you that? About *them*.'

'John doesn't write,' I said.

'How do you know?'

'I can tell. Writers know when there's another writer around.'

'Like cats, you mean?' She laughed and gave me a look.

I asked her to pass over the last biscuit if she wasn't going to eat it.

She said, 'I'll go you halves,' and broke the biscuit into two uneven pieces. She gave me the smaller piece.

'Yes, just like cats,' I said. 'You're looking very smart, darling. I like that outfit. It suits you.' I gave my piece of biscuit to Stubby. He looked up at me with gratitude and love in his beautiful eyes.

She said, 'Thanks, Dad.'

I have a dread. It's a father's dread. You can guess what it is. It is an image of Clare after I'm gone, sitting here with the newspaper on Saturday morning reading out snippets of news to Stubby, or his successor. Becoming the solitary old lady in her father's house. If that happens I will have betrayed Marie; I will have betrayed our covenant of love for our little girl. How could I do that? How could I leave our little girl alone in the world? I wanted to ask her if she'd met someone, but I didn't dare. She's been looking very attractive lately. She gets annoyed with me if I say anything.

I watched her spread the newspaper on the table. It's true. She's still my little girl. My *child*. My daughter. I owe her everything and she owes me nothing. That's the way I see it. That's the way I've always thought of it. If you bring a child into the world you owe them everything. I'm haunted by my fear that I have failed her in some way and she will be left alone.

I have a friend. He's my oldest friend. He has lived alone for more than forty years. He makes the best of it. No one does a better job of living without a companion than he does. He spends a lot of time organising his social life so that he doesn't eat too many dinners alone, so that he can look forward all day to meeting a friend for dinner in the evening. Even after forty years, he still dreads the business of having to cook something and sit there eating it on his own in the evening, as if he were a character in an Anita Brookner novel. No one gets used to that. The evening coming on and not a soul to have a laugh with or to argue the toss with, hearing your own voice debating the talkback callers on the radio while you fry some eggs in a pan on the gas. Whose idea of fun is that? What dismays this friend of mine is having no choice. I meet him for dinner once every couple of months. He's my only regular outing of this kind. He insists on it. If I don't call him, he calls me. He says to me, 'It's okay for you, you've got a family.' I don't argue. It's true, I have a daughter. I'm lucky. But it's not right for Clare to be living here with her dad at thirty-eight. I want her to feel at home here in my house, her parents' old place—the home she grew up in and will inherit one day—but I don't want to do anything that will encourage her to stay here permanently. I couldn't forgive myself for that; beguiling my daughter into being *my* company in my old age. Even doing it inadvertently.

I watched her as she carefully folded the newspaper in half on the table. That's the way she's always done things, with care, taking her time. She used to stick her tongue out, concentrating, when she was five. I wished for her sake she would meet someone and go away and make a place of her own. Maybe even have a family. Is that too much to ask? Is it too late for that? Not so that I can have the pleasure of being a grandfather, but so that she can have a bit of reality of her own. A bit of happiness with someone by her side before it's too late.

'It's what they usually turn out to want from you, Dad,' she said. 'Sooner or later. Once they know who you are. A free appraisal of their nonsense.'

'It's not always nonsense,' I said. 'Remember Caroline?'

'Caroline was the exception.'

'Exceptions are always the exception,' I said. One thing I knew for certain was that John Patterner was no writer. He had never said anything to me about writing: mine, his own, or anyone else's. He didn't talk about the books he was reading. He kept all that to himself. He had never even let on if he'd read any of my books, and I certainly had not asked him—if they've read one of your books and liked it they can't wait to tell you. And you don't want to hear the other thing. Writers talk about their stuff all the time. You can't shut them up. It's all they ever talk about. There had never been one word from John on the subject of writing. John was the quiet type, as all true readers are. Keeping their imaginary worlds to themselves. Except when he was telling me his story. Even then there was something quiet and private in the way he spoke about himself and Sabiha; as if he was telling *himself* the story; going over it to find its meaning for himself. Looking for something he'd missed when it was happening to him.

As he and I sat together at our regular table in the Paradiso on rainy days, or under the plane tree on the footpath when it was fine, or when he could no longer resist having a cigarette—he was still 'giving them up'—it was often as if I was not there with him. He needed to *know* I was listening to him, but *I* wasn't the point of his telling. Which was one good reason why he held my interest the way he did. I often felt I was eavesdropping. Overhearing things I shouldn't be hearing. I never interrupted him. Never. I never urged him on or put a question to him. I didn't dare deflect him in case he failed to find his way back to where he'd left off. I feared to miss something. Some bright detail catching the light in the monochrome intricacy of his memory and his imaginings, this thing he was making of his lost years in Paris, the story. He needed me. Of course he needed me; I was his perfect listener, his perfect audience. But he only needed me so that he could *tell* his story. So he could understand it himself and move it on. I had no active part in it. I was not his prompt. It was *his* confession and he didn't need to be told what to say by me.

When I get home from our sessions I go upstairs to my study and sit at my desk overlooking the park and I write up my notes. I enjoy doing this. I've never told him about it. To have my own secret life of his story is part of the pleasure of it for me. I've never quite said so, even to myself, but I know what these notes are, these lengthy summaries of my own, these diversions and reflections, into which my own life finds its way—like a cat finding its way into a cupboard and going to sleep there. These secret intrusions into his story are the assertion of my rights as a listener. My view of this is that when someone tells you a story they give it to you. The story is their gift. It becomes yours. That's the way I look at it. They place the story in your trust. And they do that because they *need* to do it. They want their story to go out from them and be somewhere else, with their listener. Just as a writer wants to rid himself of his writing and get it to a reader. I am aware that with my notes I am, in my own customary way, making something other of John and Sabiha's story than the story *they* know. Shaping it, if you like, to my own imagination. I don't know how *not* to do this.

A writer can't arbitrarily decide what to write. We can only do what is offered to us. What comes our way. I like to call it a conversation with the unconscious. Following the prompts of the imagination. But these prompts must offer themselves freely. They won't be forced. That's the nature of the gift. It's what we mean when we say some people are gifted. They receive the prompts, and they follow them. Not everyone is so prompted, and not everyone who is so prompted follows them. It can be an arduous journey. But contrary to the common belief, writing is not a solitary pursuit; it is always a conversation.

A story will suddenly get a grip, and there it is, a deeper resonance, and you wake in the night thinking about it. I hadn't reached that stage with John's story, not yet. Perhaps I never would. But it was out there. It was a possibility. It had happened to me before. Perhaps I even *hoped* for it to happen to me this time, so I could come out of my retirement and stop wandering around the house like a ghost, my days full once again with the preoccupations of my craft, gifted once again. Writing and telling are very different fish. My father was a great storyteller who never wrote a word in his life. The writer cruises in the ocean currents, and often comes to grief out there. The writer who loses his way in what Christina Stead called the ocean of story. It happens all the time. We drown out there. We go under. A familiar voice falls silent and is never heard from again. The *Mary Celeste*s of the writing world. It's not something you can calculate. The loss is mysterious and puzzling. The teller, on the other hand, keeps to a familiar stretch of the river and remains safe.

'Come on,' I said to Stubby, and I got up from the table. 'Let's go and buy some pastries from the beautiful Sabiha.'

Clare said, 'Is she being nice to you yet?'

'Sabiha and I have an understanding.'

Clare laughed. '*You* have one maybe, Dad. Get some of those semolina biscuits with the almonds on them.'

I said, 'I thought I might get some of her fried honey cakes.'

'Some of them too.'

We looked at each other.

'What kind of an understanding?' she said, rather solemn suddenly.

*T*uesday morning and it was just breaking day, a thin cold light rimming the curtains. She was lying awake beside John, watching the slow dawn and wondering if Bruno was going to bring their order and stay for his midday meal as usual, or whether he would keep away from Chez Dom. She hadn't seen him since Friday and was dreading the thought of having to face him. But she also wanted to see him. It was true. She wanted to see him not in the real world, but in some kind of ideal place, where they would be accountable only to each other. But where was that? If he was going to sit there in his regular place in the dining room today, giving Nejib and his grim companion a hard time of it as usual . . . She couldn't think about it. And when he walked into the kitchen holding a box of Grosse Lisse against his chest, how was she going to meet his eyes?

Her thoughts were in a mess. Hopefully Bruno would be too ashamed to show up. He might even be so ashamed of what they'd done that he would *never* show up again; his disappearance from their lives a puzzle for everyone but herself. Was it just possible she and John might sail on peacefully together with the child now? Her child and her husband unsuspecting as the years went by? Like an episode out of one of the novels John forever had his nose in. But there was still Bruno on his knees weeping. *That* was surely a portent of something terrible. A big strong man like Bruno brought to his knees. She couldn't shake the image from her mind. She wasn't in control of her thoughts. Since last Friday she had been living inside the mind of a frantic stranger, desperately looking around for something solid to grab onto, something to steady herself with.

John drew in his breath sharply and made a noise in his throat. She turned her head on the pillow and looked at him in the dim light. She loved his profile, the reassuring and familiar intimacy of him, his beautiful strong nose. John was her man. As they'd lain in each other's arms on the bank of the river at Chartres that day he had whispered to her, *You and I are like the two wings of a butterfly.* She had cherished his image as a token of their enduring love. She had soon discovered that John was a gentle and romantic man. An old-fashioned man, she thought him. But she had never really understood what he thought of his own life and had often imagined him living his real life in the secret world of his reading; shy, thoughtful, saving the best of himself from the ordinary world of cheating wine merchants and butchers. Men whose language he would never learn to speak, not in *any* language.

She turned over and closed her eyes. Had she betrayed John's delicate image of the butterfly wings? She didn't know whether she had done absolutely the wrong thing or absolutely the right thing. Thinking about it exhausted her. There was no one she could talk to. No one to confess her story to. She was on her own with it . . . Except for Bruno, who would understand what she was going through? He would not be man enough to listen to her quietly and make sense of it with her. The weeping man!

She opened her eyes. She hadn't *seen* him in the darkness of his van, but had felt the touch of his hands on her naked thighs. Despite herself, despite everything, the touch of his hands on her nakedness had aroused her. Coupling with him she might have been a blind woman. There was something exciting, something of fantasy, in this thought that blindness must intensify the mysterious pleasure of sex. Pleasure wasn't the word for it. She knew that. There was another, bigger word. *The blind woman and the stranger.* She wanted to say it out loud—to hear it and know its meaning. The stranger's naked manliness as the blind woman takes him into her body, strong and gentle, giving pain and pleasure, a pleasure beyond words, her strong hands holding him, possessing him with her strength, gripping him! A small sob escaped Sabiha.

Surely the old gods had her now? Would she ever be free of them? Would she ever again be a woman with a quiet mind?

She got out of bed and put on her slippers and her dressing-gown. Her throat was dry and burning. John turned over and murmured something into his pillow. She looked back at him from the door and went down the stairs. In the kitchen she bent to the tap over the sink and drank the cold water greedily, letting it run down her throat and into her nightdress, its cool fingers between her breasts. She stood and wiped her mouth and lit the gas under the milk. John must never suspect. He must never know. John was too gentle, too trusting, too quiet in his nature to defend himself against despair. There was something intractably innocent, something deeply vulnerable, in John's nature. She had seen it from the beginning. That first day when he came into the café out of the rain and looked up at her from his book, his gaze was without calculation. No man had ever looked at her that way before. This shy unknowingness in the stranger had attracted her to him immediately, and she had wanted to be with him, to be protected within the charmed circle of his masculine innocence. Of all the possible kinds of innocence, and she knew there must be a great many, John's was the innocence of *hoping for the best from everyone*. It was this she had sensed in him that first day, and she had trusted him at once.

She poured the coffee and carried their bowls upstairs. On the third step from the top she stumbled. Coffee spilled from the bowls onto her hands, scalding her, and she cried out with the pain.

Sabiha dipped the ladle into the big cooking pot and filled the next bowl with the fragrant lamb ragout. It was the ladle Dom Pakos had dipped into his *sfougato* all those years ago, the last thing Dom's hands had touched in this world, a riveted iron ladle that had seen more than fifty years' service. Sabiha filled the green and blue bowls with the spicy stew, a cloth in her left hand, wiping the splashes of gravy from the rims of the bowls as she set them down on the bench. There was a livid coffee scald on the back of her right hand. The men all arrived for their midday meal within minutes of each other. They had less than an hour to themselves and expected to be served at once. It was always this same mad rush in the kitchen at midday.

John came in from the dining room and picked up three bowls and carried them out. Sabiha straightened and wiped the sweat from her forehead with the back of her hand and she tucked into her headscarf the strands of hair that had come free. Suddenly she realised someone was standing in the doorway to the lane. She swung around.

A drift of pale sunlight fell across Bruno's bold Roman features. He was holding a box of tomatoes against his chest, his gaze fixed on her, his shirt sleeves rolled to the elbows, the veins of his forearms standing out.

She saw how truly splendid he was. At the intimate touch of his gaze she felt the warmth come into her cheeks. I have become two women, she thought helplessly.

A sheen of exhaustion on his sleek skin, heavy purple shadows under his eyes.

He said, 'I must speak with you, Sabiha.'

'I'll come and see you at the market on Friday.' She was astonished to hear herself offer him this. 'You can say what you have to say to me then.' Her tone was severe. She had said she would see him again!

He didn't move, but stood looking at her.

'Put down the tomatoes and go in and have your meal at once!' she ordered him gently. 'Do it, Bruno!'

John came in through the bead curtain and stood looking at them. 'Do what?' he said.

Bruno bent down and set the box of tomatoes on the floor. He stood up and looked at John levelly.

Sabiha felt a weakness in her stomach and turned to the bench and leaned her weight against the cold marble. She closed her eyes—the blind woman again, retreating into her dark. She prayed Bruno would not betray their secret.

John said, 'Are you okay, Bruno?'

Bruno said insolently, 'Yes, I'm fine. How are *you*? Are you fine too, John?' He laughed.

John said evenly, 'Yes, I'm fine too, Bruno. Is everything all right with you?'

Bruno snorted and stepped past John roughly and pushed his way out through the bead curtain.

Sabiha turned from the bench.

John stood looking into the dining room after Bruno, as if he was going to follow him and demand an explanation. He took a deep breath and let it out. 'What was that all about?' His colour was heightened with anger.

She picked up Dom's black ladle. 'You'd better take these out before they get cold. The men are waiting.'

John didn't move. When she ignored him he lifted the bead curtain aside and looked out into the dining room once again. 'I'll speak to him,' he said.

'About *what?*' She didn't like the sound of her voice but she could not control it.

'If he said something to you, then I should know.'

She met his eyes and saw he had reclaimed his composure. That was so like John. Might he even be prepared to be reassured that there was nothing serious for him to worry about? But he *did* want to know. He was not dismissing this. He was not going to let it slide past. She saw the firmness in his eyes and in the way he stood. He might be vulnerable, but it was a vulnerability of the spirit and had nothing to do with a lack of resolve. She had lived with John for more than sixteen years, yet she wondered if she really knew him.

'Please, John,' she said, her tone softer, pleading a little. 'You know very well Bruno would never say anything disrespectful.'

'Why do you keep calling me *John?*' He was more puzzled than angry. 'What *is* it?'

'I'm tired,' she said. 'I'm sorry.' She was struggling to retrieve herself. She could do it. She *would* do it. She would cast out the demons and regain the ordered routine of their days somehow.

He went up to her and kissed her on the cheek. 'It's okay, darling,' he said gently. 'I'm sorry too. I *do* understand, you know.'

She turned away and looked down at the bench, touching the redness of the scald on her hand.

He waited, but she did not look up and meet his eyes. He stepped across to the other side of the kitchen and reached for a pile of bowls on the shelf above the timber bench. He set the bowls on the bench beside her and stood with his hands resting on the bench, leaning there and looking to his right into the dining room, Sabiha with her back to him now over to his left, filling the bowls with her spicy stew. She might have been a beautiful stranger still, a woman from a world he did not understand, thinking thoughts he could not begin to imagine.

He could see Bruno in three-quarter profile. He knew Bruno to be a decent man. Reliable and cheerful. They were not friends, he and Bruno, but they respected each other and valued the association between them. John thought of Bruno as a contented man.

He had never seen him so agitated as he was today. Bruno was looking down at his hands, which he was clasping and unclasping in his lap, his entire body concentrated on this nervous action. He was not *wringing* his hands, as an old man might, with anxiety or sorrow, but was flexing the joints of his fingers, one hand gripping the other turn and turn about, as if to ease the stiffness out of them in preparation for some action.

Nejib and his silent companion came through the front door. John watched them. The pair greeted their friends and walked across to their usual table and sat down; Nejib facing Bruno, as was his custom, his friend side on to the Italian. They both looked at Bruno, Nejib's friend turning in his seat in order to do so, registering that something was amiss. They looked away again, exchanging a glance but not speaking. Bruno appeared to be unaware of them. John did not know the origin of the antagonism between Bruno and these two, but it was already well established by the time Bruno first came to the café, the paths of these men evidently having crossed in some other quarter of life. Bruno never let a Tuesday go by without offering Nejib and his companion a provocation of one kind or another. It was invariably Nejib who fielded these comments, but it was clear to John that the deeper issue lay between Bruno and Nejib's companion. It was as if Bruno wished to remind the quiet man that he had not forgotten their old issue and was ready to settle it with him at any time he cared to choose. A matter of masculine pride. It was Nejib who kept things at a low temperature between his silent friend and Bruno, and for this John was grateful to him.

John let the curtain fall and picked up three of the filled bowls from the bench. He backed through the curtain and went out into the dining room. He greeted

Bruno and set a bowl in front of him. Bruno did not respond to his greeting, but continued looking down at his hands, which were now still. John was turning away when suddenly Bruno was looking up at him; staring directly into his eyes with the look of a man surfaced from a deep dive and struggling to utter a prophecy, his lips parted but no sound coming from them. In his eyes John saw a man drowning in despair and he was shocked.

He waited beside Bruno's table, knowing the men were watching him. He thought he was about to hear from Bruno news of some terrible diagnosis, untreatable cancer of the pancreas or some other death sentence, delivered to him in the mid-stride of his vigour. But Bruno was not able to speak of his trouble, and instead he looked down and examined his hands again, as if it were his hands that presented him with the terrible features of his dismay; a sly and difficult knot, it might have been, that he struggled with, a knot composed of knuckles and joints, a complicated and intricate thing. John thought of his mother's *Here's the church, and here's the steeple, look inside and see the people.* The old nursery rhyme suddenly acquiring for him a sinister meaning.

'Take it easy, Bruno,' he said. He moved away and greeted Nejib and his companion and set their meals in front of them.

There was bread and wine on some tables, but on this table there was never a wine jug. John had offered wine to Nejib and his companion when they first came to the café. Nejib politely declined his offer, but John still remembered the tone of the other man's response. It was cold and contemptuous and filled with pride, as if his claim made him superior to other men. He had smoothed the hairs of his beautiful moustache and said, *Alcohol has never passed my lips.* It was a claim that set him apart. John had dismissed him as ridiculous, a fanatic. He didn't like him. The man hardly ever said a word and seemed to come to Chez Dom with Nejib on sufferance, his manner making it plain that he did not consider himself one of these workmen.

One of the men waved to John and asked him to refill their water jug. John took the jug and went behind the bar and refilled the jug under the tap. These men all lived without the softening influence of their families, existing in cheap lodgings, their days precarious, their official standing with the state undecided. They stood on the rim of things, their lives vulnerable and filled with uncertainty, daily reminded by a thousand small things that they did not belong, their presence transient and uncertain. John felt he knew their condition and understood them. He had advised some of them over the years to emigrate to Australia. Two had achieved this, taking their families with them. Whenever a letter came from one of these men they gave it to Sabiha to translate for him.

The front door slammed and he looked up from the sink to see Bruno going past the window, his head down, his hands thrust into his coat pockets. John turned and looked at his table. Bruno's meal was untouched. The men had all stopped eating. John carried the jug of water over to the table. Someone said something in Arabic and they all laughed and went on eating, the café suddenly filled once again with their talk.

John went into the kitchen and stood in the doorway looking back out at the dining room.

'Bruno's in big trouble,' he said. 'I don't know how we can help him.' He looked at Sabiha. 'What did he say when he came in?'

Sabiha continued chopping a bunch of coriander intently with minute strokes of the knife, as if she was too engrossed in the familiar task to have registered his question. The rich aroma of the fresh herb filled the kitchen.

She didn't go to see Bruno at the market on Friday, as she had promised him. She didn't go to the market at all, in case she ran into him by accident. She couldn't bear the thought of facing his distress, or being confronted by the confusions of her own fragile emotions. She was tense and wasn't sleeping well. Tuesday came around and she held her breath, but Bruno didn't turn up with their order. She couldn't eat her lunch and pushed the plate away.

John asked her gently if she was all right.

His question irritated her. A spasm of anger shot through her and she closed her eyes.

He looked at her. 'I asked around at the market.'

She opened her eyes. 'What for?'

'Bruno had gone home early. Or was on his rounds. No one could tell me anything.' John took a drink of wine. 'It's a puzzle. But like you said the other day, Bruno's not the only tomato-seller we know.' He smiled but she did not respond.

•

On Sunday afternoon the weather was cold and wet and John went fishing with André. He kissed her on the cheek and went out through the bead curtain. She stood at the curtain watching him cross the dining room. He was wearing a heavy brown rollneck sweater under his blue parka, as if he was trying to look like a real ocean fisherman.

There was a painful creaking in her head. John reached the front door and opened it, and as he did so he turned around and gave her a wave. There was a sudden cracking noise inside her skull and she shouted, 'There's something wrong with *you*, not me!'

John went on out and closed the door behind him.

Had he *heard* her? Was he pretending he hadn't heard? She wanted to run after him and force a reaction out of him, to scream in his face, *There is something wrong with* you, *John!*

She stood at the curtain looking into the empty dining room, waiting for the trembling to cease. She was glad she'd shouted at him. The truth never hurt anyone. There *was* something wrong with him. She looked around the silent dining room in despair. She had betrayed John. She couldn't talk to him. She was on her own. She had isolated herself. She was so tense she wanted to vomit.

•

In bed that night, she lay awake beside him. He was sitting up reading his book as usual. He seemed to have been reading the same old red book for months. Every minute or so he turned a page. The sound of the page turning seemed to touch a sensitive spot in her brain. She waited, counting the seconds, waiting for him to turn the next page. She could hardly bear it. To break the awfulness of it she said, 'When I shouted at you this morning, why didn't you tell me to shut up?' She turned her head and looked at him. He went on reading, as if he hadn't heard her.

After a minute he looked up from the book thoughtfully. 'I wasn't sure I'd heard you right,' he said, then smiled. 'There probably *is* something wrong with me, darling. You're probably right.' He laughed and went back to his book.

She turned over to face the wall.

When he closed his book later and kissed her neck

and said a soft goodnight, she could hardly bring herself to reply. What would it take to provoke him? she wondered. Was that what she was trying to do? To provoke a crisis between them, so she would have cause to scream her confession at him in a moment of fury? A light sweat covered her skin and she shivered. If she was not careful she would make a complete disaster of their lives. The trouble was she couldn't think. She couldn't think what she should be doing. He was right, she was not herself. She was so anxious it was making her blood pound in her ears. She breathed in and out slowly and tried to relax her body. John was already snoring lightly beside her. How could he be so blind and so stupidly relaxed?

When my story is known to other women they will condemn me, she thought. Except her grandmother and the women of the old days. *They* would not condemn her. They would take her in among them and defy her accusers and protect her. The Berber women had always been haughty and powerful and feared by their men. To this day they refused to take the veil, but stared down their opposition bare-faced. The spirit of defiance is in my ancestry, Sabiha thought. It's in my blood. John has no defiance in him. His blood is cool and still. Mine boils.

She was not the first woman to have visited a man to get with child. If her grandmother had been alive she would have told her of many occasions when wives had secretly resorted to this dangerous solution. She wondered then, suddenly, if it was necessary for the woman to experience pleasure with the man if his seed was to take root in her? What would her grandmother have said to this?

John snored contentedly beside her, as if everything was normal and comfortable and settled between them. She reached across him and picked up his book and read the title, *The Autobiography of Benvenuto Cellini*. Its covers were stained and warped. He had picked it up at the second-hand book market, which had been set up where once the horses had waited for slaughter. Why did he read such things? Did anyone else read these forgotten books? He never said anything about them. He stirred in his sleep and she looked at him. His loyalty bound him to her, his calm unquestioning loyalty. His love, his quiet decency, the modesty of his self-belief, and of course his unfailing, maddening, infinite patience and goodwill; with her, with his life, even with the wine merchant. She could imagine him as a teacher, gently amused by unruly children, waiting for them to settle and to look at him and to ask him what it was he wanted to teach them. His students would love him. He would respect them. He would be gentle with them. To see him sleeping beside her, her stranger, her husband, made her sad. Terribly sad. She replaced his book carefully on the chair and got out of bed and went downstairs.

She opened the back door and stood looking out into the empty lane. Above the roofs the yellow glow of the great mysterious city. In all their years in Vaugirard, they had never really got to know Paris. The Paris she lived in was not the Paris people thought of when they said the word *Paris*. That beautiful romantic Paris might have been somewhere on the other side of the world for all she knew of it. André's cat was watching for a mouse to cross the cobbles. It observed her disdainfully, resenting her intrusion. The temptation to tell John everything frightened her.

She went inside and closed the door and locked it and stood resting her back against it, her arms folded under her breasts. If she had been religious she would have said a prayer, for them all. Her family had had no religion. Had prided themselves on it. Only the remnant of the old beliefs of her grandmother's people had survived. Her father had made fun of the old beliefs, but gently, never coarsely, always with a smile, always with an undisclosed respect. She had *always* been two people, divided between her father's beliefs and the beliefs of her grandmother. It was her fate to have forced her way against convention in order to reach her child. She looked back over the years and saw that she had never had any other choice. She placed her hands on her belly and whispered, 'My baby!' The tears ran down her cheeks. 'You are no longer alone, my darling.'

*T*wo weeks to the day after her seduction of Bruno, Sabiha woke in the night to feel the blood seeping from her. She knew at once it was not a miscarriage but was her period. The shock of it numbed her. Her body had rejected her. She cringed, bleeding into her nightdress and onto the sheet, the seeping issue of her blood and tissue, carrying away the wastes of her failure. She felt mocked. Emptied. Defeated. It had all been for nothing. She had lost.

She wanted to cry out, to curse and to weep wildly, to destroy something fine and beautiful, to purge this bitter sorrow from her life and have done with it. She wanted to be dead. She had invited the savage gods into her life, and now they mocked her. To them she was no more than just another unhappy woman. She was not a warrior, but a victim. She had not killed a lion. What

ridiculous arrogance it had been to imagine herself the
heroic woman of her grandmother's song!

John touched her shoulder and lifted her hair and
kissed her neck. His lips were warm. 'Time to get up,
darling,' he urged her softly.

She cowered in the bed, the blanket gripped tightly
around her shoulders. She would kill herself and be
done with it.

'Come on, get up!' John laughed uneasily. 'You're
getting lazy in your old age,' he teased her.

She pushed his hand away and dragged the blankets
tighter around her. *You* go to the market.'

He tried to pry the blanket away from her face.

'I don't feel well! Can I be ill? Just for once?'

He asked her gently, 'Shall I get the doctor?'

'Please, John! Just leave me alone!'

He got up and put on his sweater over his pyjamas
and went downstairs.

Alone in the cold kitchen he told himself he must
be patient with her. He must help her through it.
He struck a match and the flame flared against his
unshaved cheeks, and he leaned to the flame, as if he
peered into a dark place and searched for something
hidden or lost. He lit the gas and set the milk on the
stove and stood warming his hands over the pan.
André's cat came in from the laneway and rubbed

against his legs. The cat's fur was damp and chill from the night. It gave its confident cry and he bent and stroked it and it purred and pushed its hard little head against his hand. When the chill was off the milk he poured some into a saucer and set the saucer on the floor.

He watched the cat lapping the milk. 'What am I going to do?' He looked at the cat. 'I had a cat when I was a boy,' he said. His cat had lived to be eighteen. It used to hold Tip's face between its paws and lick the dog. Tip closed her eyes with pleasure. The cat—it had no name—was a large ginger female with sleepy green eyes. It followed him and Tip about the farm, but never crossed the creek. When he and Tip crossed the creek the cat sat on the bank and watched them go, like a wife waiting for her boys to come home. She would be there when they returned in the evening. He had saved her from a wild litter his father found in the blackberries at the bottom of the pig paddock. His father put the other kittens in a sugar bag and swung the bag above his head and brought it down onto the anvil in the shed. In the evenings John watched from the verandah as his cat lay in wait for rabbits, her body flattened in the kikuyu grass beside the blackberries where she had been born. He watched her spring, uncoiling her body high in the air over a grown rabbit and coming down on it, snapping its neck with her powerful jaws. She brought her kills home and butchered them under the tank stand, bringing a portion to Tip on the verandah, depositing the warm meat in front of Tip's nose, pushing it forward with her paw. When she died John wrapped her in his best jumper and buried her under the orange tree next to the cattle yards. He wept for her. Tip with her head on her paws watching him. Her remains must still be there. Tip's was a more tragic end and he did not care to think about it just now. It was too sad. John did not like to think about sad or tragic things.

The coffee was steaming. His mother had named Tip for the white tip on her tail. John had not given names to his animals. His father's old horse had been a big lumbering brown gelding named Beau. A great farter. A monumental farter. When his father spurred Beau up the bank of the creek the horse let out a series of mighty farts. Real stinkers. It would take your head off if you were tailing him too closely.

John mixed the coffee, the smell of Beau's farts in his nostrils.

He was thinking suddenly of André's story. André's wife, Simone, was now sixty-five and had gone through her change years ago. 'She tried to kill me,' André told him. André was sitting on the gunwale of his boat puffing on his pipe and squinting across the dark water. 'I had almost closed the door when she swung around and thrust the door open so violently it hit me in the chest and I fell back into the passageway. She jumped on me, stomping me and screaming at me. When she got home with the shopping later, she asked me if I wanted the veal or the chicken for dinner. Not a word about the attack. And I wasn't game to mention it either in case I started her up again. I had bruises all over me. It was weeks, months, before she said to me one night when we were watching the television, *A sort of madness came over me.* That's all she's ever said about it.' André looked at John and said cheerfully, 'Let's hope your Sabiha doesn't try something like that on you.' He laughed and sucked his pipe.

•

Lying in Houria and Dom's old bed upstairs, the blood seeping out of her, the word *sullied* came into Sabiha's head. Everything—this bed, their love, their memories, her body. It was all sullied. Their lives. She got out of bed and took a pad and a fresh pair of underpants from the top drawer of the dressing-table and put them on and got back into bed.

John came in and he smiled at her and set the tray

on the bedside chair, the coffee steaming in the bowls. He sat on the side of the bed and stroked her hair. 'You've never been ill,' he said, his hand resting on her hair, his fingers spread, as if he blessed her.

After a minute he got up and went to the window and stood looking into the street. He could see one of the Kavi boys in his store on the corner. They worked all hours of the day and night, those two. They would return to India as millionaires one day. The young man was leaning on the counter by the cash register reading a newspaper. He straightened and put a hand to his back and then leaned again and turned a page of the paper. He was smoking a cigarette and had an open bottle of Coca-Cola on the windowsill beside him. There were no customers. The street was deserted.

'If anything ever happened to you,' John said, 'this place would be finished.' It had begun to rain. The Kavi brother yawned and straightened again and scratched his balls, then he leaned and took a swig from the Coca-Cola bottle and set the bottle back on the sill and yawned again and turned another page of the newspaper. John turned now, looking at her. Her eyes were open but she did not move. 'Do you think you need a doctor?'

She spoke from the cover of the blankets. 'Just please go and do the marketing and leave me.'

'Drink your coffee then, before it gets cold.' He felt the sadness close around him. 'You'll have to write me a list.' He got dressed in the dim light of their bedroom then went down to the kitchen to fetch a pad and a pen.

When he got back she was sitting up, her knees raised, holding the bowl of coffee in both her hands, her forearms resting on her knees, her eyes closed. She looked drawn and exhausted. She was not drinking, but was holding the bowl as if it contained a sacred libation, which she was offering to her gods.

He would have been happy to have adopted a child, but she would never hear of it. It was her own child she had wanted. It struck him then that the phrase *the change of life* must contain a powerful and mysterious meaning. It was such a familiar phrase. He had never really thought about it until André told him his story. Did it always happen suddenly and violently, as it had with Simone? Or were there signs that warned of its approach? Strange upsetting moods? Fierce blind rages without cause.

He had an image: Sabiha far off on the edge of a field, on the other side of a high stand of ripening wheat, her head and shoulders showing above the crop, walking alone and preoccupied. Unaware of him watching her. The scene like a painting. The sun

239

shining and the clouds distant and hardly a threat of change at all. *My beautiful man*, she had called him once. It had been enough in those days for him to touch her foot with his foot under the table in a café for her to sigh and close her eyes and reach for his hand and implore him breathlessly, *I want you to kiss my breasts!* Would they have to raise their voices now, to call out to each other across the broadening divide? *Oh, so it's you! John Patterner. My God, yes, I do remember you now. Of course. The man I married and with whom I spent all those empty pointless years at that silly café in rue des Esclaves. How stupid that all seems now. What a squalid little ghetto of an existence we had. How trivial our lives were. We filled our days with nothingness. Now look at us. We were always strangers, you and I. It is only now that we have at last begun to see the truth of it.* Her laughter at the absurdity of who they had once been, her physical disgust, dismissing him, dismissing their lives, their memories. Everything worth nothing after all. *Don't touch me, John!* Without her, without their sixteen years together, he *was* nothing. He had expressed nothing with his life. Standing at the window of their bedroom looking down at the young man in his lighted store on the corner, John began to think that perhaps Sabiha's change of life was going to destroy them. The truth was going to come out and show them they were nothing.

He turned from the window and stepped across to the bed and sat beside her. He touched her cheek with his open hand. She flinched at his touch. 'I love you,' he said. Was that fear in his voice?

She drank her coffee and breathed and looked at him and tried to smile but the smile withered on her face. 'I don't *know* what's wrong with me,' she said. 'I would tell you if I knew.' She had lied to his face. Was there anything she would *not* do to him?

They sat looking at each other.

For a fleeting instant then it might have been possible for them to fall into each other's arms and beg each other's forgiveness. It might have been possible for her to tell him everything and for him to understand and to forgive her. But the moment was gone before they had time to grasp it, like the shadow of a cloud passing swiftly across a field.

Sabiha said, 'You'd better go if you're going.' She put her hand on his. 'You don't want to be late.'

She watched him go. She would rather die than be a barren wife. The thought of her own death calmed her. It was there. It waited for her and could be taken when she chose to take it. Just as her father had accepted the approach of his own death, calmly, with dignity, even amused. And who could say there was not as much meaning in choosing to die as there was supposed to be in choosing to live? Who could tell another what to think of their own death? Death is as sacred as life, she thought. How it might be approached, how it might be welcomed. The gentle, private, final ceremony of acceptance.

She slept again and dreamed of home, the moaning of the wind in the powerlines outside the courtyard, the great dark bulk of the ruined amphitheatre looming through the dust like a dream of itself. Her father's house.

Saturday evening and the men had finished their meal. John was running around clearing away the dishes, serving more wine and sweet mint tea, and doing his best to field the banter of the men. The dining room was noisy with talk, the air thickening with cigarette smoke. In the kitchen Sabiha took off her apron and hung it beside her overcoat in the alcove and went upstairs. In the bedroom she took off her blouse and slacks. In her underwear, she sat in front of her mirror and looked at her reflection. She had not turned on the ceiling light but had turned on the small Chinese lantern that stood on the left-hand side of Houria's old dressing-table. The stem of the lantern was green bronze. It was fashioned in the style of a stick of bamboo, its shade a cluster of numerous filaments of amber glass. The soft glow of the light modelled Sabiha's bold dark features, making her a beautiful enigmatic stranger to herself.

She sat there looking at her image in the mirror. There were many things in life the handsome woman in the mirror might have accomplished, but that one thing she had wished for more than anything else. 'Why?' she asked the mirror. 'Why is my child to be denied its mother's love?'

She looked at the lamp. She loved the little lamp. She had admired it in the window of an antique shop one Sunday more than ten years ago, while she and John were out walking by the river. They stood with their arms around each other looking in the window of the shop, and she said to him, 'That is a beautiful lamp.' Without telling her, he went back to the shop during the week and put a deposit on the lamp. And month by month, he paid it off. Then one day, almost a year after she had first admired the lamp in the shop window, and long after she had ceased to think about it, she came home from shopping to find it on the dressing-table, its beautiful shade glowing with the lovely amber light. On Saturdays after the evening meal she often sat here on her own looking at her lamp, letting her day in the kitchen recede, readying her mind for the world of the old songs.

She looked at her reflection again. The woman she knew so well. The woman she knew not at all. The stranger in the mirror. The enigma of herself. The good woman. The childless woman. The loyal wife. The loving wife. The lost woman. The defeated woman. The adulteress.

She sat in front of her mirror in the stillness of the bedroom, gazing at her strong handsome features for a long time, her hands resting on her bare thighs. The sound of the men's voices from downstairs in the dining room came to her from another world, the clatter of John at work in the kitchen, answering the calls from the men for wine or coffee or mint tea, were distant and unreal.

It was not until the strings of Nejib's oud began to sing to her—the delicate serenade of a familiar voice, hesitant as yet, a small voice venturing a modest opening to the evening, melancholy and filled with the promise of dreams and memories, the music of an ageless hope and desire—it was not until she heard Nejib's fingers caressing the strings of his beautiful instrument that she began to feel the strength of the old songs come into her mind. The music of Nejib's antique oud and the words of her songs were a blessing in the midst of the chaos of her mind.

A tear slid down her cheek and she lifted a hand and brushed it away.

She unpinned her hair, dropping the pins one by one into the little green dish that had belonged to her mother. The only possession she had from home. Nejib had begun to play with more confidence, and every now and then she paused while brushing her hair to listen to him. She was thinking of her father and wondering how long he would wait for her to bring the child to him. The child was still there. It might not be in her womb, but it was still in her mind. The child persisted. It was the only innocence left to her.

•

When Sabiha came through the bead curtain into the dining room, the men stopped talking and looked at her. All except Nejib. Nejib did not look at her but leaned closer over his beloved instrument, fingering the strings so sweetly he might have been caressing the cheeks of his sleeping son.

She walked across to the door without looking at the men and stood gazing into the empty street. She was wearing a dress that reached to her ankles, a heavy woollen weave of deep russet shot through with metallic threads of gold and blue, a high collar of black silk, her hair braided and coiled. Outside it was raining. She watched a car go by, saw it slow at the corner, then turn right, and it was gone. Another car followed the first, its lights sweeping the darkened fronts of the shops, then the street was empty. Now there was only one of the Kavi brothers leaning on his counter smoking a cigarette and reading a newspaper, the white light from his store reflected in the wet road like a sheet of translucent ice. The blue light of the television above his turbaned head. His turban a deep maroon. He had told her his name meant *poet*.

She turned from the window and began to sing.

Nejib lifted his head and met her eyes. She smiled. He bowed his head again, his fingers falling silent. She sang a song for him in the silence he had opened for her. It was a woman's song of home and children. It was for him, for his homesickness, for his memories of his wife and his longing for his children who were growing up without him. She sang for his dreams. Then he began to play again, so quietly at first the plucked strings of his instrument seemed to vibrate in the mind. *I shall go home*, he had confided to her one evening. *When I have saved enough money to buy my uncle's olive grove and his farmhouse from his widow, then I shall go home.* Sabiha had asked him, *Where is your uncle's farm?* And he looked into his memories and described for her the view of the Medjerda Valley from the stony hill of his uncle's farm, nestled immemorially in the shadow of ruins, set among olive trees so old they had not changed for hundreds of years. When he had finished telling her, he thanked her for her songs and for listening to his dreams. *When there is no woman to listen to our dreams*, he said and at this he glanced at his silent companion, *it is then that men cease to dream and become embittered. I know this. I have seen it. I saw it in my father when my mother left us. My father grew old in his mind long before his body was old. I was a boy when I saw the light of my father's dreams die in him.*

She knew the kind of man Nejib's companion was and she could not understand why Nejib kept him close. At home this man would have worked for the government and worn a uniform. But he would not have frightened her father. She was not afraid of him either. When she looked at him now he lowered his eyes and fingered his glass of tea, a smile of contempt curling his lip beneath his beautifully groomed moustache. She saw how he understood that nothing of his vice or his malice was hidden from her. To be so exposed to her bold look made him anxious and he could not meet her eyes. That was the kind of man he was. He stretched his legs under the table and lifted his glass and took a sip of tea. It was bravado.

He was afraid of her. He despised her. She knew it. Such a man did not need a reason to hate. Hate was in his nature, just as love and gentleness were in the natures of other men.

While she sang, Sabiha's gaze touched first this man then the next, singing her grandmother's songs for each of them, singing for herself. When John came out of the kitchen and stood at the bar, enjoying a moment of leisure and smoking a cigarette, a glass of wine by his hand, she looked at him and smiled. It was for John too that she sang. And as the evening wore on, and she lost her fears in the grace of her grandmother's songs, Sabiha began to understand that she must go again to Bruno. She would race across the desert in the night, speeding like a mother falcon over the cold white sand under the stars, a mother aroused, and she would defeat whatever stood between her and her child. She must persist. Her voice filled with the spirit of her mood and the men looked at her and were astonished by her beauty and her strength and the richness of her song.

She knew now, with a rush of optimism, that she was not going to give up. When the time was right she would go to Bruno once more and seduce him again. This time she would give herself to the pleasure of the moment and his seed would take within her and she would get her child. She laughed and sang and the men were delighted and moved all at once to see her confidence, her beauty and the aching melancholy of her song.

Five

*I*t's happened. Clare's met someone. He's not what I've been dreaming of for her. I got home from my swim on Saturday and he was sitting in the kitchen on my chair with his head on his arms, spread over the table listening to the football, an open tinny from my stock of Carlton Draught beside him. There was no sign of Clare or Stubby. I came into the kitchen and he stayed down on the table, looking up at me with his head on the side, his right eye looking out past the peak of his baseball cap.

'I'm Clare's dad,' I said, wary.

'Hi,' he said.

'Who's winning?'

'*We* are. Shush!'

Clare told me later, 'He's a mad Hawthorn supporter, Dad. You just have to accept it. He wasn't being rude.'

I've never been to a football game. None of my books have football heroes. Everyone I know in Melbourne has been telling me for years I'm missing one of the greatest emotional experiences of life. But I don't go.

I asked Clare, 'What does Robin *do*?'

'He's a stand-up comic.'

I was deeply shocked.

'Don't start on him.'

He's younger than Clare. It worries me. How is it going to work in twenty years' time when she's nearly sixty and needs a loyal companion and he's still a flighty fifty-five-year-old making the girls laugh at the stand-up place where he works? Wherever that is. I've never seen a stand-up comic either. Local stand-up comedy is as arcane to me as the footy. It's everywhere these days, except where *I* am.

I went up to my study and poured a large scotch and read through my latest notes on the saga of John and Sabiha. My refuge! I wrote some stuff that I thought had promise. It felt good to get it out. Moving it on towards an eventual reader. That's the good old feeling. It didn't last, but I enjoyed what there was of it. I'm prepared to be thankful these days.

John's story was keeping my mind off the fact that there was nothing much *on* my mind. John was my weekly visit to the therapist. He had seemed a bit depressed the other day when he was telling me some of the tough stuff about his wife's activities with the Italian. I felt sorry for him and asked him if he'd like to bring his wife and daughter around for dinner one Saturday night. He said they were always busy Saturday nights with the pastries. Sunday trading was wearing them out. I said, 'So what day would suit you?' He said he'd give it some thought, and would speak to Sabiha. An image of Sabiha sitting at my dining table, her hair up and wearing one of her gowns that she wore for her Saturday night singing at Chez Dom, was deeply interesting to me. I knew in my heart I was never going to see this for real, so I made the most of imagining it.

Asking John to dinner was my attempt to push our friendship to another level. And maybe it wasn't the right thing to do at that point. I felt him backing off. So I said no more. Anyway, I'd begun having visions of him and Sabiha and their little girl and the baseball cap and Clare and me all sitting around our dining table looking at our food and wondering what the hell to say to each other. The Cap, I guess, would have one ear and one eye to the television replays. He doesn't take the cap off while he eats.

I told Clare I didn't think he was funny.

She said, 'He's only funny when he's working.'

'So he's a professional? No free stuff for us, eh?'

'I love him, Dad.'

This really knocked the wind out of me. I got up and drew the cork out of a bottle of Henschke and drank a whole glass before I thought of offering one to Clare. Stubby was lying under the table giving me a warning look. I was on the point of saying something— I forget now what it was—when Clare cut in with, 'I know what you're thinking. Don't say it. This means a lot to me.'

I drank some more wine. Clare was cooking something. It hadn't struck me till then that she was actually cooking at her mother's cooktop. It was evident, now that I started taking notice of the kitchen, that she'd been shopping, for *food*.

I said, 'Is he coming for dinner tonight?'

'His name's Robin, Dad. And yes, he's coming for dinner after the Geelong game.'

'I thought he was a Hawthorn supporter.'

'He's interested in all the football. He follows it in detail.'

'Is that the area of his jokes?'

'He doesn't tell jokes. That's your area.'

'What's that you're cooking?' I stood beside her and looked into the pan. 'It smells great. You're making bolognaise sauce! How do you know how to do that?'

'Everyone in Australia knows how to cook bolognaise sauce.' She turned to me. 'Please be nice to Robin, Dad.'

'I will. I'm always nice to people. I don't have any enemies, do I?'

'Promise?'

'I promise.'

'Hand on your heart?'

'Hand on my heart, darling.'

She leaned and kissed my cheek. 'I love you, Dad.'

'I love you too, honey pie.'

'Promise you won't call me that when Robin's here.'

'I can't promise that,' I said. I was dismayed. Maybe I would go back to Venice and die there, do a Gustav Aschenbach after John had finished his story. Venice was always an option. I like to have an option.

Clare said in a let's-change-the-subject voice, 'So how's your friend John?'

'He's been dealing with some tough stuff. He's a bit down.'

She stirred oregano into the pot and we were silent for a while, watching the sauce bubbling along nicely. I looked around the bench. 'Did you get parmesan?'

'Of course.'

Of course! Suddenly she was the complete *hausfrau*.

———

She stirred the sauce thoughtfully for a half-minute, then said in a dreamy voice, 'I wonder if *I'll* ever have a baby?'

I couldn't believe what I was hearing. 'You've never said anything before about being interested in having babies.'

She looked at me and smiled, the certainty in her eyes that I would not understand what she was experiencing. It was an infinitely soft smile and made her look at least five years younger than I knew her to be. 'I'd like to have *Robin's* babies, Dad. I've never wanted anyone else's babies.'

'Does *he* want babies?' I imagined a row of half a dozen dwarfish stand-up comedian babies with Clare's eyes and wearing baseball caps. I don't know why they were dwarfish.

'He wants *my* babies.'

I was lost for something to say.

She laughed and said, 'Dad! Cheer up. It's okay. It's normal. You and Mum did it.'

'Does he have a house to put this family of his in?' I asked gloomily.

'No one has houses these days, Dad. We'll live here till we can get a flat. We both love the beach. We'll get somewhere in Elwood. It's expensive, so it'll be a while.'

I drank most of a full glass of wine and wiped my mouth with the back of my hand. The health benefits of my swim had all been used up and I was suddenly feeling like a very old man.

She looked at me with little-girl eyes and said, 'Is that okay with you, Dad? Me and Robin staying here?'

'Of course it is.' The idea of having the Cap around the place day and night terrified me.

'You're sure?'

'Positive. It's what your mother would have wanted.'

'Is it what *you* want?'

'Yes, darling.'

I could see she wasn't convinced.

'Are you glad for me, Dad? Really?'

I pulled her against me and gave her a big fatherly hug. My throat was tight with emotion for some reason. 'I'm just a little bit puzzled, darling.' I sounded as if I was being strangled.

She broke away impatiently and stirred vigorously at the bolognaise sauce, splashing it on the back of the cooktop.

'It's just very sudden,' I said. 'Where did you meet him?'

'It's not sudden. Anyway, love *is* sudden. In a pub. He was doing stand-up. I thought he was hilarious. I was laughing louder than anyone else and he started playing his jokes to me. We fell in love.' She stamped her foot. 'We *did*! Don't say anything, you bastard!'

The image appalled me. My beautiful little Clare falling for this weirdo in a pub, half-pissed and laughing her head off at nothing, desperate to move her life along, ten years older than the rest of the audience. My poor little Clare! What would Marie have said? *Babies!* If I lived, I could yet become a grandfather. My baby time of life was long past. I thought of my room in the little hotel on the Lido where I'd been staying before I came home. I could pick up the phone tonight and give Signora Croce a call and be back there in a day and a half.

I climbed the stairs slowly, Stubby at my heels looking serious, and I went into my study and closed the door. I sat at my desk and looked at my notes. I needed to be in someone else's story for a while.

Sabiha's fourteenth day fell on a Friday again; the rhythm of her body figuring her life in Fridays. She walked out into the chill morning air, leaving the café by the back door. The smell of the garbage bins strong and cold in the dark laneway. She had left John in bed warming his hands around a bowl of coffee and reading his book, savouring his precious solitary hour of the week. When he was alone reading like that, did he imagine himself to be a man endowed with the liberalities of a finer life than this one? she wondered. Did he imagine himself to be Benvenuto Cellini, the hero in his book?

As she walked along the early-morning streets towards the *métro* at Porte de Vanves she was hanging back in her mind with the innocence of her husband and his book. She told her stories in her songs, as her grandmother and her father had told them, by the fire in the evenings when she was a girl. She did not *read* stories. Books were too solitary for her. With her grandmother she believed that stories needed the company of listeners; the story finding its life as a gift, passed from teller to listener. For Sabiha the spirit of story was in the community of its telling. Unlike John, she saw no advance in writing over telling. She would sing her stories to her child; and her child, its warm sleepy body against her breasts, would come to know the stories in the intimate interior tones of its mother's voice. John's books seemed mean-spirited things to Sabiha; too private, too secretive, too solitary. Books, the silent interior lives within their closed covers, made her feel lonely.

She came up out of the *métro* and turned into the street of the market. Here the city had been awake for hours. She could never approach the brightly lit entrance to the market without seeing a kind of Aladdin's cave, a flicker of her original excitement at the sight of it even this morning. Such an incredible abundance of food! There had been nothing like it in her childhood. She could never take the market for granted. It would always be for her a place of enchantment.

Her purpose this morning did not have the grand simplicity of her first visit to him. It distressed her this time to visit the smelly toilet and prepare herself. The sheer cold-bloodedness of it. The calculation. The possibility of failing again. The grimness of her surroundings. She felt like an animal crouching over the open pan. But she went through with it. She was not going to give up. She would not face her life as a barren wife.

She came out of the toilet and walked along the main aisle, her underpants in the right-hand pocket of her overcoat, a pad in the left. Bruno's stall was at the back of the market, several aisles across to the left, in the far corner. As she walked along the aisles between the fruit and vegetable stalls, the skin of her thighs was shivery and goose-bumped. She felt as if she had a mild fever of the kind she used to suffer from when she was a little girl, her fear of her schoolteacher inspiring the shivery spasms, her longing that her mother would let her stay home from school. She knew nothing would come of it. This was not a symptom of bodily disease.

She saw three women pushing prams, one after the other, as if they had been put in her way on purpose as a sign to her. But she had never envied other women their children. She had never doubted that the motherhood other women experienced was different from the motherhood she would experience herself one day. Other women's babies did not interest her. The world of mothers and babies did not preoccupy her. It had never occurred to her to ask herself why this should be so. She and her baby were unique. They were inseparable. It was a mystery to her. A sacred mystery. She did not want an explanation for it, she just wanted to fulfil it.

Would Bruno be enraged when he saw her? Would he shout at her to get out of his sight? Would he accuse her of trying to destroy his marriage and his life? Her mind seethed with these anxieties. But she kept going. It was either that or turn around and go back . . .

To the respectable world, when it came to know what she had done, she would seem no better than a whore. Going to see Bruno a second time was not the heroic project of claiming her child it had been the first time. There was desperation in this visit, a sense that she was approaching the end of something, the enterprise sliding into a deep entanglement from which she would never be able to extricate herself; this was the moment when a sweet dream turns into nightmare, casting the intricate net of her illusions into the depths of herself—to snare what monsters?

They saw each other at the same instant.

She stopped. Her hand going to her throat.

He was standing on the far side of the divide between the end of the fruit and vegetables and the bulk stores. He was talking to a man, looking over the man's shoulder and holding her with his stricken gaze.

The man Bruno was talking to turned now and looked at her. Had Bruno said something to him about her? She felt a rush of shame. Was Bruno telling him, *See that woman standing over there looking at us? She comes to see me. You know what I mean? She can't resist. I'm onto a good thing there, hey?* The two of them sharing their joke. Men. She, the woman. But the man turned back to Bruno and they shook hands and he walked away and did not look in her direction again.

Bruno was walking towards her, making his way around the end of the last bays of fruit stalls, his figure lost to her briefly behind a pyramid of golden melons, then reappearing. He was not hurrying. Despite the chill of the morning his red checked shirt was open at the neck, his sleeves rolled above his elbows, his black curls falling to his shoulders, his leather apron the attire of a man who might hold a great wagon horse by the halter and make it kneel to him. Master of his place here.

There was a sudden sharp pain in her bladder, as if a blunt knife dug at her insides. She flinched and put a hand to her side.

He came up to her. Unsmiling. His eyes on hers. And he reached and took her hand and led her back the way he had come.

At the touch of his hand dizziness swept through her. She walked with him to his van without feeling the ground under her feet. She wanted to cry out and tear her hand from his grip and run away.

•

He took her lovingly, gently, with soft words of desire, with sobs, with laughter. For an insane, fleeting instant she envisaged another life for them, a life in which they lived out their story to the very end. A story without his eleven children, without his Angela, without her John, a story even without her child. A love story it was, herself and Bruno, the impossible, exquisite agony of sex. In that terrible blissful moment her mind could hold nothing else . . .

She gasped as he withdrew, emotion sweeping into her chest. This time it was she who wept.

While she fumbled about in the dark, sniffling and wiping at her tears, putting in the pad and rearranging her clothing, she felt him waiting beside her, something of the animal in his calm, his patience, his unnatural stillness, his silence but for his breathing. When she had finished, she straightened and looked to where he stood beside her. She found her handkerchief and blew her nose and wiped her eyes. The light from the crack between the doors of the van behind her was reflected in his eyes, two points of light in the darkness.

'Don't say anything!' she said. She buttoned her overcoat.

'My Sabiha,' he said softly, a tender sadness in his voice. He put out his hand, his touch on her shoulder, his voice an entreaty. 'I think of you all the time. I would have been all right if you had not come back to me again today. I would have been changed forever, but I would have been all right.' He laughed softly. 'Now I am lost. Now I am damned. I don't care.' He kissed her gently on the lips. 'I love you, my beautiful Sabiha.'

She permitted the kiss then drew away. 'You and Angela have eleven children. I have none.' She wiped at her tears. 'Why can't you just be a man?'

'I am tortured.' He spoke quietly, calmly, as if he had not heard her. 'I no longer sleep at night.' His voice was low, little more than a murmur. He held her arm, holding her to him. She did not resist. 'I get up in the night and walk about the streets of our town,' he said. 'I look at the clouds and at the moon and I speak your name and ask you what you are doing, and if you are thinking of me, and if you, too, are sleepless and looking at the moon.' He laughed quietly. 'You would smile and think me a fool to see me standing in front of the butcher's window under the streetlight, looking at the reflection of my own lips speaking your name. I see in myself the ghost of a stranger who has come to haunt me. Someone I knew long ago, but no longer know. I am lost, Sabiha. I have a great need to say your name. I want to say it in the presence of Angela and the children. There is a torment in it that I delight in. How can this be? I want so badly to know what your name means to me. What it *really* means. Sabiha? I repeat it again and again. It is a riddle. I try to find the answer to it.' He broke off. 'Forgive me, my darling Sabiha. I can't help it. This is the way I have become. I am no longer Bruno Fiorentino. If anyone of our town sees me from behind their curtains in my nightly wanderings, everyone will soon hear that Bruno Fiorentino is mad.' He laughed quietly again, as if the thought amused him.

She reached for the door handle but he gripped her arm and held her.

'Sabiha! Without you I'm finished.' His tone was quiet. He drew her close and held her against him. 'I don't care if I am mad,' he murmured into her hair.

'I don't want you to be worried. They are nothing to me, Sabiha.'

She was drained of will. She was exhausted. She rested her head against his chest and gave in, just for a moment. His broad chest, the smell of him, strange and familiar, so unlike John. 'Bruno,' she said, but could not go on. Had she been about to ask him for his forgiveness? What did he understand of her?

They stood together in the dark, the sounds of the market outside.

'That is not the worst of it,' he said. Again he spoke so calmly, his tone so confiding they might have known each other since they were children, and this just another of their childhood escapades, him telling her his secrets.

She waited.

But he said no more.

She withdrew from his arms and wiped her eyes with her handkerchief. 'I'll never love anyone but my John.'

Bruno said, 'The worst of it is, I can't make love to Angela anymore. I think of you, and I can't touch my wife.' He made a sound of disbelief. 'Angela is silenced by it. I was going to tell her about us. I was going to tell her everything. I prepared my thoughts, but when I saw the look in her eyes I couldn't speak. She doesn't

know what to think. What can I say to her? My eldest
son looks at me across the table while we are at our
evening meal as if I have become a stranger to him and
am no longer the father he loves. I ask myself, with the
greatest anguish I have ever known, my Sabiha, has my
dear son learned to hate his father? He sees his mother's
unhappiness and is shamed and bewildered. I am not
able to decide whether I see in my son and my wife my
own guilt looking back at me, or whether I see what
they are truly feeling. I don't know. I can no longer
distinguish between what is real and what I fear to be
real.' He paused and expelled the air from his lungs.
'Or that what I most fear will suddenly break out and
become real. I live in two worlds, Sabiha. Theirs and
ours. This is the truth. Talking to you here, now, I see
this clearly. I understand it. When I am not with you
I am confused and filled with doubt and uncertainty
and I think of you all the time. At night and during
the day. But now you have come back to me I see it
clearly. In my heart I know I am faithful to Angela,
and will be faithful to her until the day of my death.
I know it must sound strange to you to hear me make
such a claim. In this world of yours and mine I love
only you.' He fell silent, the faint creaking of the van's
springs. 'When these two worlds meet, both will be
destroyed.' It was his conclusion. It was simple. It was

real. It was not to be disputed. He might have been speaking of a surprising and impressive phenomenon of nature that he had happened on by chance.

Sabiha had her eyes closed. She was waiting for him to finish.

'Promise me you will come to me again next Friday.' He stroked her cheek with his fingers.

'I can't.'

'I have dreamed of this and now it has happened to me and I am glad. I can never go back to being who I was.'

'I came to you to get with child,' she said. 'That's all. Not because I love you. I love John.'

He said nothing.

His breath on her cheek. The sound of his breathing. His hand cupping her breast.

'Why can't you just be a *man*?' she said. She removed his hand from her breast. He offered no resistance and placed his arm around her shoulder, lightly holding her against him. 'Why can't you accept what I've given you and go on being yourself? Other men would do that.'

'What other men? Have there been other men?'

'No! Of course not. You are the only one.'

'Ah,' he said. 'Yes, I believe you. But if I don't know when I'm going to see you again,' he said, his voice calm, as if their situation was commonplace and manageable, 'it will be a torture for me. But if I know when I am going to see you again, I can dream of our meeting and count the hours.'

'I'm going home,' she said.

There was a sudden stillness. An expectation of something. A little shock travelling between them. She did not pull away from him but waited for what was to come.

He laughed. A soft laugh it was, gentle and filled with wonderment. 'You have changed me. I am a man I hardly know.' He laughed again at this, a low, private laugh of deep amusement, sharing his astonishment with her. 'Just a little of this man I know. The new man, I call him. You saw him in me. You saw him waiting for you and you called to him and he came to you.' He was silent for some time. His arm around her shoulder, holding her against him. He said quietly, 'I think this new man is to have a very short life.'

She said, 'Don't say that! Please! You mustn't say things like that.' She had a horror that his saying it would make it real.

'I have seen it,' he said simply. 'I know where it will be. Now I am unable to go to my priest and make my confession faithfully. Now I am no longer faithful. I keep us secret in my heart. I lie to God.' He said, 'When I wept at your feet, it was from despair. He saw it then, the old Bruno, grieving for the loss of his virtue. He knew he was lost. The new Bruno, the man you have made of me, had not yet stood up. Now he knows there is no way back to the man he was.' He was silent again, his fingers absently stroking her hair.

She pulled away and straightened her coat. 'I'm going,' she said.

'Will you come to see me?'

'No. It's finished.'

'*This* will never be finished, my Sabiha.' He spoke easily. 'Until you and I are finished. It is everything else that is finished. My Angela. My family. I can never reclaim them now as they were for me. It is all lies and deceit at home when my children clamber on me in the evening and my wife looks at me across the room and fears to smile.'

'Please let me go!' she pleaded. She was beginning to panic.

'Of course,' he said. 'I'm sorry.' He reached past her and opened the van's doors. Suddenly she was Madame Patterner again. The doors swung back, screeching on their hinges, letting in a blaze of light from the market.

He stood to one side and held out his hand to help her step down.

She hesitated, blinded for a moment, then thanked him, as if he were a stranger who had courteously opened a door for her in the course of an ordinary day. She took his hand and stepped to the ground.

He released her hand. 'Come on Friday,' he said. 'We can talk. There is no one else I can talk to.'

'I can't come,' she said. She walked away. She could feel him watching her. As she was turning the corner of the last fruit counter she looked back. He was standing at the open doors of his van. What did he mean, *I have seen it*? She was afraid. If only there was a place where she could hide and never be found until it was over. He was like a man on the scaffold who has accepted his fate and turns to his executioner and smiles and says, *It was worth it*.

On Tuesday, just after midday as usual, Bruno came in the back door of the café and set down their box of tomatoes. He said nothing but walked straight past Sabiha and through the bead curtain into the dining room. Sabiha and John looked through the curtain. Bruno was sitting at his usual place waiting for John to bring him his lunch. Sabiha thought of a little boy behaving himself. Not making any trouble. Being good. Being invisible. He sat there, still and silent, looking down at his hands in his lap, ignoring Nejib and his companion. The good Bruno.

John took his meal out to him and set it in front of him and Bruno said, 'Thank you, John.'

John said, 'No worries, Bruno. It's a pleasure.'

Bruno ate his meal and left at once, not lingering as he usually did.

John said to Sabiha, 'Whatever it was, he seems to be dealing with it.'

She wasn't so sure. Where was the bad Bruno hiding? The lost man?

The following Friday she went to the market but avoided Bruno's area. On Tuesday he came again. The good little boy. Saying nothing. She longed to ask him what he was hoping to achieve, behaving like this. How long could he keep it up? It couldn't possibly last, it was too unreal. If only he had been the *real* man she had mistaken him for, an ordinary immoral man, instead of this innocent. Was he waiting for a sign from her? Was he waiting to be told by her what he must do? Or was it a sign from his *life* he was waiting for? From his god, or his intuition? She had a horrible feeling he was going to come out of this ridiculous pose suddenly and do something violent. His physical beauty made him seem absurd to her now. A god pretending to be a good little boy. He had lost his dignity. She was deeply ashamed to think of what they had done together. Her child, if it were ever to exist, couldn't possibly have anything to do with that Friday at the market in Bruno's van.

•

She was out shopping when John answered the telephone. It was Sabiha's sister, Zahira. She said she was calling from the box outside the post office in El Djem. John found it hard to understand her. The line was not very clear and she spoke so softly and with such a strong accent he had to ask her to repeat herself several times.

'Can you please speak a bit louder!' He felt as if he were instructing a child.

But she did not speak any louder. She just repeated her message in exactly the same murmur. In the end he asked her to call again later when Sabiha was home.

When Sabiha came home he told her, 'Your sister called. I couldn't understand a word she said.'

Sabiha was hanging up her coat and putting her apron on. The back door was open, André's cat watching them, as if it was also hoping for some news. Tolstoy stood off on his own looking down the lane.

She was alert all day for the telephone, but her sister did not call back. She waited up in the evening, standing out in the empty dining room with the lights off, her arms folded under her breasts, looking into the street. There was a steady stream of people coming and going at the Kavi brothers' store. It was becoming a new world out there. Houria would not have recognised the street these days. The Indian boys were the only ones who seemed to know what they were doing. André's and Arnoul's shops were unvisited antiques from the old days. Nothing was French anymore.

She turned around and looked at the telephone where it hung on the wall behind the bar, as if looking would make it ring. It stayed as silent as if its wires had been cut. She almost went over and checked that they had not been cut.

At eleven she gave up and went out to the bathroom and had a wash then went upstairs. If her father had died, John would have understood that much from Zahira, or Zahira would have telephoned again. It wouldn't be her father's death, Sabiha was sure of it. His condition had probably deteriorated unexpectedly. It would have taken something like that to have made Zahira walk to the post office on her own and make the call. She would not have done it if she had not needed to. She must have woken this morning to find their father much worse. Or had he asked her to make the call on his behalf? At the thought of her father asking for her, a surge of emotion caught Sabiha in the throat and she gave a helpless little cry. She would not let herself weep, not yet. She prayed to someone's god that she was pregnant this time. It had been almost two weeks but there was no sign yet. Nothing. There were moments when she truly believed she would kill herself if her period came again. She could hardly stand the suspense. Her body was silent. Unchanged. Empty. She wanted to scream, *Give me my child!*

How much easier it would have been if Bruno had been an ordinary cynical man. What was he thinking? What was he waiting for? *I have seen it.* What did he mean? Her grandmother was no help to her. She had gone too. Into the silence. This emptiness of waiting day after day, night after night, without a sign.

Going up the stairs she felt like an old woman. She paused halfway, one hand on the banister, her eyes closed, gathering her courage to face John. She had the feeling he knew.

He was in bed with the lamp on. He had a new book. Benvenuto was still on the chair beside him, as if he could not bear to part with his old friend just yet. She got undressed. She didn't look up but knew he was watching her. She was careful not to catch his eye. If she caught his eye she would be required to smile, and then he would expect to have sex when she got into bed. She couldn't bear the thought of making love. No one but herself could see the ruin she had brought on them. She would never tell him. He must never know what she had done. She put on her nightdress and went around to her side of the bed and climbed in.

'Goodnight, darling,' she said. She tried to put some gentleness and warmth into her voice. She closed her eyes.

John reached over and put his hand on the rise of her hip. 'I love you,' he said quietly.

'And I love you too.' Bruno was right: she was never going to find a way back to herself. Her old self was lost in this labyrinth.

John's hand remained resting on her hip, his thumb and fingers massaging her lightly.

She kept her eyes closed and willed him not to ask her anything. If he asked her now she knew she would not be able to make up a lie. One minute she was vowing never to tell him, and the next she was ready to tell it all. There was no certainty anymore, no solid ground for her to stand on. She didn't know what she was thinking. To lie to John now seemed almost a greater evil than betraying him with Bruno. To lie to the one you love! The one who trusts you! How terrible! Her chest felt thick and heavy.

The weight of his hand through the blankets. At last he patted her and took his hand away and she heard him turn a page of his book. He cleared his throat. It was something familiar that he always did whenever there was an awkwardness between them. A little clearing of his throat. A quiet reassurance to himself that all was well, or that things could be mended at least. That much of him she was certain of. He was not going to press her for explanations. He was going to let her decide when it was time to let him back into the intimacy of her life. How would it be if he did insist? If he took her by the shoulders and turned her towards him and told her he was putting up with no more of her mysterious nonsense. But he would never do that. He would respect her feelings and not question her, until she invited him to. She was safe with John. John would wait. She could rely on him to wait. For how *long* would he wait? For a year? Forever? Yes, she knew it was quite possible that John would wait forever. That he would be prepared to go to his grave in ignorance, rather than hurt her in any way. They still slept in the same bed, but she had abandoned him.

There was a loud crack downstairs and she jumped.

John said, 'It's just the stairs, darling. Go to sleep.'

A cat somewhere gave a distressed yowl.

The street outside was deeply quiet.

She listened. There was not a sound. It was as if everyone had crept away, she and John were the only ones left in the neighbourhood, the only ones not to have heard the warning, *To stay is certain death.* If she slept now she would have a nightmare, she could feel it waiting for her. She remembered when she was a child forcing herself to stay awake in case a strange creature came in the night and took her away. The creature had come. She had been taken away. She was beyond help. She was afraid of the good boy Bruno.

John said gently, 'Are you crying, darling?'

She sniffed. 'No.'

A minute later he turned a page.

Sabiha woke into the night stillness. She lay listening to the silence. Had an urgent shout called her out of sleep? Everything was quiet. The thin light around the edges of the curtains from the solitary streetlamp on the corner. John snoring steadily beside her. No disturbance on the street. No dogs howling. Nothing. Just the steady hum of the night. Had her father died and called to her as he left this world? She felt a chill at the thought of it. Calling to his favourite daughter, so far away from him, his daughter lost to him, blaming himself for the loss of her, regretting sending her to help his sister all those years ago. Her father breathing his last sorrowing for her, longing for the clasp of her hand in his, her lips against his forehead. Her sweet breath in his face. Her dear father. Why hadn't Zahira called?

Sabiha felt a terrible regret that she had not gone home to see her father. Now she would never see him again.

Then the truth suddenly struck her. It wasn't her father who had called to her at all. It was her grandmother! She slipped her hands under her nightdress and felt her breasts. They were tender, as if lightly bruised, her nipples hard. This was not the fleeting tenderness she often felt a day or two before her period was due—her period was due on Friday—but was something else, something more lasting, something far more substantial. She was certain of it. It was a feeling that was entirely new to her. It was a feeling she had never experienced before. She knew it, she was pregnant!

She gasped, emotion flooding through her, a rush of warmth sweeping through her brain and her body. It was the warmth of another being inside her. She had conceived. The child was with her. She caught her breath and wept. If only she could have woken John and told him her news! She was to have her little girl beside her! She could feel her grandmother smiling on her. She had risked everything and had rescued her child from oblivion. There could be no regrets now, no loss of faith, no uncertainty. No matter what she was called on to confront now, she would be strong for her daughter's sake. She wept, with relief, with gratitude, with the astonishment of disbelief. At last she was to be a mother. She thought of that summer night years ago with John, when she believed she had conceived. In her mind now this child was that same child. It had always been the same child. *Her* child.

She laid both hands flat on her stomach and closed her eyes. She would wait until Friday, then for another few days, a week more maybe, before going to the doctor to have it confirmed. But she knew already this was not a false sign.

She whispered, 'I am a mother.' What could go wrong now? She would go home and see her father at once. He had not died in the night. She would sit beside her father's bed and place his hands on her stomach. Those strong hands of his that held her when she was a little girl, her father's quiet courage making the world safe. They had been each other's champions. How fiercely she had loved him when she was a little girl. How greatly she had admired him. Had understood him so perfectly it was at times as if she *was* him. Her dear father. She had never believed so confidently in the continuation of the old people as she did at this moment. When she thought of her father dying, she was certain the voices of the ancestors persisted. Out there somewhere. In the mysterious uncanny silence. Why should it not be so? The voice of her grandmother had woken her from her sleep. She had not imagined that call.

She would go with her child in her womb and see her father and for a brief time the three of them would be together in the old home. She would set her father free to take his leave of this world. Wasn't it the same heartbeat in her child that beat in her own breast? Sabiha could see her father's smile as he placed his hands on her belly and closed his eyes, the new life under his hands. Now that her child was coming, she was sure that her father's death was not to be the end of him.

She slept. And when she woke again she began to ask herself the impossible questions, questions for which she had no answers, but for which she would soon be required to provide answers. John must be the first to know. And was she to tell Bruno he was to be the father of her child? She saw Bruno now as a strangely unstable and even rather infantile man. She had ceased to see him as the man of *the perfect score*. It had been John's taunt that day that had begun this whole thing; *Did you know Bruno's got eleven kids?* How could she not have flung it back in his face? Her patience with him reached an end that day and she felt she had to go and find her own answer. There was a great blast of energy in her head and in her chest that day. She could still feel it. She had known from that moment that she must either take matters into her own hands or remain without her child for the rest of her days. Well, she had done it. Her child was safe in her womb. So why was she afraid?

She turned her head on the pillow and looked at John. Would she tell him everything, from the beginning? How was she going to navigate the contradictions of her life now? The dangers that were ahead of her, she began to see as she lay there in the dark, were far greater than any that were behind her. The child, like the death of the lion, was a beginning, it was not an end. The thing was not done yet.

Looking at John it seemed to her that men are forever alone. Men, she said to herself, are not like women. Their aloneness is in their souls. In their deepest place, men remain solitary all their lives. No matter how well loved they know themselves to be by a woman, men are always on their own. We never touch them in the place of their solitariness. John is alone now, lying here beside me sleeping. And when he reads his books, then he is also alone. He looks in those old dead books for the answer to his own aloneness, seeking a confirmation of his solitariness in the thoughts of other men, hoping to hear in their thoughts an echo of his own deepest aloneness. And when he meets it, he says to himself with satisfaction, *There! I knew it already.* And when he drinks too much wine he embraces his aloneness as if it were a punishment that he has deserved. And when he goes out on the Seine at night with André in his boat and they fish together and share their friendship, then they are alone in their hearts and they know it and it afflicts them, and they can't be honest with each other. And their dishonesty twists their thoughts around each other and around their friendship and makes them dissatisfied, and they withdraw into themselves and into their solitariness for the grain of solace that is there for them. Solitariness is a man's only truth. And that is the difference between us and them.

But the woman who has a child growing inside her body is not alone. The man has no companion for his soul. He is always looking for something he can't have. He is always discontent. But the woman who is a mother has a companion for her soul. Woman is not singular, she thought. Man is singular and always remains so. It is an illusion for Bruno that he has become a new man, but for me it is a reality that I have become a new woman. The truth will destroy Bruno's illusion and leave him alone and sorrowing. But the truth of my motherhood will confirm the change in me.

She felt sorry for John and for Bruno and for poor silly old André, and for all men—even her father. It is not just Bruno; they are like children, she thought. Men never meet the perfect friend they dream of meeting. The hero they long for. They dive deep into themselves, hoping to find a companionable meaning, and they find only themselves.

She drifted among these thoughts until she at last fell asleep again. In her dream the sun shone on a field of ripening wheat in the Medjerda Valley and she was a girl. It began as a happy dream. The figure of her grandmother, dressed in black, walking ahead of her through the golden wheat. Sabiha was hurrying to catch up with her grandmother in order to show her a beautiful flower she had found among the stalks of wheat. As the dream went on a little, Sabiha began to realise that no matter how fast she went, and no matter how slowly her grandmother seemed to be going—and her grandmother was going along very slowly—she was never going to catch up with her grandmother. Her frustration at not having sufficient strength of will to overcome the forces holding her back became so strong in the end that Sabiha woke, suddenly, with a feeling of alarm.

She lay there wide awake seeing her dream and feeling as if something terrible was about to happen to her.

She realised John was not beside her.

Then she heard him coming up the stairs and smelled the freshly brewed coffee. Her heart was thumping in her chest. With a shock, she remembered she was pregnant. How *could* she have forgotten? Even for a second? She sat up. Yet she had forgotten. For far more than a second. She wanted to feel her breasts to reassure herself she had not dreamed her pregnancy, but at that moment John came into the bedroom and put on the light. He was carrying the tray with their coffee and biscuits.

He said, 'Good morning, darling. How did you sleep?' He set the tray on the chair beside the bed and reached for her dressing-gown and draped it around her shoulders. 'It's freezing outside. Wet and freezing.'

She must have been staring at him with a peculiar expression on her face. He laughed and said, 'What is it? You look like you've seen a ghost.'

She burst into tears, spilling coffee over the blanket.

John jumped up and took the bowl from her, then put his arms around her and held her against him. He rocked her gently backwards and forwards. 'There, there, darling. It's all right.' The lovely smell of her hair. He smiled. She was like a child who had woken from a bad dream. 'I love you so much, my darling,' he whispered into her hair.

She couldn't stop crying. When she did finally pull herself together she blew her nose and wiped her eyes. He was sitting there smiling at her and looking pleased with himself. She decided to tell him everything.

As she went to speak, the words forming already in her head, she met a powerful resistance. It was the same force that had prevented her from catching up with her grandmother in the dream. It was as if she finally stood at the lip of a precipice and could not make herself jump. A deep unbidden urge of self-preservation, it was, preventing her from telling John the astonishing fact that she was carrying Bruno's child. It was just too enormous to put into words. She couldn't do it.

John said, 'You have to go and see your father at once. You mustn't leave it any longer. If your father were to die before you had a chance to say goodbye to him properly . . .' He shrugged. 'Well, you know you'd never forgive yourself.' He put his hand on hers and leaned and kissed her on the forehead. 'You're exhausted worrying about it all. I can see that. Get Sonja to come over and do the cooking for a week. She's got those two big lumps of girls of hers to look after the spice stall. She can't sing, but she *can* cook. The two of us will hold this place together till you get back. You mustn't worry about it anymore.'

He put his arms around her and held her close against him. 'I'll do the Friday morning run from now on. I should have offered ages ago. I'm a mean bastard, lying in bed here reading these useless books of mine every Friday as if they're some kind of necessity, while you go traipsing off in the rain to drag yourself around that rotten market week after week. From now on I'm doing it, and I don't want to hear any arguments from you.' He sat back and looked at her. He reached over and wiped a tear from her cheek. 'Okay then? All better now?'

She thanked him.

He got up off the bed. 'It's all right,' he said. 'It's nothing. I feel ashamed of myself for not offering before.' He leaned forward and looked into her eyes and lowered his voice. 'You're a strong woman. I know you'll get through this and come out the other side smiling.'

The following afternoon, after the customers had returned to their places of work and the cleaning up was finished, Sabiha went into the sitting room under the stairs and lay down on the couch and covered herself with a blanket. John was on his own at the table by the window in the dining room. He was reading. He turned a page, lifting his cigarette to his lips and narrowing his eyes against the smoke, the murmur of activity from the street, the grey rain falling steadily in the November light. When André walked past the window, his pipe in his mouth, his umbrella held aloft, Tolstoy on the lead, he looked in the window and saluted John with a dip of his head.

The telephone rang and Sabiha woke with a start and threw the blanket aside and got off the couch. She steadied herself with a hand to the arm of the couch, dizziness washing through her, then stumbled out into the dining room. John had already taken the call. He held out the receiver to her.

'It's Zahira,' he said and went back to the table by the window and picked up his book, which he had set face down on the table when the telephone rang. He held the book open in front of him but did not resume reading. He watched Sabiha. She was speaking Arabic and he could not understand what she was saying. A change always came over her whenever she switched from French to her mother tongue. It was not only the larger range of tones, but a change in the way she carried herself. The sound of the Tunisian dialect was familiar to him. He thought of it as a kind of music. He loved the sound, its strange familiarity. He had once made a half-hearted attempt to learn it. But Sabiha had proved to be an impatient teacher and he was not a good student. That had been during the first year of their life together, when Houria was still alive. The Arabic lessons had usually ended in hilarity. He smiled now, thinking of those days.

Sabiha was half turned away from him, leaning down a little and speaking into the telephone, as if she was straining to *see* something. While she listened, her head moved slightly, registering the message. Then she spoke again, her voice calm and unhurried.

He had forgotten how to say *I love you* in Arabic. It was the first phrase she had taught him. He was lying on top of her on the bed in their old room under the slope of the roof, looking into her eyes and repeating the words over and over, she softly correcting his pronunciation. 'You'll never get it,' she told him, her voice breathless with his weight on her chest. 'You make the sounds but you don't make the meaning. You speak Arabic as if it is Australian.' They laughed and made love. She already knew how to say *I love you* in English. She said it beautifully. Her whispered accents when she spoke English always delighted him.

She hung up the telephone and filled a glass with water at the sink behind the bar then came over and sat opposite him at the table. She drank from the glass and looked at him over its rim, her throat moving with each swallow. When she had drunk all the water in the glass she set it on the table in front of her and said, 'Zahira said my father is waiting for me to come home.' She met his eyes. 'So he can die. He's impatient. He's ready.'

John placed his hand over hers. 'I'm sorry, darling.'

'Do you know what he said to Zahira? He said, *Everything will be all right when Sabiha gets here.*' Her throat tightened on the words as she thought of her father saying this to her sister: *Everything will be all right when Sabiha gets here*! She had been away so long. There was something broken in her connection to home that would never be repaired now. It was not only the death of her father. It was the conviction that the last link with her childhood was about to disappear. Had perhaps disappeared already, even years ago, and she had only just noticed. She thought of the news she was to give her father. The beginning of the new life in her womb, news she did not have the courage to tell her husband. How she had longed for years to have this news for her father, and now it was to be filled with sadness. Her dream had become the dream of something long ago.

John got up and walked around the table and stood behind her. He rested a hand on her shoulder and with the other he gently massaged the tight muscle below her neck. She felt his touch deep in her chest and she closed her eyes and did not resist.

*I*n the morning John brought Sabiha a bowl of coffee and a sweet biscuit. He sat on the side of the bed and sipped the hot milky coffee. The bedroom was cold and it was too early for conversation. They might have been brother and sister, hugging their steaming bowls and gazing vacantly before them. She knew it would happen soon now. She could feel it building behind the stillness. She was waiting for it. The end of this.

John got up off the bed and collected their empty bowls and brushed the biscuit crumbs from the front of his shirt. 'You'll only be gone for a week,' he said. 'You'll be back before we know it.' He had booked her a return flight to Tunis for Monday. Not sure how long she would need to stay, he had left the return date open.

After he had gone to the market she got out of bed and dressed and went downstairs into the kitchen and began the routine of her day, preparing the sweet pastries for the weekend. André's cat pressed its cold fur against her leg. She moved her leg aside and it gave a little cry. She straightened and poured the *smen* into the pan and turned the gas on low.

Her period was due today. There was no sign of it. Her breasts were still sensitive and firm, aroused by the secret tensions in her body. She had goose bumps on her arms. She turned and dropped a piece of broken biscuit on the floor for the cat and whispered, 'Minette! I am pregnant!' There, her secret was out! She had told it.

The cat sniffed the biscuit, nudged it disdainfully with its nose, then looked up at her and miaowed unhappily. She felt the cat's dislike of her. A scavenging god! She tipped the almonds and *smen* into the food processor. Her grandmother would have made it all clear to her. When your little child is in your arms, everything will be forgiven you.

Thinking of her grandmother made Sabiha feel calmer.

How could anyone ever see a little child as a mistake? A mother and child! Or as evidence of an evil act? It was true. Her grandmother would not have panicked, but would have waited patiently, until the answer came to her, as she knew it would. It is written, my dearest child. Just as the Berber women never roused their camels to hurry when they crossed the highway to Tunis, but crossed as if the highway was not there, following an older road, a road visible only to those who shared their memories. A sacred road that would always be there, no matter what new things people put in its way. She took two large handfuls of dates and put them in the processor with the almonds, then added dried figs. She poured in the orange flower water and switched on the processor and stood watching as the mixture formed a thick paste.

•

That evening she and John were watching television. She was sitting on the green couch and he was sitting in the big brown armchair. It was a cold night and they had lit the gas fire. It was a film about the war. She was not really following it. The smell of fresh pastries still lingered in the air. When she went across to the grocery store before the midday meal to get some milk, a woman in the queue had stared at her. When she met the woman's eyes the woman had smiled and looked down at her. How could the woman have known? Sabiha had felt naked to the strange woman's gaze and had been forced to look down out of modesty. Would other mothers know as soon as they saw her that she was one of them? Were there signs she did not know?

John made a sound and she looked across at him. The air was stuffy with the gas fire. He was sunk in the deep old chair. His eyes were closed and his chin had dropped to his chest. She saw how he was going to look when he was an old man. Perhaps he was already an old man. She ached with a sudden tenderness for him; to be close to him again as they had once been, as if they were part of each other, one and the same person. She got up and switched off the television and sat down again.

John opened his eyes and heaved himself upright against the back of the chair.

'I was dreaming,' he said. 'Did I say something?'

'You made a little sound.'

'We were out in the bush together. It was rolling country. Open country.' He frowned at the gas fire, recovering his dream. 'The sun was shining and there were little white puffs of cloud.' He looked at her. 'You were with me in Australia. Nowhere particular. Just home with me. It was a race. We had to jump over these red and white striped hurdles, like the horse jumps at the Braidwood show when I was a kid. It was easy. We looked at each other and smiled with confidence as we floated over the jumps.' He put his hands on the arms of the chair and, with an effort, stood up. 'God, that chair swallows you.'

She wanted to tell him, *I'm pregnant, darling.* She wanted to say, *The world has changed. A ball of fire has struck our house and devoured us. My dearest John, my good man, my quiet Australian, we have stood together for more than sixteen years you and I, and tonight we stand among the ruins of our lives.* She wanted to say, *I have betrayed you, and I love you.* It was hurtling towards her now out of the silence. Nothing would prevent it. No power on earth could prevent it . . .

He came over and held out his hand. She took it and he helped her up.

They stood looking into each other's eyes. Very gently then, as if he had never dared touch her before this moment, he put his arms around her and drew her close and kissed her on the lips. He drew away at last and looked into her eyes. He did not speak. Did he know?

A scene presented itself to her mind. They were out there in the ungovernable future. She was at his bedside. He was old; the little girl in her womb today was already the young woman of the future standing by the door looking in at the scene. And he, John Patterner, the young woman's beloved father, was dying.

In this imaginary scene Sabiha held his hand and he looked up at her from the pillow of his deathbed.

And in this imaginary future she told him quietly, 'Your daughter, my darling man, is not your daughter.'

He smiled, and squeezed her hand. 'I've always known it.'

How simple it was, through the lens of a radiant future time, to speak the truth and be forgiven.

Here, now, in the terrible present moment, she said, 'I love you, John Patterner.'

He wiped her tears away with his fingers, and smiled and looked into her eyes. 'And I love you.'

'I'm so sorry,' she said.

He put his arm around her shoulders and led her from the room. 'You're tired. It's past your bedtime. You and I have nothing to be sorry for, my darling. It has all been worth it.'

*J*ohn came into the kitchen from the back lane. He kissed her on the cheek and she flinched from the touch of his cold lips. 'Everything's there.' He set the shopping bag on the bench beside her. 'Sonja will be over on Monday morning and I'll take you to the airport.' He took off his overcoat and scarf and stepped across and hung them on the hook under the stairs.

At the market Sonja had looked him in the eye and said, 'You're not cheating on Sabiha, are you?' She was a short sturdy woman in her middle fifties. She looked as if she had always been this big solid woman of fifty-something, the mother of two grown-up daughters, both unmarried. Her skin was as youthful as her daughters' skin, her cheeks and hands like those of a teenager, creamy and smooth.

He had laughed.

'It's not a joke,' she said. 'Sabiha's not herself. You should take better care of her. You're not getting another one like that woman. So don't go fancying you are.' She was measuring out her blend of *ras el hanout*. Sabiha claimed it was the best in Paris. 'You stay home and do the right thing,' Sonja told him severely. She handed across the packets of spice, naming the contents of each packet as she handed it over, her eye going down Sabiha's list. And last a big glass jar of the aromatic honey that could not be bought in the French shops.

'You're not a Tunisian,' she said. He asked her what he was supposed to think of that, but she just repeated it. 'You're not a Tunisian.' As if her meaning was self-evident. 'I'll see you Monday morning.' She was a woman who could not absolve herself from motherly responsibility for almost everyone she knew. 'Look after her!'

Sabiha said, 'Did you happen to see Bruno?' The sound of his name on her lips startled her.

John came over to the bench and stood beside her. 'He wasn't there. His stall was covered with a tarpaulin.'

'What about his van?'

'Not there.' John shrugged. 'Maybe I should call Angela? What do you reckon? Is it really any of our business?'

She felt a sick stab of fear. She would have to make her confession to John. She could not keep it from him any longer. He must not hear it from someone else. That would be too horrible.

•

Somehow the hours of the day passed and Sabiha did not make her confession. They were busy and her panic subsided. They both slid into the familiar routine, and before they knew it it was evening again and they were tired and ready for bed. By midday on Monday Sabiha would be in El Djem with her dying father and her sister.

On Friday afternoon she went to the hospital. She waited two hours to see a woman doctor. The doctor confirmed for her that she was pregnant. On the way home on the *métro* she felt a sense of anticlimax. She told herself she was taking her baby home to El Djem but the claim didn't ring true. There was a deadness about it. She and Zahira would say goodbye to their father. It was the end. She should have felt elated and happy, but instead she felt flat and sad and strangely empty, as if even her child could not possibly be all she had dreamed it would be. Was it possible, it occurred to her, that motherhood would be a disappointment?

Back at Chez Dom she rolled out the pastry for a fresh batch of honey-dipped briouats for Saturday evening. It was the quiet triumph of a commonplace life that her tears mixed with her pastry. Before the *samoom* there is stillness. This stillness is so perfect it sucks the moisture from the air and from the lungs and from the mind. Her grandmother called this stillness the laughter of the gods. Sabiha had always wondered why. Now she understood. This was a day on which Sabiha knew with her grandmother the laughter of the gods. Whichever direction you decided to go, it could not be the right direction. For there was no right direction.

*T*hat night a freezing wintry rain began to fall. It continued all through Saturday. There was talk on the radio of the rain turning to snow and of the roads becoming hazardous. By the time the men started arriving for their evening meal on Saturday night there was a touch of sleet in the air. John was behind the bar preparing the bread and the wine. He watched the men come in alone and together, each of them known to him by name, their clothes smelling of damp, lifting their hands to push back the hoods of their jackets as they came through the door and responded to his greeting, then going to their usual tables.

By eight o'clock most of the tables were occupied and John was busy going back and forth from the dining room to the kitchen serving the meals, the window steamed up and the talk loud now, the crowded café warm and cosy, the icy rain outside forgotten.

When the meal was over and John had cleared the plates and bowls and the cutlery from the tables, Sabiha came out from behind the bead curtain. She was wearing her dark plum gown, her hair coiled on top of her head, a necklace of her grandmother's old silver coins glinting at her breasts. Nejib had already begun to finger his oud, beautiful sounds floating out among the cigarette smoke and the talk, his silent companion seated beside him.

John saw how none of the men looked openly at Sabiha, and once again he knew the pleasure of this gentle place, the tact and quiet respect of these working men. There was something of home for him in the familiar dignity of this Saturday night gathering at Chez Dom, something for which he was grateful, something he would miss. He was reminded once again of the day he arrived there by mistake and heard Sabiha and her aunt singing in the kitchen behind the bead curtain. There were some nights when there was still for him a touch of the exotic magic of that first encounter. Some sense of having been admitted and made a part of their lives by the goodness and generosity of Houria and her beautiful niece. A sense that had never quite left him of being a guest in this place. And for this he felt grateful. He had never taken it for granted. He was smiling with this thought in his mind when he caught the eye of Nejib's companion. Nejib's companion did not change his expression, but looked away, his eyes sliding towards the door.

It surprised John to see then that Sabiha was facing the men and waiting for their attention. He wondered what she could be up to. Usually she began to sing and the men fell silent. Tonight there was a restlessness among them. And tonight she was standing beside the street door, closed against the cold night, and was having to wait for them to settle. When they realised she was waiting for them a hush fell over the room and Nejib's fingers ceased to pluck the strings of his oud. The sound of the rain rattling against the windows came up through the silence.

'Good evening to you all,' Sabiha said. She spoke French, her manner formal, as if she was not the cook who had just prepared their meal, or the singer who was about to sing for them, but was some other woman who needed to approach them from a place that was not familiar. There was a perfect silence while they waited to hear what she had to say, every man's gaze on her.

She said, 'My father is dying.'

The men shifted uneasily and one or two murmured a word of sympathy.

'I am going home to El Djem on Monday to say goodbye to my father. I shall not be singing for you next Saturday, and I will not be cooking your meals during the week.' She waited, her features softened now by a smile, and she looked from one man to another. 'My good friend Sonja, whose spices you all enjoy, will be cooking for you. But she will not sing for you.' There was laughter. 'Sonja is a better cook than I am.' There was a murmur of disbelief. 'But I am a better singer. I ask you, friends of Chez Dom, please don't desert us while I'm away.' They turned to each other and said how impossible such an idea was, to even suggest they would ever desert Chez Dom! 'Sonja and John will take good care of you until I come back.' She turned to Nejib and he took her signal and began to caress the strings of his instrument.

John watched Sabiha turn at the door and look at Nejib, their eyes clinging to each other. She began to sing, singer and musician animated by the other's perfect register of the music. It was *this* place in her heart to which John knew he would never be admitted. He felt a little tug of envy for Nejib's perfect favour with her. It was not something that could ever be learned. One had to be born with it. To know it in one's heart as a child, the way he knew the bush and the sounds and smells of his own childhood home.

Nothing would ever replace it. And it could never be shared. Except with another born to it.

The men watched her openly now, for as a woman she was masked to them by her singing. They smoked their cigarettes and sipped their wine or their mint tea, the lament of Sabiha's song holding them in thrall to their dreams of family and their fathers' sacred stony fields.

The street door crashed open, catching Sabiha on the shoulder and spinning her around, then smashing back against the wall, sending flecks of paint flicking into the air, the window glass trembling, a gust of icy air and a stutter of rain on the boards.

A man at the table nearest the door stood up.

Bruno stumbled into the café. He stood swaying unsteadily and looking around, his eyes fierce and bewildered, like an animal that has been hunted and does not know where to turn to escape its tormentors. He was soaking wet and cast around him as if he was trying to locate his tormentors so that he would know which way to face.

Nejib made a small gesture with his hand to the man by the door who had stood up. The man sat down again.

John carefully set the jug of wine on the bar and stepped across and took Bruno by the arm.

Bruno woke from his trance and flung John away from him violently and stepped forward and stopped at the table he regularly occupied for his midday meal. At a gesture from Nejib the two men sitting at the table stood up and moved away.

John recovered himself. He was alert now to the whole room. He felt calm and knew he would deal with this. He noticed that Nejib's companion had the same expression of faint bored contempt on his face that he always wore, and he had a sudden intuition that the man was not surprised by Bruno's violent arrival, but had been expecting it. No one had ever seen the Italian either drunk or in Chez Dom on a Saturday night.

When the two Arabs stepped away from his table, Bruno grasped the back of his usual chair. The chair tipped and he took an unsteady step backwards, still holding the chair, then lurched forward again, the chair describing a wild arc behind him. In one long movement, neither quite falling nor quite sitting, Bruno managed to bring the chair down on two legs behind him and get his backside onto it. Someone laughed. Bruno sat perfectly still, his weight dangerously forward, his head sunk on his chest, as if the effort had exhausted him. Then he slowly eased back and set the two back legs of the chair on the boards and he lifted his gaze to Sabiha.

Sabiha had closed the door and was standing with her back to it.

Slowly Bruno spread his large hands on the table in front of him, as if he meant to rise from the chair and go to her, or as if he was about to deliver a judgment.

In the perfect stillness there was the light tap of the oud's staved body touching the floorboards as Nejib set down his beloved instrument with infinite care. Two of the men turned and looked at him, then quickly looked back at Bruno. Bruno had swung around at Nejib's movement and he kept looking at him now.

John saw Nejib's companion shift his chair a fraction to the left, not enough to make anything of it, but enough to free his knees from being encumbered by the table should he need to get up quickly. The man was now facing at an angle slightly away from the table and directly towards Bruno. John decided to watch him closely and be prepared for something. He was surprised to find that he was not nervous but was cool and perfectly ready for whatever was to happen; his decision to protect Bruno from harm was simple and clear in his mind. He knew he was going to look after Bruno. He was not afraid of drunks.

Bruno lifted his right hand and pointed at Nejib. 'Now you sing for this black *stronzo*!' he said with contempt. He swivelled and looked at Sabiha. 'You do it for this black turd!'

Sabiha pleaded softly, 'Please, Bruno! Please don't do this! I beg you.'

John looked at her. She held both hands clasped under her chin, as if she was praying.

She could not know it, but Sabiha's pose at this moment was a perfect mirror of her mother's pose when *she* had watched the bus taking her daughter away from her forever. John motioned to Sabiha to stay out of it, but she either did not see him or was prepared to ignore him.

Bruno looked at Nejib. 'Get up!' he shouted. 'Get up, you black bastard!'

John saw there was no fear in Nejib's eyes.

Nejib's companion stood first, taking a step clear of his chair and to one side of the table. Slowly, with reluctance, Nejib also got up. He made no move to stand free of the table.

Bruno pushed himself away from his table and stood up. His chair fell backwards with a crash. He stepped unsteadily out into the open space between his and Nejib's table. Bruno and Nejib's companion were now facing each other across a space of less than two metres. Nejib's companion looked slight compared to Bruno, whose boxer's frame seemed to be an impenetrable barrier to any possible assault by the smaller man. It was scarcely to be a fair contest.

The sound of the rain hitting the windows was loud and the front door rattled as it was hit by a gust of wind. Nejib's companion stepped towards Bruno. He did not appear to hurry, his small frame relaxed, his expression giving the impression that he considered this encounter of little consequence. Everyone was silent, astonished by the little man's daring, their attention glued to him. As he closed with Bruno he lifted his left arm and put it around Bruno's shoulders, placing the side of his head against the side of Bruno's head, as if he embraced Bruno and would kiss him on the cheek.

John had been on the point of stepping between them, but he hesitated, feeling an enormous relief and glad he had not intervened, believing that what he was looking at was a generous gesture of reconciliation from Nejib's companion.

Bruno was evidently so surprised by the man's confident approach and easy embrace that he did not react with violence. As if he imagined he was going to have plenty of time to react later.

Bruno flinched and gave a strange grunt.

Nejib's companion stepped away and walked to the door and opened it. He went out, closing the door behind him.

Bruno stood a moment, his face bloodless, then crashed to his knees. He knelt a moment, a man intending prayer, the room registering the impact of his fall, then he toppled forward onto the boards and lay still.

Sabiha was the first to move. She cried, 'Bruno!', and ran forward and knelt by him and took his head in her hands and tried to turn him over. 'Bruno!' she pleaded.

John realised the café had cleared. The last man leaving the street door swinging, the rush of freezing wind and rain. The only one who had not moved was Nejib.

John looked at him. 'For God's sake, Nejib! Who is he?'

Nejib stood looking down at Bruno and Sabiha. He said with infinite sadness, 'He is my brother.'

•

The autopsy would show that the knife concealed in Nejib's brother's right hand had expertly sliced through Bruno's abdominal aorta. Death had been almost instantaneous. Just as it had been for Dom Pakos all those years ago.

*J*ohn had just returned from the Préfecture and was still wearing his old brown overcoat and scarf. He was standing side-on to the bedroom window looking down into the street. The street was quiet now, the flashing lights of the police cars and the ambulance and the trampling of people in and out of the café had ceased hours ago. He was still *seeing* them down there. He turned from the window and looked across at Sabiha. She was sitting on the edge of the bed, her pale nightdress and bare feet, her old blue blanket clutched around her shoulders. She looked like a woman who had been rescued from the sea, only to be told her loved ones had drowned.

She lifted her head and looked at him. 'What did you tell them?'

'They just wanted to know what happened. They didn't want my opinion of why it happened. I told them exactly what I'd seen.'

There was a long silence between them.

'I spent most of the time sitting waiting in the passage.'

The cold blue light of dawn was beginning to lift the sky over Paris, as if someone was stealthily lifting the lid on a well.

Neither of them had slept.

'You never know what the police are thinking,' he said. 'I felt as if they suspected me of Bruno's killing. They suspect everybody. I think they'll probably hold Nejib until they find his brother.'

There was another long silence between them.

He said, 'I could have saved him. I just stood there and watched. I can't believe I did that.'

Bruno's murder had changed everything. She said, 'I am an evil woman.'

He looked at her. 'What's this for?' he said. 'Don't start saying that sort of thing. Not even jokingly. This had nothing to do with you. You're exhausted. We're both exhausted. Why do you say a thing like that?'

He turned to the window again and looked out into the street. The street-sweeping machine was grinding and trembling along the kerb. He thought of a wounded horse trying to find its way home, a ghost from the days of the old abattoirs trying to find its way back to the fields. There was a park now where the abattoirs of Vaugirard had been when he first came to Paris. A horse would find a field there now, instead of a slaughterhouse.

Sabiha made a strangled noise and he whipped around. She was bent over with her head in her hands. He stepped across to the bed and sat beside her and he lifted her up and held her in his arms. He sat holding her, the yellow light of the street-cleaning machine flashing on the ceiling.

He said, 'When Nejib's brother put his arm around Bruno I thought he was making peace with him. Just for that second or two I relaxed. I thought I'd completely misjudged the man. I failed Bruno. I was no help to him at all. I saw it coming and I did nothing to prevent it. They must have hated each other, those two.'

She said, 'I'm pregnant with Bruno's child.'

He leaned away from her and looked at her.

She said, 'Bruno was in love with me.'

'*Pregnant?*' He gave her a little shake. 'You can't be pregnant.'

She turned to him, her dark eyes grave. 'I am having Bruno's child.'

He made an impatient flinging gesture with his hands and stood up. He swung around. 'What are you trying to do? What do you mean, you're *pregnant*? How can you be pregnant?' He took two strides to the window, then turned. 'Why are you doing this?' he said. 'What are you doing?'

She held his gaze steadily.

'My God,' he said quietly. 'This is true, isn't it?' He laughed emptily. 'Jesus Christ! I thought you were going through your change of life.' He stared at her incredulously. 'You're *pregnant*? That's *it*? You're having a baby? Jesus! Bruno's baby.' He spun around and reached into his coat pocket and pulled out a crumpled cigarette packet and stood frowning at it, the light coming up in the sky behind him, an iridescence suddenly around his thinning hair. He took out a cigarette but did not light it. Instead he unbuttoned his overcoat impatiently and took it off and threw it on the floor.

'I can't bear it if you hate me,' she said helplessly.

'Of course I don't hate you. I'm not going to start *hating* you now.' He searched in his trouser pockets for matches and couldn't find any and gave up. He looked at her. 'I'm just trying to *believe* this. Did you love Bruno? Did he love you? Is that it? How long have you been pregnant? Are you saying that's why he came here drunk tonight?' He flung out his hands in an exasperated, helpless gesture. 'You and Bruno! I can't believe it. I mean, where? When? You and Bruno were always so formal with each other. He was always so courteous and respectful to you.' He stood there frowning. 'All this! This *stuff* with Bruno, these moods and this carry-on with you, this is what it's all about? How does it involve Nejib and his brother? What did they have to do with it?' He stopped suddenly and stared at her with a look of anguish. 'If you were seeing Nejib as well, I *will* hate you. Tell me you weren't seeing Nejib. *Were* you?'

'Of course I wasn't seeing Nejib,' she said.

'Of course *nothing*!' he said, bewildered. 'There's no *of course* about any of this for me. I mean, where *are* we? What are we doing? You and me? Bruno rushing in and out, then staying away, then getting excited. All that shit. *You*, carrying on.' He looked at her. 'I just can't believe it of you. *You!* You did this?' He went over to the dressing-table and picked up a book of matches from the glass tray, struck a match and lit his cigarette. He took a deep drag on the cigarette and blew out the smoke.

She said quietly, 'You trusted me.'

He said, 'I *still* trust you.' He laughed. 'You tell me you've been having an affair and I tell you I trust you.'

'I wasn't having an affair,' she said. She sat hunched under her blanket as if she was in physical pain or had been beaten with a stick. She was looking up at him, her features grey in the uncertain light, her hair thick and black and hanging in disarray around her face. 'I wanted my child.'

He actually felt quite calm. Strangely calm. Inside. But felt it was necessary to make a bit of a show of his emotion. In an odd way, he wasn't even surprised by any of this. That was the really funny thing. He felt as if he had known it all along. He was not deeply, shockingly, wildly surprised by it. He had always been calm in any kind of an emergency. He had felt calm before the murder. Even when he thought there was about to be a fight between Bruno and Nejib's brother he had felt completely calm. He had felt as if he was in charge. As if he was in control. But he hadn't been, not really, only of himself. But to no use. Uselessly calm. She looked so utterly at his mercy, sitting there on the bed, as if she expected to be abandoned and tossed into the street with her baby.

He said gently, 'It's the child you've always had in your dreams, isn't it? I know that. Ever since the day we met. That day we lay in the grass on the bank of the river in Chartres. You told me about your child then. You didn't have to tell me. I felt it. I knew even then.

I felt your warmth then towards this child. I still think about that feeling. Yours was different from the warmth of any other woman I'd ever met before. Your warm body pressed against mine. I remember it. I thought of you then as a mother as well as my lover.' He smiled and took a drag on the cigarette. 'I know you've never given up hope of having this baby. Through everything. I know that. You don't have to say anything.' He went over and sat beside her and put his arms around her and held her against him. 'This is your child, darling. It's yours.' He said softly, 'Bruno!'

She was crying.

They sat in silence for a long time, Sabiha weeping quietly, John rocking her. Eventually he said, 'If it's a girl we'll call her Houria.'

Sabiha gave a choking sob.

He was so tired he felt sick. He was trying to recall the details of the scene. What had he told the police? One moment it was a peaceful Saturday night in the café, Sabiha singing her songs, Nejib playing his oud, the men quiet and enthralled and happy. Then suddenly the place was empty and Bruno was lying dead on the floor. Under the police questioning he had found himself getting confused and had started contradicting himself. He had felt they didn't believe him and this had annoyed him and he'd got a bit upset with them. They had been suspicious and rude and had kept him waiting for hours, sending him out then calling him back in again. Sitting out in the passage waiting for them to call him back inside for more questions he had felt exhausted.

He said, 'We must get some sleep.' He pulled back the bedclothes and took the blue blanket from around her shoulders and helped her get into bed. He stood and tucked her in and leaned down and kissed her.

She looked up at him.

He put his finger on her lips. 'Don't say anything. I'll come to bed. It's happened. We must get some sleep.' He went over to the window and pulled the curtains closed against the day. 'The café's done for,' he said. 'None of these fellers is coming back, that's for sure. I don't even know if the police will let us open again. I could have been nicer to them. We're not going to need Sonja on Monday either. I'd better give her a call. What's today?' He stood trying to think. 'Sunday morning. I'll call her at home later. It's impossible to believe Bruno's dead. I just can't believe it.' He was thinking of Angela and the eleven children and what they must be going through tonight.

He got undressed and climbed into bed beside her and held her against him. 'When you come back from El Djem we'll go home to Australia. There won't be anything left for us here. We'll start again.' He kissed her on the cheek. 'Don't worry, we won't forget Bruno. We'll think of some way of remembering him.'

There was the slam of a car door and the sound of an engine starting. The street was waking up. The mournful howl of Tolstoy from the back lane greeting the new day—the beast waking from his dreams to find himself alone on the snow-covered steppes of his ancestors.

'There are things I've kept from you too,' he said. 'Nothing like this, of course. I'm not even sure what these things are. Parts of myself, I suppose. My ambitions. Perhaps it will all be clearer to me when we're in Australia. There must be things about ourselves we can only know properly when we're at home.' He was exhausted but he didn't feel sleepy. He would be returning to Australia after sixteen years in France, having accomplished nothing. What had he done? His mind was racing.

'Men fighting,' he said. 'It's so stupid. The cops must see it every day.' He was silent for a while, listening to the sounds in the street. 'I've wanted to be a father,' he said. He knew it would not matter to him that he had not fathered their child himself; he would *become* the child's father. He would look after them both, Sabiha and the kid. And he would find a way to dignify the memory of Bruno in their child's life. That would be necessary. One day he would tell the child about its real father. He held Sabiha close against him, feeling the warmth of her body, the tiny baby growing inside her, its perfect unknowing, the absoluteness of its innocence. To begin! The small beginning. A new life. His own life had been such a waste.

He began to drift towards sleep, images of the terrible night springing into his mind, André and Simone and their daughter, bewildered, standing in the wet street in the lights of the police cars, like refugees who have been kicked out of their home. Old Arnoul Fort, and the Kavi boys and their customers, ringed around and staring silently, their eyes bright with the mad lights, the rain falling through the lights. The strange silence of the frenzy, not an Arab in sight. The pointlessness of it all.

Sabiha's leg kicked out in a nervous spasm and half woke him. He longed to relive the night and be given another chance to save Bruno. He imagined himself quietly removing the knife from Nejib's brother and telling him to leave Chez Dom. Normality restored. Sabiha finishing her songs. Bruno sobering up and apologising to everyone . . . Sabiha was asleep. He would have to get an advance on his credit card for their fares home . . . He was dreaming Tolstoy's howl was a train hurtling towards him, its trembling light dazzling him. He could not get off the tracks as it flew towards him out of the dark. He wrenched himself awake and lay there breathing heavily, his heart pounding. Suddenly he was weeping. He couldn't stop. He wept for everything.

Sabiha arrived home from burying her father on a Tuesday. The café was silent and empty. The chairs upended on the tables in the dining room. The curtains closed across the window—for the first time ever. A few minutes after midday Sabiha was in the kitchen preparing lunch for herself and John when a shadow fell across the wall in front of her. She turned around. A young man of eighteen or twenty was standing in the doorway to the lane. He was so like Bruno it was uncanny. He was holding a box of tomatoes in his arms.

'Good morning, Madame Patterner,' he said. 'I am Bruno Fiorentino, my father's son. I will carry on his business as he would have wished me to.' He was very nervous and delivered his speech as if he had rehearsed it. 'My father greatly respected you

and Monsieur Patterner. My family does not blame
you or Monsieur Patterner for this tragedy which has
befallen us. I understand that you have just buried your
own father. For this I would like to extend to you my
family's condolences. Such a loss is terrible.' He took a
step into the kitchen. 'Please accept this box of tomatoes
as a gift from my family. I shall be carrying on the
business as my father would have wished me to.' He
leaned down and set the box of tomatoes on the floor
by the door and straightened.

Sabiha could not take her eyes from him. She had
one hand to her throat, her chest tight with emotion.
She was not sure she could speak to the young man
without crying.

'I can't accept your gift,' she said. 'There's no point
in you coming here ever again. We have no customers
left. They have fled from the police and are either in
hiding or have gone back to Tunisia.'

'New customers will come,' he said. He smiled.
'Your cooking is famous.'

When he smiled Bruno lived in his eyes. 'Chez Dom
is closed,' she said and had to turn away to hide her
tears. 'We're going to Australia. Please go,' she urged
him gently. 'Please go.' Tears were running down her
cheeks. She did not wipe them away. 'I am so sorry.

There is nothing I can do.' She turned around to face him and said gently, 'Go away, Bruno, please!'

He looked down at the box of tomatoes and murmured helplessly, 'They are a gift from my family, *madame*.' He picked up the box and held it, his eyes on her.

She saw his humiliation and went to him and put her hand on his arm, touching him as a mother might wish to touch her son, farewelling him on a long journey. She was weeping and was unable to speak.

Six

When I came home yesterday evening after a session with John at the Paradiso, I was looking forward to having a quiet drink on my own. I needed to spend a bit of time on my own digesting what John had told me. He had surprised me. He had shocked me, and I wasn't sure how I was going to deal with it.

When I came into the kitchen, Clare and her new man, were having a drink together. One of his horrible CDs was on loud. Clare was leaning against the stove with a glass of wine in her hand. She looked a bit rumpled and red in the face, as if she'd already had a few. It wasn't a good look. Her man, Robin the Cap, was sitting at the table as usual, his chair pushed back and his head down on the table, chin on his left arm—cap on, of course. He was squinting along his outstretched right arm at a can of Foster's Lager in his fist. Stubby was lying under the table, his head on his paws too, his usual position. Was the Cap mimicking the dog? Was that something a stand-up would practise? When I was young, stand up meant your girlfriend had ditched you.

Like Clare, I didn't sit down. How could I? The Cap was spread all over the table. I said hello and Clare said, 'Hi, Dad,' as if she was trying to sound younger than her years. We don't usually say hi to each other. I didn't actually hear the Cap offer me a greeting. But then my hearing is not as good as it once was and the music was very loud, so I may have missed it. I don't want to be unfair to him. Prejudice is a nasty thing. Haven't I spent half my life writing about it? In fact I have given the matter a great deal of thought in my books one way and another over a period of several decades. I poured myself a glass of wine and stood drinking it, looking down at the Cap. He was looking back at me, his head on the table. He was smiling.

I raised my glass to him and shouted, 'Cheers!'

Clare yelled, 'Cheers, Dad!'

When I looked at her she gave me a pleading smile.

The Cap was looking up at me from under his frayed peak. He yelled, 'So what did you used to do for a living, Ken?' Yelling seemed no effort to him.

I suppose it was necessary to yell in the house where he lived with his friends all playing loud rap, or whatever it is. I don't *know* what it is. I know Shostakovich's string quartets. Particularly the Sixth. That's what I know.

I looked at Clare. So she hadn't told him proudly that her dad was a famous novelist? I felt sad to know this. But why should she have? She saw my pain and leaned and turned the music down. Didn't any of this matter anymore? 'I *used* to be a writer,' I said. 'Until I retired.'

'Books? Or what?'

He was still squinting up at me, evidently intrigued by the unusual angle from which he was viewing my features.

'Novels,' I said shortly.

'Fiction novels?'

'That's the kind.'

'I might read one,' he said. He examined the can in his hand with interest, as if he had never seen a can of Foster's Lager before.

I don't think he's ever going to read a book. Him reading one of my books is not something I can imagine. There's a limit to what you can make up. He lives in a post-novel world—fiction novels or not. Not that Clare herself has ever been much of a reader. I think she read one of my books when she was in high school. And that was about it. And maybe she didn't quite finish that one either. I remember her carrying it around in her school bag for a very long time. Every now and then she'd hold it up and show me and give me an encouraging smile.

Clare said, 'Hawthorn won, Dad.'

The Cap sat up and raised his can in the air. 'We thrashed Collingwood! And *I* was *there* to see it, Ken!' He drank from the can and put it down on the table in front of him. 'We're third on the ladder.'

I realised he was waiting for a response from me. I said, 'Terrific, Robin. Good old Hawthorn! Here's to the Hawks!' I leaned and touched my glass to his beer can. '*Up* the Hawks!'

These two make me feel dumb and inarticulate. My grasp of language closes down on me when I'm with them and I stumble forward helplessly while they look on, unsurprised by my awkwardness, my fragility, the failure of my remarks to make any sense, my complete lack of a cool understanding of what's going on. They don't expect anything better. That's the trouble. When I'm with John I feel youthful and optimistic. I feel like my old self. My viable self. The man in charge. With these two I am an old man and they are telling me I am an old man in every way it is possible for one person to tell another person something without actually putting the matter into so many words. Literalism, the enemy of art, is not needed. They do it without thinking.

•

They are all coming to dinner on Wednesday evening. I know, I didn't need to do this to myself. But I'm doing it to satisfy my entirely selfish desire to see Sabiha sitting at our old dining table being a tragic beautiful exotic princess, one of our antique crystal goblets in her hand, the red wine gleaming like the blood of a bull in the candlelight. I want to set her up for this, as if I'm a portrait painter, Max Ernst setting up his model for his *Attirement of the Bride*. What a picture that is! The most unsullied eroticism. I'd like to know what Sabiha would think of it. It's in Venice. A good reason for going there. We've not had a dinner party in the dining room since years before Marie died. We stopped doing that kind of thing. How dumb is it to want to see Sabiha in this way, though? How *old man* is it of me? It's something I'm never going to confess to my daughter. There are some things we don't tell anyone.

Wednesday seems to be the only evening Sabiha can spare. I'm feeling anxious about it. But then I'm anxious about a lot of things these days. There is no flow to my life, that's the trouble. What *don't* I feel anxious about is more the question. I can't decide whether to be completely informal with them on Wednesday and just sit around the kitchen with some finger food and a dozen cans of beer, or whether to put on a grand show for them in the dining room and demonstrate my respect. I can only have my dream image in the dining room. Clare hasn't offered to cook. And I haven't asked her. The Cap will be there, with his head on the table I suppose. I asked Clare, 'Why can't he sit up at the table like everyone else?' She said, 'Dad!' So I left it at that. His legs fill the space under the kitchen table and his arms angle about all over the top. He doesn't seem to notice that there are things on the table that he might knock off. How do they sleep together? Clare must be crouched in a corner of the bed. I can't sit down when he's here without being afraid I'm going to touch him.

And he's always here. I think he's moved in. I'm not sure. I asked Clare but her answer left me no wiser. I don't understand them. We are not of the same world anymore. Venice beckons. It's not funny anymore. It never was. They can have the house. After all, what do I need a house for at my age?

It's not just Robin the Cap, however. It's not just him. And it's no good blaming him. After all, he's not intentionally rude. He's not aggressive. And he seems to genuinely care for my daughter. More than once I've noticed his expression soften when he looks at her. Is that love, or not? From memory, that's love. I should be grateful. I've never seen him drink more than two cans of beer and he doesn't seem to be on drugs. Though how would I know? Anyway, Clare has to live her own life, in my house or somewhere else. And she has a right to choose who she sleeps with. I don't want to think about that side of it. No, it's not him. This goes a lot deeper for me than my daughter's boyfriend.

I'd just about decided to make a start on John and Sabiha's story when we had our last meeting at the Paradiso. Yes, that's right, I'd decided to come out of my retirement for one last throw. This is not a surprise to anyone, I realise that. My retirement was genuine, but John and Sabiha's story seemed to be just too much of a gift from the gods for me to pass it up—Sabiha's old gods, undoubtedly. The playful ones. So why *was* I passing it up? I hadn't been able to find an answer to this question that carried any conviction. In fact I knew I was going to regret it for the rest of my days if I let their story slip past without having a go at it. So a couple of evenings ago I spent several hours at my desk reading through my notes, from beginning to end, to see what I had. It was all there. The whole thing.

•

It was a lovely Melbourne autumn day. Autumn is the best time of the year in Melbourne. The oppressive heat of summer is gone and the sun gives just the right amount of warmth to the air to make life comfortable without a jacket or a cardigan, no wind and maybe just one or two innocent white clouds going by. You have to *be* here. People are happy on days like this. Strangers say hello. Even young women smile at me. And no one's in a hurry. It's the kind of day Chinese students get up and offer me their seat on the tram.

John and I were sitting outside the Paradiso after lunch at a table on the footpath. All the tables were taken. There was a lot of chatter and laughter going on around us in about three languages. John told me he didn't know Australia when he got home, things had changed so much, but not in ways he'd expected. He laughed and said, 'Sabiha was more at home in Carlton than I was.' Every now and then a big dry leaf from the plane tree above us came twisting and spiralling down and one of the young women at the next table made a grab for it and laughed. Watching the girl grabbing for the leaf I remembered telling Clare when she was a little girl that if we catch a falling leaf our wish will come true. The two of us running across the oak lawn at the Botanical Gardens chasing falling leaves, Marie sitting on the grass by our picnic watching us or drawing in the pad on her knees. Marie was always turning her world into drawings. She never joined in our games but she loved to see me and Clare running around having fun. It was a magical time for the three of us. Clare must have been about Houria's age then. A little kid full of confidence. It used to break my heart to watch her running across the grass, her skinny little legs going like clockwork. I see kids doing that now and I stop and stare at them and my throat tightens. As a general thing I don't have a problem with being old or even with getting older, but when I see the beauty of children I do regret that life must soon pass from me and be no more. It's a dry kind of regret and I don't weep, but it's real enough.

I thought John had finished his story. He had left me with that affecting image of Sabiha and Bruno's son in the kitchen of Chez Dom, the place sad and closed up and finished, its history done with. The young man doing his best to deal with what had happened in a manner that would dignify the memory of his murdered father. I wasn't expecting a lot more after that. I had one or two questions, like did they ever catch up with Nejib's brother, and stuff like that, but I had decided these things could wait for another time.

We were sitting there saying nothing. I was listening to the conversation in Spanish at the next table. Lorca's language! It was a pleasure to listen in. I stopped thinking about myself. There was no expectation playing between me and John, and the silence between us was easy. I thought we'd done for the day, for the whole thing. Life was going on around us and I had a new story to write.

Then I realised John was looking at me steadily, a smile in his eyes. He said, 'I want to thank you, Ken.'

'Oh, there's no need for thanks,' I said. 'It's me who ought to be thanking you.'

'I mean it,' he said. 'You don't know what you've done for me. I came home from France after sixteen years with nothing of my own to show for it. Not a thing. I felt as if whatever gifts or ambitions I'd once possessed had been wasted. I felt guilty about this failure to make sense of my life. When we got back to Australia I made the mistake of taking Sabiha to Moruya. I felt sure there would be nothing for me in Melbourne. I couldn't believe I'd get a job with the Victorian education department after being away so long, so I didn't even try. I went home to Moruya to see Mum and Dad. Mum was pretty far gone with Alzheimer's and never did work out who Sabiha was. But she seemed to like her, whoever she thought she

was. Sabiha was depressed for a long time, grieving for
Bruno. For a year or so I didn't think she was going
to get over it. If it hadn't been for Houria I wonder if
she would have come through it. I don't imagine she
will ever forget him. But she's found a way of living
with it. We don't talk about it. Whatever she feels now
it's her private sorrow. We had five pretty tough years
up there. Then I heard about this teacher shortage in
Melbourne. You know the rest.'

He sat there saying nothing again and I thought this
was definitely it. I was on the point of asking him if
Sabiha knew he had been telling me their story when
he looked up at me and said, 'When you started coming
into the shop on Saturdays and then I saw you at the
library I didn't know who you were. Then I saw you on
the daytime replay of *The Book Show* and realised you
were a writer. I'd heard your name, but I'd never read
any of your books. When I found myself standing next
to you at the shallow end of the pool that Saturday I
decided it was a sign. That's when I asked you to join
me for a coffee. Remember?'

'A pool-water coffee,' I said. 'Yes, I do remember.'

'I was planning on making use of you.'

'How do you mean?' I said. But I believed I knew
what he meant, his need to move his story on and get
it out of his system had been obvious.

'I had no confidence that anyone would be interested in our story. But our story was all I had. It was all I'd brought home with me after sixteen years in Paris, and five years wasting our time in Moruya. I decided to try our story out on you. Like you said, you were my perfect listener. Your interest has given me the confidence to write it. When I get home after each of our sessions, I spend hours writing what I've been telling you.' He waited for my reaction.

I said nothing.

'I've been staying up till two and three in the morning writing it. Once you start, it's all just lying there waiting for you, isn't it? I've more or less got a draft of the whole thing.'

'That's good,' I said. 'Who doesn't want to write their memoirs?'

'I've become a writer, Ken.'

I could see he was serious.

'I'm making some sense of my life. It's this I want to thank you for.'

I said, 'I just listened.'

'Our story was written in my heart. But I needed the confidence to write it. That's what you've given me.'

He was rather solemn about it. I said something like, 'Well this is terrific news, John. Good luck with it.' I shook his hand.

He said, 'I'm not asking you to use your connections to help me get it published. I'll do that myself. It's not ready yet. I'm dedicating it to you.' He grinned. 'I hope you don't mind?'

I said I was flattered.

'I suppose you're in the middle of writing a new book by now?'

'I have an idea for one,' I said.

'Have you done much work on it?'

'Quite a bit.'

'I'm happy if you want to talk about it. I might not be the perfect listener, but you could give me a try.'

'That's very kind of you,' I said. 'But if you don't mind, I'd rather not talk about it just now.' I met his eyes. 'I've found the surest way to lose a story is to tell it.'

He laughed uneasily. 'I've *found* mine by telling it.'

I didn't say, We'll see, but that's what went through my head.

We were silent for a minute or so, then he said, 'You know almost everything there is to know about me. I know almost nothing about you.'

I said, 'There's not a lot to know. My life's in my books.' I got up and went inside the café and paid for our coffees.

I was in the pastry shop this afternoon, waiting my turn, enjoying watching Sabiha serving her customers. I love to watch her move, to witness her calm reserve, the grace of her manner, to look at her and know her secret strength, her secret tragedy, her endurance, her courage enough to face a lion. She is my hero. I love her most deeply, most secretly. I have only ever been able to write about people I love. No matter how filled with doubt about my life I am when I go into her shop, I am convinced of my purpose once again by the time I come out.

She turned from serving a woman and looked out the window. I turned to see what she was looking at, so did the woman she was serving. The traffic was heavy at that time of the afternoon and all I could see was the usual line-up of cars and trucks behind a bus, heat radiating off their bonnets. The woman Sabiha had been serving was not fretting at the delay, but was looking out at the traffic and the people on the street in the afternoon sunlight, as if she shared Sabiha's interest in the scene. It was one of the beautiful things about Sabiha and her shop, this lack of hurry, the quiet respect with which people felt called on to treat each other in her presence.

Thoughtless people, people in a hurry, young women in black suits with frenzied eyes, their new Audi double-parked outside, were not in the shop five minutes before they discovered the joys of mental calm and good manners. I loved Sabiha for it. I was going to write her story, and I was going to go on being her friend and her admirer, and the friend of her husband and her beautiful daughter, a miniature replica of her mother. My part of Carlton was so much more hopeful with Sabiha and her pastry shop in it than it had been with the derelict drycleaners and the desolate supermarket. Thanks to Sabiha Carlton was my reality once again. There was no longer any need for me to think of returning to Venice to slip away quietly one summer afternoon like Aschenbach in his deckchair. The Paris of Chez Dom was my dream now, my fiction, and for a year or two I would live it. Venice could wait for another time.

The traffic moved along and when the bus had passed I saw John and Houria standing at the kerb, waiting to cross to our side of the road. I have never dwelled heavily on nostalgia, but I couldn't help thinking of bringing Clare home from prep in the old days. A lifetime away, that, and a fine subject for nostalgia. It was not nostalgia, not a longing to relive those times with my daughter, but a pleasure in witnessing once again that these things survived. I've sometimes been tempted to cry out with despair that everything has changed and all the good things have been swept away. But that is the prejudice of the old and must be resisted. The truth, if I can deal in truth for a moment, is that the very best and the very worst of things, those primal things that make us human, have remained unchanged, the good and the evil.

Houria was looking up at her dad with an eager expression on her face, evidently asking him something that was important to her just at that moment. Her blue and yellow kid's backpack bouncing about on her back as she made her point with great enthusiasm. John was looking down, listening to her. I watched him bend and pick her up then. She was a big girl for her age and he held her against his chest, his bulky satchel making it an awkward manoeuvre for him. He stood holding her, looking along the street, frowning and ready to make a dash for it as soon as there was a gap in the traffic. Watching them I experienced again my old anxiety at children and traffic and wide streets. In fact I could not bear to watch and looked away from them and at Sabiha.

Sabiha was laughing at something the woman customer had said to her, and was selecting pastries with the crocodile tongs, offering that same considered care she had shown me the first time I came into her shop, holding the paper bag in one hand and looking into it as she positioned the pastry inside, being careful not to damage the crust.

When I looked out the window again John and Houria had made it to the centre island. John set Houria down and took her hand and they stood waiting for the cars to pass. There wasn't so much traffic going into the city, and it was only moments before they were able to cross in safety. Houria didn't walk, she jumped. She was seeing how big she could make her jumps, her hand gripping her dad's hand, he looking down at her and encouraging her, giving her an extra lift.

The woman said, 'And I wouldn't mind getting some of those too.' She was pointing at the pyramid of honey-dipped briouats on the shelf behind Sabiha. 'How do you pronounce that again? They always look so delicious. I've been meaning to try them for ages.'

Sabiha picked up the crocodile tongs and selected the two topmost briouats, one at a time, and put them into a paper bag. She put the bag on the counter next to the bag of pastries. 'Try them. No, you don't need to pay me for these. They're just for you to try.'

'That's very kind of you,' the woman said. 'Frank will love them. I'll be lucky to get a look-in.'

I looked at Sabiha and wondered if the night of Bruno's murder still flashed in her mind when she was lying awake beside John. Did she go over the details of that night again and again in her memory? Reliving the horror of it? Was she still tortured by guilt and remorse for what she had done to that man? John had said she had found a way to live with it, but none of us is master of our dreams or our night fears. To see her smiling and talking to the woman customer it was almost impossible for me to believe that Sabiha was a tormented woman. But I remembered the day I first saw her, and how I had witnessed some deep old grief in her eyes and had wondered then at the cause of it. I had her story now, but it is one thing to have a story and another to write it. How was I to articulate the delicate complexities that must give weight and depth and beauty to her story, those things that most easily elude us?

She turned to me, her eyes meeting mine as if she saw the question in my mind. 'Hello, Ken,' she said and smiled. I was aware of John and Houria coming into the shop behind me, Houria's high-pitched voice, excited about something she wanted to tell everyone. Whose idea had it been, I wondered, to call the pastry shop *Figlia Fiorentino*?

Sabiha said, 'I'm cooking for Wednesday's dinner. Something you and Clare have never had before.' She laughed.

'You can't do that,' I protested. 'You're my guest.'

'Something Tunisian,' she said. 'A surprise.' She looked at me. 'We cook for our friends, Ken. We know how to do it. It's what we do. You and Clare can provide the hospitality of your lovely home. We'll do the rest.' She held my gaze and I saw she wanted to say something more but was hesitating. 'You are part of our story now,' she said.

I was moved. But Houria was tugging at my sleeve and shouting my name over and over, 'Ken! Ken! Ken!' I turned and knelt down to her. 'What is it, darling?'

She held a piece of paper in her hand. There was a child's drawing on it.

'I got a prize for my drawing of Mum!' She was breathless with it. I scarcely had time to look at her drawing before she snatched it away and ran past me and went around behind the counter and held it up for Sabiha to see. 'Mum! Look! I got a prize for it!' Sabiha picked her up and hugged her and Houria struggled and yelled, 'Look at my picture, Mum!'

Sabiha was Clare's age when she fell pregnant with Houria. I wondered if it was just possible that Clare might have a child too. Clare had never felt Sabiha's overwhelming need for motherhood. I looked at the two of them now, Houria talking like crazy, correcting her mother's attempts to interpret the drawing. 'No, that's your nose, not your eye!' Whenever Sabiha was asked by her Italian customers, as she quite often was, Why did you call your pastry shop by an Italian name when you and John are not Italian? Sabiha always told them, Signor Fiorentino was a man who gave us something precious for which we can never repay him. But of course she never told anyone what this precious thing was that Signor Fiorentino had given them.

John and I greeted each other. He hefted his satchel. 'English assignments,' he said. 'I might not be doing too many more of these.'

I said, 'I wouldn't give up your day job just yet, John.'

*I*t's getting dark outside. I haven't switched the light on. I'm sitting at my desk looking across the road at the last of the sun slicing through the elms in the park. I have Sabiha's blessing now, her permission. One day I will talk to her about my fiction. The house is quiet. My notebook and box of sharpened pencils are on the desk in front of me. I don't use a computer. I like to lean on my desk and twist my notebook around and chew my pencil and look out at the elms. A screen in front of me would stop me from dreaming. Writing is my way of avoiding the Venetian solution, not encouraging it.

Stubby nudges my leg with his nose. I'm watching the last of the sun. It is a very beautiful sight. When I told Clare earlier that John was writing his story, she said, 'I told you he would be.' I said, 'Yes, he'll probably call it *Murder in the rue des Esclaves.*' She said, 'You might be surprised.' I said, 'I might be.' Then she asked me, 'What will you call your version?' I said, 'We'll see.' I'm not convinced by John's claim to have become a writer overnight. However forgiving he is of Sabiha, there is a sense in which he has closed off those difficult channels into himself that a writer needs. I just don't see him getting it. 'Come on then, Stubbs,' I say, and I get up. 'Let's do the walk while there's still a bit of light left to us.' Sabiha's story had come out of her and been carried to me; now, after I had lived in it jealously myself for a while, I would carry it to others, and in the end would let it go and be done with it, like all the other stories I have carried.

Acknowledgments

I would like to express my heartfelt thanks to my editor, Annette Barlow, and the team at Allen & Unwin, and to Ali Lavau.